THE PHANTOM IN THE RAINBOW

THE PHANTOM IN THE RAINBOW

SLATER LaMASTER

COVER BY
PAUL STAHR

ILLUSTRATED BY
ROGER B. MORRISON
JOHN R. NEILL

POPULAR PUBLICATIONS · 2021

TABLE OF CONTENTS

THE PHANTOM IN THE RAINBOW

*When Edmond Fletcher, broker's clerk, stepped
into a waiting limousine, he stepped into
the strangest drama that was ever staged*

1

A SHIP COMES IN

PRIVATE RADIO CODE snapped and snarled through the ether. Out of the very early morning mist, a great ship loomed up off Sandy Hook. The veteran captain, in resplendent uniform, stood tensely on one end of the bridge and closely scanned the Long Island horizon.

On that side of the huge vessel, down under the lowest deck, a freight opening was being cleared. These preparations were so far below that no one could notice them unless he was particularly curious and hung over the rail to see.

The vast promenade decks were deserted anyway at this early hour. Only a few passengers were astir, but among them was Bill Skyles, star reporter of the sensational New York *Morning Star*, returning from a European assignment. Ever alert to any unusual development, he felt the quiet tension pervading the crew and traced their interest to the skyline and the mysterious business below decks.

The monstrous greyhound of the deep gave one short blast and idled to a stop as a long dark cabin cruiser shot out of the fog which clung to the Long Island shore. The wasplike boat circled gracefully to the side of the steamship.

This was very strange, thought the reporter, for it was too

soon to take on the pilot. Skyles, screening himself behind
a ventilator, peered far over to view what might happen.

A covered bridgeway was flung to the other deck and
something which he could not make out, was huddled
across it. The gangway was withdrawn as quickly as it had
appeared and the dark cruiser disappeared into the mist
as the engines of the great steamship began to turn again.

"Now I would like to know," speculated the puzzled
reporter, "what in the Cinder Regions has come to America?"

THE NEXT MORNING, however, the newspapers carried
no mention of this misty incident off the country's shores,
nor could Skyles get any explanation of it.

The young June day, with all its fresh splendor, was especially delightful in an old residential section of New York
where lived one Edmond Fletcher. This nonchalant young
man lay tranquilly in bed, bathing in the warm sunshine
as it filtered through the curtains of his little bachelor
apartment.

Three stray cats and a large nondescript dog sat in a
row like soldiers at attention watching Edmond Fletcher.
These were friends that on various occasions he had picked
up and brought home. The dog, a shaggy individual of
mongrel mixture but very loyal disposition, had been the
latest addition to his household.

About dawn, after the nature of animals awakening
with the light, his pets invariably filed into their master's
bedroom and waited in strained postures for him to arise.
This was indeed a vigil. Fletcher was in the brokerage business, and his work did not begin until ten o'clock.

Belshasher, as his master had christened the big dog,

*He was looking into his own face, which was staring
at him through the upper sashes of the window.*

saved a scolding by holding his patience every morning
until nine o'clock, when the alarm sounded. Then in all
anticipation he would flop his tail on the floor and bark.

If this and the alarm did not bring Fletcher out of bed
he was privileged to take some liberties, such as jumping
onto the bed and licking his master's face. Out of the bed
they came together and it was a joyous romp to the breakfast eaten on the bathroom floor while Edmond bathed
and shaved.

THERE WERE SOME distinctive qualities about the young
fellow. He was inordinately two things: a gentleman, and
a gambler. He would stake everything instantly to attain
any sufficiently desired end.

But above all, he had the instincts of a gentleman born.
At present he was experiencing genteel poverty; but to strip
this youth of all the niceties of life, his pleasant little courtesies to every one, the innate refinements which distin-

guish the truly well bred, would have been as impossible as to separate the moon from its earth.

Edmond joyously led his retinue of Belshasher and the three felines, which he had chosen to call Fatima, Celeste, and Aphrodite, to their breakfast at his feet on the bathroom floor, even as if they might have been guests at a hunt breakfast.

In a few minutes Edmond Fletcher was in a fresh, well-tailored suit and clean linen. In his dress he would make no sacrifice, no matter what else poverty might force him to forego. His retinue walked solemnly behind him to the door; and his shoulders thrown back, he jauntily stepped forth to the day's adventure in the market.

At the corner some fancy moved him into a florist where he purchased a little flower and stuck it in his buttonhole, even as though the fairest and most ethereal little lady in all the land had placed it there; ethereal indeed she was, for he had never met any one who approached his ideal.

At ten o'clock his play day began and he stood immaculately dressed by the ticker in the offices of Morton, Keene & Company. Entering the customers' room and seeing him there, one would have been more likely to take him for a partner in the house than any one else present. As Fletcher reasoned, he needed the appearance more than any of his superiors.

In nearly all forms of employment, Fletcher saw others drudge. But from ten to three was for him one continuous adventure. Always there was a little catch in his throat when the market opened. To him, when the gong sounded on the floor of the exchange and the opening prices started over the tape, it was as though the barrier had sprung at the race track and a thrill persisted until the close.

But at the present time the brokerage game was not yielding him much of an income on account of certain silly scruples which he possessed in a marked degree.

The excitement and uncertainty of gauging the possible trend were like wine in his veins and he loved it personally, but underneath it all there had been accumulating a deep sympathy and sadness for the poor customers who made this last stand of legitimate gambling in America possible.

The game did not seem quite fair to the harassed customers. Since the Civil War every year or so and sometimes much oftener the market was rigged sky high, securities were unloaded on the public at silly prices; and then the market inevitably broke all to pieces and the public was cleaned out. Again and again they repeated the process with a new crop of uninitiated.

There was something rotten to this young Don Quixote in such wholesale treachery. Of course these cynical opinions were not conducive to a large income. Money was made by playing the game, not by throwing cold water on it. His love of fair play was simply developing with such leaps and bounds that he would not deign to follow expediency as a guide.

Only a small clientele, who could understand this very altruistic salesman, remained with him and kept him going. Thus there existed the paradox of a young business man apparently successful in every way, who was actually very poor.

"AMERICA'S PRINCE, VAN Mortimor," said a man standing at the news ticker, "has not been found yet. Seems to have given the newspaper boys the slip yesterday."

"That's a clever fellow," bantered Fletcher. "He and I are the same age to the day, but we live alike only in time; in all other ways our lives have been so different!"

Then a great idea came to him. If he could only get to some young Croesus like that, or any one of a dozen other enormously wealthy men, what he could do with his knowledge of this game! Think of all this great public's enthusiasm—investment loyalty and faith carried to the point of sacrifice, which was forever going wantonly to waste. What wouldn't he do if he had the opportunity to handle one of those great accounts?

To take the money of the small fellows who came to him and who, like so many sheep, always wanted to buy, was little short of larceny. Day-dreaming was his weakness and along his mind flew on how he could interest one of these great overlords of finance, in letting him unify some of this much squandered blind investment loyalty in great productive enterprise.

His eyes dropped to the decoration in his buttonhole. Truly the idea was as delightful as the one that prompted him to wear the flower. It breathed something of the same spirit.

At noon Edmond Fletcher picked up the telephone on his desk and notified the office operator that he was going out to lunch. Once on the sidewalk he rushed a little because he wished to conserve his meager funds by eating in a good but inexpensive cafeteria outside of the financial district. Financial dyspepsia was worse than the other kind down there. In the district he dared not show himself in any but the very best restaurants.

As he strolled back to the office, any one who did not know how little there was in his pocket would have taken him for a wealthy, well-bred young man returning from his luncheon club.

A gentleman of distinguished appearance, gray haired and with a professional Vandyke beard, happened to be emerging from the Bank of the Western Hemisphere. Suddenly the elderly gentleman halted and stared at Fletcher. The man seemed in some manner very much shocked and evidently surprised that he received no sign of recognition. He had met the young man face to face.

A close observer of the incident would have seen that the professional man, if such he was, attended to it that the young chap should distinctly see him again—again without obtaining a flicker of recognition from Fletcher.

"A remarkable resemblance," muttered the elder party, as out of a growing curiosity he followed Fletcher.

"Oh, Mr. Fletcher," greeted Morton, one of the partners of the house, on his return, "that funny-looking Bullard Bland was in to see you. What does he do—wear pyjamas in the day time or sleep in his clothes?"

"Why, Bullard's all right—really a fine scout!" laughed Fletcher.

"Well, keep him out of the customers' room," Morton smiled kindly. "Looks bad for you as well as us to have him hanging around here."

As Fletcher idly sat by the ticker that afternoon he took himself to task. He was about ready for anything. Prospects were not very hopeful for him. Unless he suppressed his foolish idealism and eternal consideration for others, and began to play the game in the severely practical way as others did and as he so well knew how to do, he could never expect much more than a mere living in his present position.

"MAY I SPEAK to you?" suavely queried the partner Morton at Fletcher's shoulder later that afternoon. Fletcher followed him into his private sanctum.

"Mr. Fletcher, we like you," he admonished ominously, "but you should do more business. What's your answer?"

"Nothing," asserted Edmond earnestly, "unless you wish me to sever my connection and go elsewhere."

"Fletcher," Morton coughed and paused as though he was angling for words to express himself, "you know we don't want you to leave. Honestly, my boy, what is the matter with you?"

"Morton," snapped Fletcher, and there came into his eyes a gleam of something which actually made the ever placid Morton uneasy, "you are inviting me to thrust the truth right into your teeth, and here it is: I am sick of seeing these suckers lose their money. Now fire me!"

Morton swayed as though some invisible fist had landed upon him. Next he braced himself in his chair and held up his hand warningly, as he stared shrewdly at the erect young fellow. He even neglected to relight his cigar, something never before known to happen.

"No," he blustered hotly, "don't you dare leave here! I have noticed you moon-calfing around. It's a sure sign you are starting something big!" He cocked a knowing eye to the ceiling and complacently lit his cigar. "I think you are just scorning the small fry!"

"You know more than I do," answered Fletcher a bit wonderingly as he slipped out.

Morton's attention returned to a bunch of inquiry sheets which had poured in all afternoon. They were queries on this peculiar youth to be filled out for several commercial reporting agencies. All afternoon, too, Morton had been occupied answering the most silly sort of questions about him to an anonymous inquisitor whose compelling references could not be slighted by any brokerage house.

"I wonder," he sighed, "whether this kid is patronizing loan sharks, furnishing a hotel on the installment plan, or flirting with big business. He is surely exciting a lot of interest, and, anyway, I like him."

As the word "close" appeared on the tape, Edmond Fletcher bade good night to the office and stepped out into the warm and genial sunshine. It was to him indeed an auspicious day, but little did he realize how auspicious. He strolled up Broadway wondering just what to do next. He had no ties. These late afternoons were sometimes irksome.

One day an average good man, practically unknown and unacclaimed, holds the office of Vice President; a death occurs, and in the twinkling of an eye he becomes President of the United States. An honest son of toil is elected President, due to a split in the opposition; a civil war breaks out and we have a Lincoln. A minority on some confused issue elects a scholar, who would never get much beyond theorizing but for a great catastrophe. A world war comes our way and makes him the standard-bearer for all humanity. Sometimes an individual and a circumstance do collide magnificently.

The street agencies gave Edmond Fletcher an abso-

lutely clean bill of health, a reference hard to surpass; and
he happened to saunter up lower Broadway on a particular afternoon.

A LARGE CAR of foreign make edged into the curb as
he stopped to light a cigarette. A uniformed chauffeur
respectfully touched his cap to Fletcher and jumped out
to open the car door.

Fletcher looked into the car to see who wanted him, but
no one was inside.

"Do you wish to go now, sir?" asked the chauffeur
respectfully.

Fletcher could have said "Where?" or "What is it you
wish of me?" but to have done so would have violated one
of his principles—it would have disclosed his hand, or
betrayed his lack of information in an interesting and probably advantageous situation.

Instead, he answered, "Wait a minute," while he continued to light his cigarette, thinking quickly whether he
should accept the invitation. He decided that at most it
could only be a question of mistaken identity, or just possibly some practical joke at his expense.

At any rate, this luxurious equipage seemed to be very
much in line with his desire to associate with the very rich.
If he could just make the most of this amusing little incident, maybe it would lead to some wealthy acquaintances.

So he calmly stepped into the car and nodded to the
driver. The motor made its way up to Lafayette Street,
while Fletcher noted that this was a very powerful foreign
make of car, an Isotta Fraschini; he believed it was the most
costly Italian car.

The upholstery was exceedingly soft and luxurious, and

he noted that the chauffeur's uniform had been carefully tailored in a distinctive livery. He could not imagine any one he knew who could command such accouterments playing a joke upon him. So he came inevitably to the conclusion that it must be a case of mistaken identity, and began to wonder just where this bubble would break, and, more particularly, how he could get out of the situation gracefully.

Anyhow, for the moment it certainly was a most pleasurable feeling to sink into these downy cushions while he was being so smoothly propelled uptown.

Guardedly he kept looking around, for he had perceived that another beautiful motor, a Hispano-Suiza, was following him, nosing up close each time they slowed down. Lifting the tube, he spoke to the chauffeur.

"I think there is a car following us."

"Yes, sir," replied the man, touching his cap again, "that is your second car, sir. In case of any motor trouble, you can go ahead in the other car without inconvenience."

"Ah!" he thought.

On Lafayette Street the car picked up speed and the traffic officers began to salute the equipage. At first Fletcher thought an officer every now and then was friendly with the chauffeur. Then he believed they could not all be so friendly. Soon he decided the car must belong to some one of importance. Consequently he surmised that they must all be saluting the one presumed to be riding in the car. The person in the car was no other than himself.

This gave him a little shock. He had no idea of what he was doing and he did not wish to be placed in the position of impersonating any officer of the Police Department, a

high national officer or any great person. Difficulties with
the police are as much to be feared by a gentleman as a
crook.

He was just about to ask some general questions in the
hope of adroitly getting out of all this when the chauffeur
touched his cap and spoke through the tube.

"Shall I start home, sir?"

"CERTAINLY," HE SAID gratefully, after a mere instant's
hesitation. This, he quickly meditated, settled it. If he did
not understand the situation by the time they arrived home,
wherever that might be, he would dismiss the car, or rather
cars, at the gate. The chauffeur would think he was going
in. If any one else saw him they would probably think he
was some guest using the limousine; but he knew he would
not be going in, nor would he be a guest if he could help
it. He would simply go quietly away.

The car now sped up the avenue and turned through
Fifty-Ninth Street. It ran up Broadway and gracefully
swung into the West Seventies. Very unexpectedly, and
much to his consternation, the easy gliding coach began
to wend its way down to the docks under Riverside Drive.
It seemed he lived on a ship, and you could not very well
dismiss your car and walk away from the gangplank of a
ship.

Fletcher could see that they were approaching a long
rakish yacht, her white woodwork and brass rails agleam
in the afternoon sun. At their approach a covered launch
came from the yacht. *"Put-put-put-put!"* it sang as it kept
coming toward them.

The car came up to a canvas-sided landing, at whose end,
as if by magic, appeared a trim young sailor in the launch.

The chauffeur stepped down and opened the car door; the young sailor saluted. There was nothing for him to do but step in, and *put-put-put-put!* he was carried out.

As he passed up the ship's canvased stairway he saw a captain adorned with much blue and gold appear on the diminutive bridge. The captain saluted and bowed. A steward led the way into a softly carpeted spacious cabin which gave a splendid view on all sides. The steward asked:

"May I do anything for you, sir?"

Edmond sank down on a lounge.

"Yes," he said, "draw the curtains. I am rather fatigued."

The steward deftly did this, going around the cabin and then went out softly as Edmond stretched himself out on the lounge.

No sooner had the door closed behind the servant than, like a cat, Fletcher was on his feet. First he explored a writing desk thoroughly, but he only found stationery with a Park Avenue address embossed upon it, and other letter sheets bearing the name of the yacht Sylvia upon them. It all meant nothing to him.

Around the room ran bookcases full of most rare and interesting volumes. At random he looked them over hurriedly but gently. This is an attribute of a person who really loves books. He will under no circumstances handle roughly, mar, or mutilate a good book. A lover of good literature handles a book with as much care as a woman.

After a careful search he could find no clew which would solve his identity immediately, but this did not discourage him. He sat down in a comfortable chair and took a fragrant club-monogrammed cigarette from a gold humidor.

"Evidently," he reflected, "these people are my servants or I am the guest of their master. With all these facilities at my command I should be able to obtain the information I desire without making my situation worse."

Studiously he reviewed every little detail since he had left the financial district so ceremoniously. In a few moments he straightened up in the chair, tossed his cigarette away, and pushed a button which he noticed inlaid suitably on a near by table. The steward silently appeared as if from nowhere.

"Have I any mail?" Fletcher asked absently.

"You have quite a good deal, sir," replied the steward. "We were holding it to be delivered to your secretary."

"Thank you, but you may bring it in. I wish to glance through it."

The steward returned shortly with a pile of mail matter. The personal letters addressed in longhand were first put together on the table. Now followed several neat stacks of typewritten correspondence and miscellaneous matter separated to the best of the steward's ability.

Edmond's eyes were quietly riveted upon the first letter he saw. It bore this astounding inscription:

Sigmond Van Mortimor
Fifth Avenue
New York City

AS IF BEYOND belief and just from reflex and automatic action his memory summed up what he could recall about this illustrious family. Its name alone was a magic talisman with which to conjure and in the popular mind meant unlimited wealth and power, for chancellors and treasurers of nations had actually stood humbly in line to borrow from its bulging coffers. Since Edmond was a boy its mighty power had become as subtle and mysterious as it was vast. Scarcely anything was generally known about how this tremendous wealth was handled, but its control was felt so forcibly in so many directions that it had become a sort of an octopus in the public imagination and was credited with owning well-nigh everything.

Evidently, it came to him, he was being mistaken for Mr. Van Mortimor. The readiness with which the steward gave him the mail dispelled any doubt on that score. A sort of numbness pervaded his entire person when he realized how far he had now gone in this dangerous business. He had certainly got into touch with great wealth quickly enough!

As his overwhelmed faculties returned to him, he appreciated that here was a situation fit for the gods. If he kept his head sufficiently clear and used nimble enough wits, this might become his golden opportunity to become intimately acquainted with Mr. Van Mortimor.

A delicate situation now arose in his mind. Fletcher greatly desired to know more about his second self, his great temporary identity, but his reason told him not to open any of that mail. Instead he selected at random several important-appearing letters and laid them to one side.

As he expected, the ever courteous and extremely obliging steward picked up a letter opener, slit the envelopes and smoothed out the correspondence nicely in front of him. After that Fletcher selected the other letters which interested him, laying them to one side as before, and the steward repeated the process. Whereupon he dismissed the servant.

Finally he really found himself. Letters from friends on the continent, letters from fellow hunters in Africa, letters overintimate from women and much formal correspondence gave him an excellent understanding of his supposed identity. One on the stationery of the Savoy Hotel, London, considerably enlightened him. It ran:

> DEAR SIGMOND:
>
> Just reached London today after my visit to Nice. The past year which we have spent in the jungles of Africa has brought us very close together and prompts me to take the liberty of saying that this rough life may in some measure have prepared you for taking up your position and residence in America.
>
> If you keep well no doubt you shortly will take interest as an empire builder, and fulfill your heritage in the fullest sense. Please believe that I am most sincere in my platitudes as your name is synonymous to me with great action, as against the noxious, wasteful, worthless life that you and I have lived here and in Europe since our early youth.
>
> As ever your friend,
>
> ARCHIBALD.

Another letter greatly astonished Edmond Fletcher. It was from Alexander, Cromwell & Klaton, Attorneys, New York City:

> MR. SIGMOND VAN MORTIMOR,
> Fifth Avenue, New York City.

Dear Sir:

It is indeed a distinct pleasure to welcome you home. As your lamented father's chief counsel in his many great enterprises, may we not ask your immediate consideration of the important affairs which have fallen into your hands? You will find detailed accountings of everything in the hands of your secretary, but there are several matters of pertinent importance which we wish herein to press upon your attention.

Although twenty-seven years of age, you have not been here since you were fourteen. In the meantime while you were living entirely abroad, great changes have occurred at home.

The six great railroads in which your family has control have passed through the hands of the government administration incident to the war and need your attention as to the policies of management which should now be pursued.

The banks in which you are so heavily interested have become members of the Federal Reserve System and present new problems, which are beyond our authority to handle.

Areas of real estate which you own in New York City have greatly increased in value without adequate improvements on them, and present obstacles to civic progress.

Will you please let us know at your earliest convenience when we may come to see you or have the honor of receiving you at our office?

Very respectfully,

ALEXANDER, CROMWELL & KLATON.

In letter after letter, he gleaned that he had just returned home after having spent his life, since boyhood, abroad. Now he had come to take his rightful place in American life and to assume the authority with which fortune had endowed him.

FLETCHER PUT THE mail aside. There would be plenty of time for details if this went farther. The problem which confronted him was what he should do at once. Obviously the thing to do was, the moment he met any member of the family, to explain the whole thing and to apologize as gracefully as possible. It would be ludicrous to attempt an explanation to these servants and if he tried to inform the captain of the yacht it might result in his arrest with serious consequences.

Fletcher had found that if you were in a strange city and without identification, and needed a check cashed or some favor, the proper thing to do was to go to the best hotel there. If you ever were embarrassed in your dealings with any concern or family, go directly to the most important person in it and straighten out your troubles frankly. This intention steadied his overwrought nerves.

He had the curtains opened, and calmly surveyed the placid silvery Hudson. Shortly he noticed the yacht turn in toward a little white pier. He heard the telegraph on the bridge gently guide the swanlike boat up to the pier without the slightest vibration and the next moment the captain stood in the doorway.

"Mr. Van Mortimor," he spoke, "I have not had the honor of knowing you before this occasion, but I've had the yacht thoroughly reconditioned and I trust you will find it seaworthy in every respect."

This was the first time Fletcher had been addressed as Van Mortimor, and it gave him a distinct thrill. He disliked to admit so much pleasure and distinction at the deference the great name carried.

Fletcher's answers were very guarded, anticipating the result later of what he might say now.

"Quite so," was all the speech he risked.

He passed across the gangway and at its other end stood what seemed the duplicate of the car he had just left in the city. The door was open, he stepped in, the chauffeur saluted and they were off.

Before him he could see a castle-like structure on one of the Westchester County hills, overlooking the river. Around one side of this great undulating hill ran like a ribbon, a white roadway and into this the car turned taking the slight grades as though it were on a race course. He wondered at the reckless driving and then it occurred to him that this was all a private parkway, where no other cars would be met! Carefully tended shrubbery and parklike greensward spread out to his right and left, and after a few deft turns in the bright thoroughfare the car ran under an awning before the house on the crest of the hill. As the car was brought to a stop, he saw a large motor-load of trunks and baggage coming in from another direction.

"If I don't get out of this soon," thought Fletcher, "I'll be wearing the chap's clothes."

2

GLORIA

FLETCHER HAD SMALL time for contemplation. A liveried man was swinging open a large grilled door. A venerable and stately butler was standing just inside, and as Fletcher passed the portal, he bowed and began a little speech.

"Mr. Sigmond, everybody below stairs wishes me to bid you welcome. We have long waited this day to have you again with us."

The feeble old man's emotion was truly touching and Fletcher wondered if he could really see him well.

"I am glad to be here," Fletcher vouched, watching to see if his voice would register a false note. Apparently not. As an afterthought he asked:

"Is any one to dine with me this evening?"

"Miss Gloria wishes to dine with you, sir."

"Very well," he answered as a servant led him to his apartments. Who, he puzzled, was Miss Gloria?

The main room held a large bouquet of flowers and by them lay a card with the fortunately enlightening words upon it:

"From your loving sister, Gloria."

He could hear baggage being quietly moved into the

rear of his rooms. Stepping into a convenient bedroom, he mechanically began undressing to clean up and make himself presentable before facing the patrician girl below and apologizing for his awkward position. A servant obsequiously passed into the room, opened a door and turned on the bath.

In a few minutes Fletcher was completely refreshed and upon reentering the room he found his clothes gone and in their place, carefully laid out, was a dinner suit.

"What next?" breathed Fletcher. "I hope I can get into his clothes!" They fitted him surprisingly well. With a few slight alterations, they would have been perfect.

"Bring me back the clothes I have just taken off; I wish to take some things out of them," he ordered. "And you may tell the butler I shall be down in fifteen minutes."

As soon as the man had withdrawn, he removed all of his effects to the dinner suit. Following which he put his own clothes in a chiffonier drawer and locked it, placing the key in his pocket. He meant to tell his own story and did not want any advance news released on it.

Momentarily, this young adventurer studied his expression and appearance in a mirror to make sure that he had fully regained his composure. His courage arose, and he even smiled. It was better to have lived, if only for a few hours, than never to have lived at all.

Thereupon, Fletcher descended. He wondered how he should greet this strange feminine aristocrat with the touch of Midas. He considered it better to let her greet him and then, after seeing the effect that his presence would have upon her, to explain the situation. As he reached the foot of the grand staircase, the dignified old butler led him into the drawing-room as if he were the world's eighth wonder, and so, Fletcher felt, he was!

It was a large, deep room with a highly polished floor. Period furniture and deep lustrous rugs of untold value lay scattered before him in elegant simplicity. Splendor sat unobtrusively about. Each thing was severely beautiful to his sensitive nature in its quiet perfection of detail. The very grandeur of his surroundings gave him the sensation of having unceremoniously broken into a royal court. But his eyes strained ahead for the high priestess of all this; ugly as sin, he supposed, like so many of our ultra-rich.

FLETCHER FIRST SAW her rising from a chair to meet him. There is a lithesome grace about some women which makes their every motion poetic. She was slender, and there was a soft femininity about her, a purity of breeding and beauty as though the power of the house through generations to pick and choose its women, had been concentrated in producing this utter thoroughbred.

Half dazzled, Fletcher could only make out that her hair was dark, and that her large gray eyes somehow wore a hurt look. He sensed the feeling of being a hunter who had just startled a fawn at some stream. But he only had this feeling for one fleeting instant; she was coming toward him, and the strange look had gone from her eyes.

He was so overcome by the loveliness of this girl advancing upon him that he was at loss for words. She put her arm around him and kissed his cheek ever so softly.

"Sigmond, how well you look," she began. "Really, what a wonderful brother I have! Come sit close to me. I have needed you so badly. Just the two of us and you have avoided me so long!"

How any one could long avoid this girl was far beyond Fletcher's apprehension. However, the unexpected was coming at too alarming a pace. He had every reason to believe that the mere meeting with Gloria would solve the whole thing.

He had expected that as soon as she saw him, she would look at him in horrified amazement. A cold, withering look would follow as soon as her consternation at seeing this rank impostor had subsided. He knew how to counter the expected.

A humble explanation and apology would set things right, and if he could only succeed in confessing all the little reasons for the situation fully enough, the matter might become very humorous and really result in an interesting acquaintanceship.

Now all his plans were upset. But one thing he would, must do. He must make a clean breast of the whole thing to this lovely young girl.

She took his arm, and he felt an indefinable softness, the clinging weight of a feather and a thrill of strange contentment went through him. As if here were that utmost in the world for which he had always been unconsciously seeking, and now that he had found it, he well knew how unattainable it was.

She drew him to her side on a slender divan, its dainty lines well befitting her delicate little figure. He sat as one entranced while she diffidently cuddled up to his side and looked wistfully up into his face.

"SIGMOND, DEAR," SHE spoke gently, "you must love me—oh! so much. You must be a father, a mother, and brother, and everything to me; I haven't had any of them for so long. I'll tell you all sorts of silly things, and you must listen and help me, for there are so many intimate little matters in which I do not know what to do, and in which I cannot ask any one else's advice.

"There's the count, who says the most beautiful things, and threatens to die if I do not marry him. There's Phil Vordman, who dances divinely, and is the best polo player we have, who will call this evening.

"You are my whole family. Should I drink more? Our set often laugh at me and insinuate that I am a poor sport." Her sensitive countenance changed slightly.

"Oh, Sigmond, there are some ugly rumors about you, but I could never believe them, and you are so good, I knew they were lies. You are so strong, your face seems determined; I believe in you, Sigmond. You are just different from men I know." A shadow of doubt, even of disappointment, came over her face. He felt a slight chill in her voice as she drew partly away from him: "But I must bore you. Please forgive all this banal talk. It is the desire to confide in some one, that has been pent up in me. I hoped I could in you, but you have not said a word to me. Perhaps you do not like your little sister!"

"You are the most interesting person I have ever met," he answered truthfully. "I have so much to say to you, but I do not know how to start."

"How wonderful!" she exclaimed, beaming upon him. Her changing moods were reflected beautifully in her limpid expressions like some iridescent jewel struck by lights and shadows, or the delicately tinted lights which play from deep within some pure white diamond. How like a diamond, thought Fletcher! For he fully appreciated that no less than that very same stone could this girl cut hard and deep, for him.

At last she pensively said: "But you do not have to be so polite. You are my brother!"

The butler appeared in the doorway. "Begging pardon, sir!" he said. "I have about outbowed myself in the hall. Dinner, if you please, sir?"

"You are the first one ever to nettle Parkins!" declared Gloria gayly.

Fletcher gave her his arm, as they passed into an immense feudal dining room. It was a formal affair, and scarcely seemed the place to make an explanation, especially with Parkins standing behind his, the master's, chair. Besides, they were in the presence of several other stiff-backed servants. It would have proved doubly embarrassing to the real mistress of the house, in view of her confidences.

They carried on the usual small talk of a formal dinner; he at one end of the table, she at the other, with a confusing array of glass and silver sparkling between them.

The butler pompously poured a different wine with each course, but Fletcher scarcely tasted it because that was what Gloria was doing. He had thus passed up sherry with the oysters and the soup, his sauterne with the fish. With an entrée and claret Gloria incredulously asked:

"Don't you drink at all?"

For once Parkins had his whole soft-footed crew out of earshot, and Edmond seized this opportunity to answer boldly:

"I am drunk enough on your eyes!"

"Oh!" was all she said, and settled back in her chair, badly startled.

SEVERAL LEADING QUESTIONS put by her now, probably in all innocence, badly confused him. He noticed her
studying him intently. He did not wish a public explanation of his ignorance of matters, and he thought he would
give an excuse until he could get her alone again.

"I do hope you will excuse me if I act queerly at times,"
he pretended. "I experienced a slight injury at Ypres, and
I do not remember as well as I should."

"I did not know that you were in the war!" she exclaimed
in surprise.

He flushed crimson. Instantly she was by his side.

"There were lots of things we didn't know about you! Of
course you were! I am dreadfully sorry," she pleaded.

"It is of no importance," he said, mentally detesting
himself for having used such a distasteful excuse. Only
his dire risk of premature exposure had forced him to do
so. "Forgive me if I am absent-minded. I'll tell you about
it later."

She excused herself immediately after dinner, but not
before he had entreated:

"I have something of great importance to tell you—may
I speak to you alone?"

"No," she smiled sweetly. "Join Mr. Vordman and me
on the east terrace a little later. The moonlight is beautiful,
and I shall need a member of the family. After he departs
we can talk all night."

As one enthralled he went into a large library which
opened conveniently where she had left him. There a telephone came to his notice, and he was reminded of something. He gave a New York number and heard a familiar
voice.

"Mrs. Kelly," he spoke softly, first looking carefully around, "you know who this is. Use your duplicate key and take my dog and cats out for an airing and everything they can eat. Treat them as though they were your own children. I am compelled to be away a little while. Fine! Good-by!"

Then he sat and smoked. Absent-mindedly he ran his eyes down the wall of books nearest him. French authors they were, Baudelaire, Flaubert, France, Maupassant, and so it went, volumes in French and in English. Surely he could explain everything to her on the terrace later in the evening, he meditated, when they would be all alone as she had promised.

Eventually he noticed a collection of American authors and further observed that they were not in alphabetical arrangement as others in the room. Poetry and prose were mixed as well. Rather interested as he was always keenly observant of anything unusual, he noted that the first five authors from left to right were the works of, first, Poe; second, Walt Whitman; third, Thomas Paine; fourth, Nathaniel Hawthorne; fifth, James Huneker.

He started. By the strangest coincidence he ranked American authors in this order himself. Although he had never tried to graduate authors in order of preference beyond the fifth place, he ran on through the list and was practically compelled to agree with the arrangement. This was uncanny. Did he think like these people, too?

Being in the mood he read at random, mostly poetry. He was so absorbed that he did not hear Parkins until he spoke at his elbow.

"Excuse me, sir. Miss Gloria would like you to join her on the terrace."

HE AROSE AND followed until at the far end of the house he came out on a long stone terrace, gray in the pale moonlight of a warm summer evening. Great trees in the gloaming made it look singularly cool and inviting. Just a sufficient amount of light came through a French window casement to illuminate the faces of the couple sitting there. They instantly became a study to Fletcher.

The young man arose. Gloria remaining seated, murmured simply: "My brother, Mr. Vordman."

Mr. Vordman replied: "I am indeed honored to meet Mr. Van Mortimor," as though he were being presented to royalty. Fletcher bowed, and did not offer his hand for fear he might have been supposed to have acquired Continental manners.

However, he indulged in a pleased smile—not of politeness, as it was taken, but at the idea of a Vordman feeling honored in making his acquaintance.

Vordman was a very handsome young fellow, well mannered and apparently likable in every respect, but Fletcher could not help but mark up a mental reservation against him before he began talking. Fletcher did not feel that the words "Too soft" were fairly descriptive of him, but they were what rang in his mind. One unfortunate result of great wealth, he had observed, was that after a few generations it, time and again, saps the stamina of the family, and leaves its young men rather colorless.

Here, too, he found an entirely different Gloria, superficial, coolly polite.

The talk ran on, and Fletcher listened attentively and as politely as he could. Since he did not interject any remarks, the others, in deference to him, asked his opinion on the topics being discussed—sport, yachts, the doings at smart resorts. But Fletcher feigned a lack of familiarity with the local society, which was true enough.

Throughout the conversation he could not help but notice the constraint in Gloria's manner. She was affable, she was exceedingly charming in her little affections, but it was just as though a beautiful Dresden china doll was mechanically performing.

She was vivacious, but in no degree spontaneous; nothing flowed from her real self. Letter perfect were all her petty little conventionalities, but there was an icy barrier, beyond which one could not peer. Fletcher could only reflect that earlier in the evening he must have had a peep into her real heart.

Soft, melodious chimes within struck eleven o'clock. Vordman arose and excused himself. In a burst of cordiality, his parting words were:

"Come over and get potted; have a cellar of wonderful liqueurs."

Fletcher returned to the terrace. Gloria had undergone another transformation. She simply glowed her happiness at being alone with him.

"Freeda," she commanded in a kindly tone, "you may go." A herculean woman appeared from just behind the French casement, where she had evidently been the entire time. Fletcher was astonished. She was a giantess, and he thought how puny the ordinary man would be in her hands. She looked at Fletcher searchingly, but respectfully, laid a Spanish shawl on the arm of a chair and smiling in a stolid way silently withdrew. The duenna of the household was a good one.

3

UNDER THE SHROUD OF NIGHT

"OH, SIGMOND," GLORIA began, "come close to me!"

The winsome girl had moved over on a cushioned settee, and he sat beside her. She nestled up to him and put her head on his shoulder. Her soft body intoxicated him. Her hair breathed a most delicate perfume. He felt her dainty little fingers close on his and then his arm was pulled around her. He looked away lest she read his expression.

"Isn't it beautiful this evening?" she sighed. "I love the view from this terrace, but it never was so lovely as tonight. I suppose it is because I am very happy, but I am more than happy, I am contented—that is the only way I could feel, now that I have you here, my very own big brother to love me, and cuddle me, and help me."

Fletcher felt her warm cheek against his as she again lightly kissed him. Her face was damp with tears. She relaxed upon his shoulder.

"I am so happy," she sobbed softly! He could understand, for deep emotions, which were very rare with him, affected him similarly.

"Hold me tight," she said tenderly, "I am just a silly little baby. I have been so lonely and my heart is so full tonight because I have you."

This was the proper time, but how could he tell her now? To disillusion her at the moment would be like bowling in a cathedral. He must turn the conversation into other channels and prepare her for what maybe he had to say.

"It feels so good to be myself," she confided. "To have some one with whom I can be unreserved and just human. I shall try hard to please you so that you will never leave me again for long."

Her tears were gone as quickly as they had come. The deep emotions which swept her were as April showers. He expected her to excuse herself to remove the traces of them. But this did not concern her. Evidently she did not dab at her face as much as the usual run of womankind. Eagerly she looked up into his countenance and asked:

"Do you like your little sister?"

This afforded him a splendid opportunity to talk.

"Gloria," he said, "most people and things are named inaccurately; but you are perfectly named. Every moment since I have seen you I have been struck with the thought that you are indeed a glorious little creature."

"Oh, oh!" she interrupted. "All women are vain, and I am going to be frank with you—go ahead, I just love it!"

"You seem as exotic as though you were a lovely flower growing in some tropical paradise—a thing apart from human mediocrity." But the fascinating glow of her soft eyes was dazzling him. Putting a brake on his ardor, he continued:

"I cannot make up more poetry, but I'll tell you a fairy story."

"How delightful!" she exclaimed. "I'll be a little girl and listen."

"This day has been the most wonderful one in all my life. Once upon a time, we shall say this very morning, I was a listless young man working in a brokerage office. We shall call myself, for instance, Edmond Fletcher. Nothing out of the ordinary happened in such a person's life until after the market closed at three o'clock this day. I see myself arising in a little bachelor apartment about nine o'clock this morning. Aphrodite, Celeste, Fatima, and Belshasher are with me."

"Who are they?" She looked at him startled.

"They are my cats and Belshasher is my big shaggy dog."

"Oh!" she said with apparent relief, and settled her head back contentedly on his shoulder.

"THEY WERE MY loved ones. Outside of them no one loved me. There were relatives who loved me sincerely but they were far away. Some I had thought cared for me and maybe one in particular."

"Who was she?" asked Gloria, placing her dainty little ear near his lips as though it was a great secret.

"She was a little girl who liked to dance all the time and always was demanding things to be done for her or given her."

"She loved herself," decided Gloria, and settled her precious little head with its mass of hair slightly disarranged, back again upon his shoulder.

"So it went. Outside of a few lifelong men friends, there was no one to care for me. But often I dreamed of a slender ethereal little creature—oh! so sweet and tender—who would stand apart from all other women."

"Only men with blue eyes can think like that," murmured Gloria, and she playfully kissed his fingers.

"Isn't it getting rather late?" inquired Fletcher solemnly. "And we are all alone."

"What does it matter? Can't I be up as late as I wish with my brother?" she questioned, and stretching her fascinating little body out on the settee, she pillowed herself on his breast and arms and asserted contentedly:

"I am simply too happy. Go ahead with the fairy story!"

"So I had gone to the office and after the close of business was sauntering up Broadway, when I met with a great adventure. A coach of a fairy princess was waiting for me just around the corner. I stepped into it and was whisked to a fairy boat which conveyed me to a great castle.

"I didn't know that the princess was waiting for me at the end of the journey, and not being accustomed to her station of life, I was somewhat embarrassed. By a happy coincidence I was mistaken for her brother, which gave us some happy hours together. The little princess was very lonely and—perhaps I entertained her for a little while."

Gloria was holding one of his hands tightly as though he were about to slip away from her, and in the semi-darkness she was looking wide-eyed into his face.

"Shall I finish the story?" he asked. He felt as though he was sounding his death knell, for what could ordinary beauty be to him now, after the superlative vision of Gloria's smile? Bitter indeed must this disillusionment be for him!

She buried her face on his breast that he might not see her and one little slender hand caressed his cheek as though she expected to read his expression as the blind do.

"Yes," she assented, almost inaudibly, as if she were afraid to finish it, "it is all a puzzle to me."

"All fairy stories do not end happily," he informed her sadly. "This one must end miserably for one of its characters, but he will feel better for having been truthful with the little princess. I am not your brother—I am Edmond Fletcher!"

She clutched him to her tightly. "Sigmond, dear," she gasped, "are you trying to frighten me?" He felt a tremor of fear run over her and sensed the same feeling of having hurt her that he experienced at their first meeting.

"You should not say such things. I need you desperately," she beseeched, as she looked up at him pleadingly. "Please do not scare me any more, as I am very nervous from what happened here last night."

HE GATHERED HER tightly into his arms.

"My wonderful sweet little girl, I have only done what I thought was right. I would willingly do anything conceivable for you. I am going to do one more thing that bears on this subject and ask you a question, and then I shall never mention it again to you."

Tenderly raising her head, he implanted fully upon her soft warm lips a kiss, and he felt her relax in his arms as if her very soul were going out to him. She had innocently made no attempt to resist him, and she lay in his embrace for a long moment before he spoke.

"Who am I?" he asked.

"You are my brother—and do not kiss me so peculiarly!" She straightened up.

"You are Sigmond Van Mortimor," she answered, again defiantly, "and of course it was only a fairy story. Please don't tell any more like that one. I have your promise!"

"Ah-h well!" he sighed. "What's the use of my arguing

with you?" and a deep silence seemed to wrap them in a dark cloak.

The moon had set; the trees loomed up like great black patches. He made her comfortable in his arms, for she had entreated:

"Just a few moments more, before I must give you up."

Fletcher looked out into the darkness supremely happy, holding in his arms the most entrancing bit of femininity that he had ever imagined. It was so very quiet. He was thinking what a miracle the day had produced; how adventure and romance were just around the corner to him who sought it.

Cuddled up to him she was asleep, he noticed, asleep with one of his hands pressed to her lips. What an exquisite sensation it gave him to have this surpassingly lovely creature dreaming in his arms.

For a few moments he just sat there before disturbing her, marveling at how hushed and peaceful it was at this late hour of the night, so far out in this ideal country. The darkness out beyond was like velvet, and where his hand had touched the balustrade he could feel the night's cool moistness.

Suddenly there came a plaintive, ghastly cry, from somewhere far down in the hollow among the trees, something gruesome, swelling louder as his flesh began to creep. He was not a coward, but this sound seemed inhuman. Never could he recall having heard such a weird and ghoulish wail. For strangely intensifying the dread voice and commingled with its shrillness was a trace of tune or song, some fiendish hopeless dirge of the unknown, scarcely understandable.

Gloria was awake and shaking. A convulsion of fear was

sweeping over her. Terror-stricken, her little hands broke into a cold sweat. Fletcher sat frozen with fright. For fully half a minute the eerie wail rent the night, its undulating sound breaking into horror-laden notes, abounding in some sort of inhuman torment, which infected the listener.

Some inconsolable appeal, it seemed, which levied painful sympathy, as though its maker, having run the full gantlet of human emotions, sought a further and unearthly thrill in its own torment.

Fletcher suddenly remembered, in a dazed way, having heard of drug habitues, particularly users of hashish, who in their hallucinations gave forth such excruciating agony.

This was suggestive of such a fiend and more. Its bitter melody savored of the sigh of dank winds through valleys of tombstones and myrtle! The morbidity of a lost dead soul was haunting the earth to some other than natural purpose! As suddenly as it had come it stopped, leaving the dismal darkness ringing with an oppressive silence.

HE WAS CHILLED to the marrow. Gloria weakly straightened up, clinging tightly to his hand. Her heart was beating frantically as the old butler and several servants, hastily dressed, appeared in the light.

"Is Mr. Sigmond there and safe?" asked Parkins, the butler.

"I am here," he spoke, and, supporting Gloria, he stepped into the doorway. "What is this noise?"

"We do not know, sir," the old man quavered. "Will you both please come in out of the lighted doorway? You can be seen for miles in the light. Pardon my suggestion, sir."

They went, Gloria huddled against him, to the foot of

the stairway, while Parkins, with all the starch out of him, in a trembling voice went on:

"We heard it last night, sir. Miss Gloria has been panic-stricken. We have had the woods all round and the valley searched, but have found nothing unusual. Thank God you came today, sir! We have been apprehensive of your safety."

"Bring me a revolver," demanded Fletcher. "I am going down in the valley. The sound cannot be far away and we shall find some simple explanation of it."

Gloria clutched him hysterically.

"Sigmond, for any love that you may have for me," she begged, "do not go out of the house. Something dreadful would happen to you, I can feel it. You must be near me so that I may call you if it comes again."

Her entreaty was so serious that, without any argument, he took her to her apartment as she hung on his arm quivering, and with pallid face.

They met Freeda on the steps. A bare arm of huge proportions protruded from her hastily donned clothes. "Forgive me," said the giantess, "I slept after you sent me away, Miss Gloria."

Fletcher had some coffee served in the living room of Gloria's dainty little quarters, and shortly had her back in normal spirits. She did not wish to discuss the occurrence of the evening, and he did not hurt her by insisting on it. Finally he departed and Gloria called after him:

"If I send for you, come. If you wait to dress, I'll send Freeda to bring you."

Smiling, he sought his rooms. But when all alone in them he seriously looked out into the velvet night.

Between fresh, cool sheets he fell asleep. Exhausted but

undaunted, he still smiled. If Fate would thus so mightily jest with him, he would laugh too. His last thoughts were, would he be able to literally wear the other chap's shoes? He expected them to be placed out for him when he awoke. Another's clothes might fit passably, but another's shoes had their problems, and might not fit so well as the pumps he had worn at dinner.

4

HIS OTHER SELF

FLETCHER AWOKE ABOUT nine o'clock. His first impulse was to dive for the bathroom that he might not be late at the office. He put up one arm to ward off the advances of Belshasher, who was wont to leap up and lick his face about this time. Instead of Belshasher, he saw his valet enter.

"Do you wish to arise now, sir?"

"Yes," he announced, and he could hear his bath running. He bathed and, with the aid of the valet, was soon dressed. A pencil-striped suit practically fitted him. The shoes were full instead of tight, and he thanked his stars for that. The valet placed in his buttonhole a bud from the bouquet outside. He smiled his pleasure, went downstairs, and was about to start for a walk when Gloria joined him.

She was delightfully refreshed and wore a charming, simple little morning dress.

"Good morning, my dear," she greeted him. "I could not breakfast until you arose."

She kissed his cheek, and together they went in. No reference was made to the night before, and, enthralled by her charming little mannerisms, he dallied over his breakfast for half an hour, an amount of time which he had not spent that way in all his days.

A clock chimed ten. In olden times when the alarm sounded in the firemen company's house the horses pranced and were nervous to go and firemen dressed automatically without any thought to it at all. Before the clock struck Fletcher was about the most languid and contented young man imaginable. The first chime rang; his body became taut as if a current had passed through him.

Down in the Street, the prices were coming over. Force of habit and an overpowering sense of duty brought him out of his chair. His customers were making and losing money, and God alone knew where he was!

"Excuse me," he said, "very important!" There was preoccupied terseness about him that left an anxious expression on her face.

A few quick steps brought him into the library. First looking guardedly around him, he gave his office number in a low voice. At least, long practice had made him perfect in talking into a telephone so that others could not hear. The answer came back:

"Morton, Keene & Company."

"Mr. Morton, please. Fletcher speaking.

"Mr. Morton," he began, "this is Fletcher. I shall not be able to get in today, and maybe not for several days. Real business is in prospect. Give general quotations by phone today to Sigmond Van Mortimor, Cleborough, New York."

"Repeat that, please, Mr. Fletcher," said the astounded partner. Then he added: "Congratulations. I trust for your own sake that you are not joking with me."

"Never so serious in my life," he replied. "Explanations later. Have somebody give me quotations, please." Fletcher listened while they came over, intrusted his customers to the partners of the firm and hung up the receiver.

Gloria and he went riding. It was one thing he could do well, having come from a range country, where much of his equestrianship had been bareback. Gloria marveled at this, not understanding his prowess.

All nature seemed to be striving to paint a beautiful picture while they rode through bridle paths which were deep woodland trails.

They rode all morning, and he carefully led over the entire estate; but whenever he approached the deeply wooded valley which lay below the terrace Gloria tried to keep him from riding through it.

"I am superstitious," she said piteously, "about your going through the valley. You can guess the reason!"

In deference to her he did not insist, but he succeeded in gaining an eminence which commanded a better view of the lower part of the valley than the terrace afforded. From there he saw a sort of lodge, or bungalow, which aroused his strongest curiosity. Could that be the habitat of this ghoulish creature, or sound, or whatever it was? Only Gloria's entreaties took him back to the house.

"MR. MORTON, OF Morton, Keene & Company, brokers, on the phone, sir," Parkins gravely announced. "They have been calling you for some time."

Fletcher picked up the instrument.

"Mr. Van Mortimor," the voice came, "this is Morton, of Morton, Keene & Company. Our Mr. Fletcher, who is detained out of the office, informed us that you wished general quotations. May I personally give them to you?"

"Yes, thank you," said Fletcher. There was a moment's

hesitation at the other end, as though Morton, one of the shrewdest room traders in the Street, smelled a mouse upon hearing Fletcher's crisp and familiar voice.

Then the quotations came. As Morton finished, trying with his usual canniness to hear a little more of this suspicious voice, he said:

"Mr. Van Mortimor, we are indeed pleased that you should call upon us through our Mr. Fletcher. May we ask you at first hand what you think of conditions abroad, since your opinion will help us in rendering you such service as you may require?"

Such a question, in any way that Fletcher could answer it, required more than monosyllables.

He said coldly: "Sorry, Mr. Morton, I am really out of touch with business conditions. I am afraid my opinion is of no value."

"Now, Mr. Van Mortimor, would you not say that there is a good deal of hypocrisy in what we get over here from the other side?"

"Mr. Morton," said Fletcher, "I am not interested in your opinions. Is that sufficiently clear?"

"Certainly, sir," apologized old Morton. "We are brokers, not prophets, and glad to serve you. I trust I did not offend you, Mr. Van Mortimor?"

Old Morton was playing safe on big business, but it was obvious that he thought it queer how similar this voice and Fletcher's were.

"No. I appreciate your interest, but I will not be quoted," answered Fletcher as he hung up the telephone and turned to the door.

On the threshold stood Gloria, her face wreathed in

smiles as though she had made some pleasantly surprising discovery about this brother.

"You are interested in business," she exclaimed, "aren't you? I know now why you left breakfast so hurriedly. How remarkable! You must really like it from the way you act."

"Dear," he said, "I should like business if I had a million dollars"—then, as he saw a puzzled look on her face, he waved his hand and added, quickly—"to invest every minute."

"You make me very happy," she answered. "I can only conceive of a real man doing some kind of useful work. You are not in the least like what I have always heard you were."

IT WAS A narrow escape from the consequences of his momentary slip of the tongue. Every moment he feared that the bubble would break, but until it did he decided he had just as well play the game.

After luncheon with Gloria he spent the afternoon with his new secretary, Floyd. This young chap was a wizard for figures. In concise statements Fletcher had the enormous ramifications of the Van Mortimor fortune laid at his finger-tips. With Fletcher's financial knowledge he got an excellent understanding of the condition of everything; but he did not express opinions, lest his own secretary should wonder at his insight. At the conclusion of the conference he merely said casually:

"Prepare for me a statement of how many human beings work for enterprises in which there is Van Mortimor control."

The secretary had innumerable appointments and conferences to press on his attention. These Fletcher waved aside temporarily.

Altogether he was having a glorious week-end. The enormous castlelike house, its spacious grounds, the feeling of grandeur which permeated everything about him, and the adorable little Gloria, were all so charming that Fletcher's over-acute sensibilities were highly satisfied. He was happy, delighted, no matter what horror might be lurking in the valley below them.

The evening passed quickly with his soul-satisfying companion. Some subtle sense told Fletcher not to stay up too late with Gloria. He succeeded in getting her to retire early, and it must have appeased the voice below, for they were undisturbed. Sunday morning broke bright and clear upon two gay young people who had slept serenely in the very shadow of some dread which they did not understand.

At last he came to the conclusion that there was no use in delving into that weird business anyhow. If he did get into the vicinity of the thing, it would only terrify Gloria. Rather than pain her, why not just let the situation solve itself. Naturally, however, he would be ever alert to protect her.

One evening, much to their mutual regret, Gloria went out after dinner, having previously accepted an invitation. She begged him to come along, since he would have been welcomed, but he pleaded fatigue, for he did not wish to risk a public appearance.

FLETCHER KNEW NOT how long he had slept, for it had been particularly sound and deep. The isolation of the house in its vast estate gave a singular quietness during the night.

Fletcher felt himself suddenly awakened by that plaintive sound of the first evening. It was very near. Involuntarily a cold chill ran over him. He felt that he was probably all alone in that part of the house and about to face something supernatural. Just under his window was the roof of a stone portico which had been made into a little garden. Steps ran up to it from the end of the east terrace which overlooked the unexplored valley. All this flashed through his mind as he lay in bed as if paralyzed.

The sound now came low and soft, but, oh, so weirdly! He knew it was the unearthliness of it alone which had awakened him, for it was so low that surely no one else could hear it. Evidently this was a personal message. He wanted to rush to the window, but he could not move.

On second thought, he remembered how the butler had urged him in out of the light the first night, and realized that it would have been very foolish to have exposed himself in the window. He thought it better to lie still and watch the window in the hope that the thing would appear within his vision, so that he might get some idea of what he was up against.

On came the anguish-stricken notes, nearer and nearer, as though it were groping along the side of the house to his window. Transfixed by fear and unable to move so much as his head, he stared through the casement at the portico. A stone balustrade ran along the edge of it, and the low, waning moon threw gray shadows between the little columns of the balustrade.

By the setting of the moon he judged it must be close after midnight and about the hour when this ghoul had called before. Why did not the marauder come within his vision?

The anguish-laden notes came low, but clear, yet they

seemed to hesitate at the verge of the window. Was this fiend or incarnate voice waiting for the moon to set and leave the world in pitch darkness ere it entered? Was it trying to fill his soul with horror in the interim? His thoughts raced along with this ghastly accompaniment, this dying swan song of unearthly desire.

Some details in the room suddenly stood out vividly in his mind. A chair was sitting by his bed facing him as though something had been sitting in it studying him, probably a little earlier in the full moonlight. The window was wide open from the bottom, and he would have sworn it had been half up from the bottom and half down from the top.

Something had been in the room. For what was it waiting? Why did it now hesitate?

The suspense was as horrifying as if a hangman were trifling with the gallows after the signal had been given to spring it. The haunting notes came fuller, and then something moved silently full into the window and stopped just in front of the sill as if it would send its plaintive song straight through as it peered in.

The moonlight came a little brighter, and the thing did not draw back as Fletcher had anticipated it would. Instead, it looked searchingly in, as if this strange, ghastly thing sought something by the moonlight, or, having finished its morbid errand, turned back for one last look before departing.

The moon must have been behind a cloud, for now the gray light flooded the stone roof, and Fletcher looked full into a pale face, a blanched and ghostly face—but, for all that, his very own!

His heart seemed to stop, he could not breathe. He was looking into his own face, which was peering at him through the upper sashes of the window. He did not move a muscle—he could not. This could not be a reflection, for the lips of the apparition were puckered up. Now it was whistling that weird tune again; Fletcher was motionless, and helplessly aghast.

FOR A BRIEF moment while he faced the apparition, he felt himself dead. This, his physical body, was dead in bed, so that he had no physical use of it; but it still retained the faculty of perceiving what went on about it. To the strange accompaniment of the weird notes, he was perceiving himself disentangled from his present body and clinging to the window, taking one last look at his old mortal body before his tormented soul departed for parts unknown.

He wondered if he had been murdered as he slept and that this was his soul really departing to that bourne from which no traveler returns. He had no physical power to investigate whether there was any wound on his still form. Pie could not move; he could only stare at himself there at the window, the face blanched and agonized, but unmistakably his own. It was turning away from the window now.

He could see himself silently crossing the portico. That music of the dead—nay, dirge of the more-than-dead, was growing fainter. It was himself leaving, his very stride; and *this apparition wore his clothes*, the very clothes that he had worn to this house on that memorable day.

Strange sweet thoughts flitted through his mind. At least he was going in his own clothes. Even if he were dead, he had died in his own raiment and not as an impostor.

There was something consoling about being honest in death.

The weird, ghastly music was nearly hushed; no such supernatural funeral chant had mortal ever had before, and the spirit was stopping by the balustrade again to look back.

His great climax of happiness with Gloria had ended in sudden tragedy. The dismal end was tragic and quick as the joy had been great and sudden—such were the jaws of compensation in life. Needs be that he would once more look back at the scene where he had lived the sensations of an ordinary mortal's life all in two days and now he must pay as quickly with the penalty of his life.

The moon shone full on the figure by the balustrade. How often he had worn that old suit, how he had romped with his dog and cats in it; what simple pleasures with his friends he had wearing it down town. Those with whom he had lived in it came back to him, the simple life that he might have lived on for his full span, if he in these same clothes had not been led out of his old surroundings into the glorious adventure now so tragically closing.

"Where do I go now?" he pondered, for he had lost all sense of feeling. His spectral body was leaving the balustrade outside and gradually fading away. "I can scarcely see myself any longer," he thought, "so it is to nothingness—oblivion."

He could not see; darkness engulfed him, and he knew no more.

When he awoke about nine o'clock in the morning, he found himself lying identically in the position he had occupied earlier in the night. His gaze in a sort of a fascinated way went through the window. The lower sash was fully up, and he knew it had not been left that way by his hands on retiring.

He was tremendously happy that he could see, but a horror seized him that if he attempted to move he would find himself incapable of action as in the night. A delightful breeze through the trees outside wafted into the room the scent of blossoms from the garden. His servant came in and adjusted the curtains at the window and seeing Fletcher looking at him mutely, asked:

"Do you wish to arise now, sir?"

Beyond his fondest hopes he could also hear; three of his senses had returned.

"Yes, indeed," he said joyfully.

Then as the servant stepped into the bath, he pinched himself, with the results most to be desired. Hurriedly examining his body he found he was not injured in any way. But beside the bed sat the telltale chair, and on the floor was a small envelope, empty and without any markings.

Arising and stretching his limbs, inordinately happy to feel life pulsating through his lithe young self and deeply thankful for each breath of the pure invigorating country air, he felt that he had miraculously escaped death.

He bent over and picked up the little white envelope beside the chair. It gave off a pungent perfume, and on holding it close to his nostrils he experienced a most nauseating sensation. He dropped it with a shudder, and went to his bath.

WHILE FLETCHER DRESSED he dismissed his servant on an errand. From among his effects he hastily took the key to the chiffonier drawer where he had locked up the clothes worn on his arrival. Fletcher opened the drawer quickly and found it empty; all of his personal clothes and effects were gone. His own wallet, his watch, some personal papers which had been carried by him—in short every possible vestige of identification of his former self— had vanished. Some of these things he had worn in Van Mortimor's clothes for fear of detection by the servants, but they, too, were missing.

"Who am I now, anyhow?" pondered Fletcher as he descended the stairway. "If some unknown authority is depriving me of my former identity and conniving to make me Sigmond Van Mortimor, surely this can only be with the assent of Van Mortimor, and if I find that he is robbing me of my identity and placing me in his position, it is only a fair exchange that I become Van Mortimor with a vengeance! I'll feel out my way a little farther today; and if I am actually made Van Mortimor, I'll be a real one, and the world will know it!"

Gloria joined him at breakfast, charmingly fresh and delightful.

"Gloria," he cheerfully smiled, "I am getting restless. I think I should like to get to work. Would you care to go into town with me a few days?"

She was overjoyed at the prospect of being with him, and he had decided that in feeling out the strength of his position, he had better keep as many anchors to windward as possible, by having around him the most important allies with whom he passed muster as Van Mortimor.

"You know I want to do that," she said laughingly. "Indeed, you will have to put up with having me near you at all times."

Nothing could have suited his plans better. The more

important servants were sent to her Park Avenue apartment, at her suggestion, instead of opening his town house at—Fifth Avenue. Floyd, the secretary, was instructed to meet him at the apartment, and Gloria and Fletcher drove down together.

"Now we set out to conquer!" she exclaimed as they stepped into the car.

How little did she realize the truth of that, thought Fletcher.

They swept into Manhattan at lunch time and ate publicly at the Alexandrian. Word quickly spread around.

People bowed to Gloria, who recognized their greeting with a slight inclination of her head. Occasionally she smiled an invitation to some one whom she presented to Fletcher. In this way he met a severely dressed old lady, two blase young men, and a charming young lady who was lunching with a distinguished foreigner.

"Only those," she said *sotto voce*, "whom we really care to know."

They were all playing the game. He noticed a little cold glint in Gloria's eyes as she glanced over the crowd. A few spoke to her when she did not seem to see. Fletcher realized that Gloria was now Miss Van Mortimor; although occasionally he caught a sly little smile when her face was turned so that only he could see. How superficial and cold this girl could be!

After lunch he drove Gloria to the Park Avenue address, and without entering excused himself for the afternoon, pleading that he wished to familiarize himself with the old city. Picking up his secretary, they fared forth.

THE DAY BEFORE, Edmond Fletcher had superficially

informed himself with the life he was supposed to live downtown, and now, having given up the safe escort of his sister, whose introduction surely could not be doubted, he drove to the National Club, the most exclusive one in town, accompanied only by Floyd. As he was riding there, he asked innumerable but guarded questions, which this accommodating fellow painstakingly answered and in detail; for since his employer ventured no opinions, Floyd presumed Mr. Van Mortimor had only the faintest conception of business.

Several times Fletcher caught veiled suggestions in some of the replies which might lead to feathering the secretary's nest. This, thought Fletcher, was a perfectly natural trend in human nature, especially considering the character of the man the secretary was supposed to be serving. Incidentally, a way occurred to him of handling this fellow's natural avarice, for he really wished to keep Floyd on account of his quick grasp of affairs and his veritable genius in accounting.

They entered the National Club. Fletcher merely indicated the register to Floyd who signed: "Sigmond Van Mortimor."

He knew that he had been elected to this and other clubs in his absence. Several governors of the club and old friends of Van Mortimor's father introduced themselves to him or were presented. He was careful in his remarks and only carried on the lightest type of pleasant, mutually respectful conversation. This endeared him to the old chaps who were ultra-conservative.

He noticed however, one tall gentleman of distinguished appearance, with a gray shock of hair and a professional Vandyke beard, who seemed to be watching him intently.

Something intuitively told Fletcher that this man was too much concerned over him. Otherwise, everything was proceeding beautifully. His plan was merely to present himself quietly but openly and see if he could be accepted.

From the National they drifted on to the Polo and Racquet Club, where they went through about the same formulae, but Fletcher got away from here as quickly as he gracefully could.

This was a younger set of men who insisted on discussing sports, even European sports rather than none, and he did not wish to feign too much indifference. Also they had been followed by the distinguished gray-haired gentleman of the National Club. Fletcher decided now that this fellow would absolutely bear watching.

As they left, an hour or so later, Fletcher bade the chauffeur stop on a pretext that he wished to look in a shop window. As the gray-headed man emerged from the club, Fletcher went directly up to him and, trying to put it as politely as he could, demanded:

"I do trust you will not misunderstand my concern in inquiring why you have been following me. May I ask for an explanation?"

"Certainly," smiled the stranger. "I am greatly interested in you. Allow me to introduce myself: I am Dr. Wendell Bates, the Van Mortimor family physician. The fact is, I am supposed to have brought you into the world, but I haven't seen you since you were about fourteen. No wonder you didn't remember me!"

The words "supposed to have brought you into the world" gave Fletcher a start. That was a point on which a physician ought to speak positively. If the man was sure of Sigmond's identity, why did he happen to use the word "suppose?"

Fletcher's mind began to work quickly. Here was a clew to something if he could only trace it. Why did this man follow him? Surely not out of idle curiosity. With this in mind he answered:

"This is indeed fortunate. Only today I was thinking that I should like to consult you."

"That will be a pleasure," said the doctor. "My offices are just around the corner. Would you care to come with me now?"

"Certainly," agreed Fletcher, and he indicated to the chauffeur that they were to follow him with the car.

FLETCHER WAS PARTICULARLY on the alert. He was convinced this doctor knew something. Going up on the elevator he fenced carefully with a very polite but meaningless conversation. With an open avowal—that must never be made to any one but the principals—he wished to convey that he knew the doctor had some knowledge about him and elicit from the doctor some sign as to whether he was friend or foe.

They went into the consultation room and Fletcher stripped off his coat and shirt for a physical examination. The suave physician began an examination in a perfunctory way. All this time Fletcher watched him intently for some sign of suspicion about his identity. None came.

"Am I doing all right?" asked Fletcher casually. It was just a simple question that any one under examination might ask; and also it was the natural question from a blind pawn to his principal, or from one in doubt asking guidance from one in a position to give it.

"Nicely," answered the physician, just as noncommittally without the slightest noticeable added meaning.

Yet Fletcher could not help but believe the physician knew something about him. He decided on a broadside question.

"Doctor," he said, "the duties that I am about to take up will be quite extensive—possibly a little wearing on just one human being! Will you please advise me how I am to live?"

"Young man," said the doctor, as he looked him fully in the eyes, and it seemed that his heart was now in his words, "great things depend on you. Just be your natural self, above all be natural. Much more than I can tell you depends on it. Keep your mind clear above all things."

After this oracular advice, which Fletcher seemed to believe was given sincerely, he passed down into the street, reflecting that the doctor was a pretty good old chap, and wondering whether his interest in him was other than professional, lie looked in his—or, more exactly, Van Mortimor's—wallet, and found money, crisp American bank notes. Some little money would be necessary for what lie had in mind, and the paradoxical idea had just come to him that with all of his wealth, he might not have a cent in his pocket.

Driving to the Forty-First Street entrance of a building on Lexington Avenue, he directed his secretary and the car to wait for him, saying he would be inside some time, he passed through the lobby of the building to the Forty-Second Street entrance where he knew there was a subway station. He took the subway and in a few moments stood in front of the building in which was his little bachelor apartment. Realizing that he had no keys he rang for the janitress, Mrs. Kelly.

"Mrs. Kelly," he explained, "I have lost my keys. Would you lend me your key, please?"

"Sure," she said. "Do you think you left them inside or did you just this minute lose them?"

"No," he answered, "I am certain I didn't do either."

"For the love of Mike!" she gasped. "How have you been getting in and out today? I saw you several times."

Fletcher kept his face under control.

"Where are the dog and cats?" he asked anxiously.

"Up in the apartment," she avowed, both hands upon her hips.

Getting Mrs. Kelly's passkey, he took the steps several at a bound.

AS HE APPROACHED his door, he heard a low dismal bark or moan. Belshasher was whining in a pitiful sort of way.

"Here is where I find out something about my other self," Fletcher reasoned as he noiselessly used the key and carefully closed the door behind him. He didn't want anything to rush by him and out.

His rooms were very dark. It rather nonplused him to find all the curtains drawn.

He waited awhile, his back to the door, for Belshasher to run to him as he knew he could not enter the apartment without the big dog knowing it and greeting him.

Instead, there only came the low but plaintive howl of the dog, seemingly from back in the bedroom. A feeling of horror passed over him. He knew that sound. Out in desolate countries he had heard a dog howl in that manner when some one was dead, and it usually was the dog's master. A creepy feeling spread to his fingers and toes. Was Belshasher already mourning him?

It connected up only too sinisterly with his nightmare of the night before. Was it a warning to go no further with this high-handed adventure in which he was so wildly engaged? Steeling himself to confront the horrible unknown, he advanced cautiously down the hallway, and peered through the portieres, into his living room.

A strange sight met his eyes. There was a black rug on the floor, how black only he knew from trying to keep it clean, but it never had looked so weird as now, for near the center of it was just one murky splotch of sunlight shining through an aperture in the window curtain. Stretched out stiff and stark in the patch of light lay Celeste, apparently dead.

Across the patch of light slowly came Aphrodite placing each foot with measured funereal tread. From a corner gleamed softly two dull lights, which he took to be Fatima's eyes. They moved in dizzy solemn circles. The low, pitiful howl of Belshasher came dismally from the bedroom.

BELSHASHER'S KEENING SET Fletcher's teeth on edge, and a nausea was seizing him. He detected a peculiar odor in the room, such as that of crushed peach pits. He must get to the door or window; he felt about to faint.

Marshalling all the strength that he could possibly command, he lunged for the window, hit it with a bump, and raised it somehow. He had stepped on one of the cats, but she made no sound, although he must have hurt her. Filling his lungs with fresh air he turned back into the room and opened the curtains. He feared an attack and braced himself for it, but nothing sprang at him. Instead an unnatural sight swam into his view.

The cats were walking about with stately tread oblivious of their surroundings, with the melancholy accompaniment of Belshasher's weird howl. They walked here and there in a mystic and spectral saraband, each foot placed carefully and slowly and then withdrawn heavily, as though it stuck to the floor.

Passing through between the cats, which paid no attention to him, he looked into the bedroom. He must find out what was making Belshasher howl so dismally. Reaching into the room carefully he pulled the shade and it snapped up.

The big dog was huddled in the corner, his back arched and bristling. Both eyes were closed as if he were dreaming some horrible thing, and he continued to emit the mournful sound in the sunlight. Fletcher called to him, but he did not awake or show any signs of recognition. He feared that his pets had all gone mad, so he did not touch them. Instead he opened the other windows, letting in as much air as possible.

After their antics had subsided somewhat he took a basin of cold water and threw some of it into Belshasher's face. The dog jumped, seemed to come out of his trance. He yawned deeply a few times and became playful, making a demonstration at seeing his master again. Belshasher was a little nervous and shaky, but he followed Fletcher back into the living room; and, as the cats were still walking around in their stately tread, he began to push them over with his nose. They offered no resistance, but just tumbled over like mechanical toys and lay still. Soon they were opening

They walked in a mystic and spectral saraband.

their red mouths with deep yawns, and something like normality was restored as Belshasher and the cats became more natural.

First Fletcher thought some one had tried to poison his pets, but if that were true, they would be sick, and they were not in the least ill now. They did not now show the least ill effects of their strange performances. To a superstitious person, it would have appeared that some occult force was at work. Fletcher did not like the subtlety of all this.

HE TOOK THE dog and cats, for which he had a genuine affection, down to Mrs. Kelly and asked her to keep them out of the apartment, as it would be more healthful for them in his absence. Then, retracing his steps to his apartment, he took all small things of value: an insurance policy, letters from various friends, a bank book, returned checks and, in short, a great number of little things that would serve to identify him, and these he made into a neat bundle. Putting this under his coat, he hailed a taxi and drove to the Merchants Safe-Deposit Vaults, where he asked the driver to wait.

Here he took a box in the name of Edmond Fletcher and deposited in it his neat bundle. When he was offered keys, he asked the official to keep them, saying, "I am rather absent-minded." They agreed to accept his signature for opening the box, and he signed signature cards in the presence of the official. He had a premonition that it was well to have proof of his real identity somewhere. Then he smiled and mumbled to himself: "Now, ghosts or dope, come get me if you can!"

Driving on to the Forty-Second Street entrance of the building from which he had taken the subway an hour earlier, he walked through to the opposite entrance. As he entered the building he noticed three men converge upon him and respectfully follow about fifteen feet to each side in the rear. As he neared the car, he saw his secretary nod to them. Two went away and the largest of the three, took the seat by the chauffeur.

"Who are these fellows?" asked Fletcher.

"They are detectives, sir," the secretary explained. "You left so suddenly that I only had time to find that you went in the subway and as you immediately stepped on a train as the doors were closing, I lost you."

"Is it necessary to have them follow me?" quizzed Fletcher.

"I should feel very badly, sir, if anything happened to you through any oversight on my part. I would particularly beg you not to go alone into the subway. Your picture is familiar to the worst characters in the city. Your life has been threatened repeatedly, sir."

"Oh!" ejaculated Fletcher as he speculated on unthought-of contingencies.

The car ran uptown a few blocks, and turned into New York's most gilded avenue. He glanced at his watch, an elegant thing, a thin and beautifully adorned time-piece of the "Pompadour" reign; no doubt once worn by some powdered dandy amid lace and silk at the castle of Versailles.

It was only about five o'clock. His movements had been hurried, for he dared not tarry long anywhere until he acclimated himself to his new condition of lordship.

He glanced out upon Park Avenue. Often he had passed along it enviously. Now he came to live upon it. The motor stopped. He passed through what might have been the nave of a cathedral, and the hushed lift conveyed him to the apartment. He could not have announced the floor, but that was wholly unnecessary. His arrival had been heralded over the house and, for that matter, the city. The elevator door opened silently, and the old butler was there to receive him with a deferential bow.

5

THE PLAYHOUSE

"**PERHAPS YOU WOULD** have preferred the old town house, sir. This is a fancy of Miss Gloria to whom we all bow, sir," Parkins said, smiling.

Fletcher started walking around at random to get a better insight into this elaborate apartment. He found a drawing-room, several living rooms, a library, a picture gallery, a large dining-room and several others he didn't explore, and then he noticed a stairway. Although the building was a large one, he knew by the staircase that it was a duplex apartment, or perhaps had more than two floors. Aimlessly he wandered up the stairs.

A mezzanine floor with doors opening off it ran around encircling a rotunda. He sank into a silken lounge and looked about him, letting his eyes gloat longingly on the quiet magnificence.

A dainty little French maid gracefully approached him, extravagantly curtsied and spoke in French.

"Miss Gloria wished to see you as soon as you came in. And Minnette," she touched her heart demurely, "is anxious to see you at any time."

He looked at her blankly.

"*Oui, monsieur?* she exclaimed, noting his confusion,

"I am very grateful for you sending me to America, but they have all been so kind to me, but where the heart is concerned, *voilà*. Only to see you occasionally—nothing more I ask."

"I do not seem to remember," stammered Fletcher. Minnette blushed furiously.

"Oh, *non, non, monsieur!*" she said, believing he did not wish to recognize her. "Pray do not fear me. My lips are sealed, it is my heart which is open. Miss Gloria is in her boudoir, sir."

She opened a door, opened it silently and very prettily, as though there were an art in opening doors, and passed down the steps, eyes straight ahead. Apparently I am a Don Juan, he pondered as he collected his wits and crossed the dainty threshold.

Mauve carpets and soft, luxurious draperies enhanced the loveliness of the interior. He was in a specious little lounge, with rooms leading off it. Gloria was sitting by a window.

She arose and, rushing up to him, kissed him daintily on the cheek.

"It is so good to have you. I saw you come in below," she began. "What a thrill there was in waiting for you. I wanted to be the first to see you when you entered here. How satisfying it is to have some one all my own who comes home to me! I have never had any one."

Fletcher felt the sincerity of her impetuous welcome and experienced keen delight at her interest in him, a joy which he could only dimly understand or recognize after his desultory, lonely life of the last few years.

"There could be no sweeter hearthstone," he said.

"You do like this place?" she asked, as she rang for tea.

"It is charming," he replied. "It is so like you."

SHE SMILED HER pleasure, started to speak, and then stopped as though she had some reason for hesitating. Fletcher did not press her. Long ago he had learned that the way to get a beautiful woman to talk is not by asking her questions. If they like you, and you do not prove inquisitive, they will tell you themselves what you wish to know.

She was very lovely in her little clinging tea gown, and he sat indolently watching her. Soon she spoke.

"I do not know why I should hesitate in telling you this. I suppose it is because in their fulfillment some plans take on such a beautiful hue, become so much lovelier than one could expect, that it gives me, almost, a feeling of reverence."

He knew not what to say, and scarcely were any words required. He just enjoyed looking at her and hoped that he might ever do so. She paused, and with her delicate hand gently touched his hair.

"I love this place because it is my little playhouse. I do not like the big old home on Fifth Avenue. It reminds me too much of the years of loneliness since I was a little girl when papa died. I had this place built just to suit me and my own dear brother I trusted.

"When you did come I wished to make you so contented that you would not wish to leave me again. This was to be my little playhouse. I should play at running our home, you know—keep house for my big brother, look after him and take care of him. To one brought up all alone there is a deep yearning to have some close relative or family which is all their own to love and cherish. I made this place just for that, and many times have I come here and day-dreamed of the time when you would make me so happy. Now I have been tremendously overpaid for all my longings."

She daintily poured tea and handed it to him. As he took it, she arose and went around to him. She hesitantly started to put her arms about him. Then, as he looked up at her, she caught his hands.

"Come see your rooms!" she cried, as if it were an excuse for not hugging him just then, and out the door of the little boudoir she led him. Down to an entrance in the center of the mezzanine floor they went.

Gloria opened it, and they stepped across the threshold. It was a square, cool, huge living room in harmonizing blues and browns. Luxurious overstuffed chairs and lustrous old woods gave it a comfortable appearance. To his right was a room containing a diminutive library, a desk and two telephones. As she saw him looking at the telephones she said:

"One is a private line and unlisted. I just had it put in for you today. You are so secretive at times, I imagined it would please you."

He smiled his appreciation at her thoughtfulness and he glanced into a most inviting bedroom and bath as they returned from the library to the living room.

HE FELT HER hand touch his. "You draw out the best there is in me," she said softly. "You say very little, and yet you inspire me to tell you everything even when I am reluctant to do so. You seem to understand me so thoroughly that I want to put my whole self in your confidence. It is wonderful to have such a splendid brother on whom you can rely.

"The morning after you came I arose early. I wanted to

sing and dance—maybe you heard me singing. Most of all, I wanted to get downstairs ahead of you to greet you again; not miss a minute of being with my big sweet brother."

A blush gradually crept over her face.

"Then I began to think of the playhouse down here, and I wanted you in it so badly, but I could not ask you to come. It seemed so bold, I don't know why. You brought me such happiness I wished to do something to delight you."

"You always delight me, dearest," he interposed.

"Oh, but I wanted to do something for you! There was nothing I could do for you up in the country; but if we came here, I could show you what I had prepared for you. But I could not ask you. It was too romantic. It seemed somehow that I had built a little cottage for my love and myself, and that entering it was a very sacred matter. Well, I must dress now," she said lightly and flitted out the door.

He sat down in an odd chair of rich velvet and contemplated his fortunate condition, while he looked at the panorama from the window. Each hour brought its new sensation. His secretary had told him many queer ways that newspaper feature writers had suggested of illustrating his income. One was, that if champagne were poured night and day continually, by relays of waiters, the expenditure would not materially affect his income. "And that would apply at prohibition prices," Floyd had said smilingly.

Practically anything the world offered was his for the mere asking. He tried to think of that which he most desired, and his thoughts from all directions focused on Gloria. All else seemed trivial.

But what about all this wealth and position which was being showered upon him? He was shrewd enough to know that you get nothing in this world without paying for it, no matter how much it may appear otherwise. What price would he have to pay? What would be the terms of this stupendous stewardship?

Very shortly it came to him that Gloria was dressing. He stepped into the dressing room, and there were his dinner clothes. His man came in silently, ever waiting an opportunity to be of service, and began to assist him. What a life this was!

He went down into the library. A few moments later Gloria entered. More than ever was she ravishingly lovely.

Her hair was done smoothly against her head, except here and there, where its natural waviness could not be confined. Her creamy bare arms and delicately curving breast flashed against a clinging silver gown.

Lithe and supple, her slender and erect little body poised on her dainty feet for one moment as she stood framed in the doorway. Here was something of the grand air, another Gloria scintillating in the high lights of life which converged upon her from every direction.

"Do you like me?" she asked coquettishly.

"You are incredibly beautiful," he gasped sincerely.

She reached up and kissed him, saying:

"You are a dear, my wonderful brother. All women love to be told that they are pretty, and you tell me so sweetly. It is so restful to be frank with you."

"No matter who you were, I would adore you," he said.

"Wonderful boy," she queried, "are you not getting too romantic?" She appeared slightly distressed. After a moment's hesitation she changed the topic. "You made me your mistress of your social affairs. Tonight we shall have dinner out. It is well for us to get accustomed to appearing together. I thought we should dine somewhere publicly and later go dancing. If it is agreeable we shall start now."

HE OFFERED HIS arm, and, taking his hat from Parkins, followed Gloria. They descended, and, walking under the marquee to the curb, stepped into the car. The car turned down town and soon stopped at a famous hotel which was known only by name to Fletcher. Their passage through the lobby occasioned quite a little comment. Eyes glanced politely from several directions when they neared the elevator.

They were to dine on the roof, and here Fletcher came face to face with Ralston, one of his best customers, who affected this hostelry occasionally. Miss Van Mortimor evidently had been pointed out at some time to Ralston, for he took a sharp look at her and Fletcher and floundered to one side as though he had been stabbed. Ralston made no attempt to greet him, much to Fletcher's relief.

They came out on the roof, gay in its bright awnings and fashionable atmosphere. The distinguished couple were seated at a very good table which was awaiting them. The head waiter called them Mr. and Miss Van Mortimor as though he had served them often. He marveled at the delicate compliment in ascertaining his name so quickly. Gloria thought he of course might know from previous visits. Fletcher's astuteness now came into play.

"Since you are in charge of my social life and we are so frank with each other," he said naively in an undertone, "you may indicate what it is your pleasure that we have for dinner. Just make your wishes known and I shall order accordingly."

She made suggestions for the complete dinner as he had hoped she would. Each course she mentioned he silently photographed on the menu before him with all the mental agility of a mountain goat sighting herbage.

The waiter came up and he ordered easily, having been forearmed. This had required no little finesse on his part and he had not attempted to look over the diners as yet. Now that the tedious part was over, he noticed that Gloria was occasionally recognizing acquaintances at other tables.

He glanced farther afield and half across the roof directly facing him was Morton, his boss!

Fletcher recognized that Morton had been doing a little private espionage on his big new prospect. He had probably had "Mr. Van Mortimor" shadowed all day!

But it was evident from Morton's perturbation that his mind was well confused. He leveled one look after another at Fletcher until he was evidently exasperated. Fletcher was careful to not look directly at him for fear the old broker would speak to him.

Fletcher could see out of the corner of his eye that Morton was talking to the head waiter, undoubtedly discussing him. Fletcher could understand how the broker was completely adrift. First he would have thought that it was Fletcher himself whom he saw dining with Miss Van Mortimor. Now, no doubt, he had just been authoritatively informed that the gentleman was Sigmond Van Mortimor himself. Morton would feel that Mr. Van Mortimor was a customer of the firm now, or any moment would be! Yet these two not only talked alike over the telephone; they looked alike so deucedly much so that Fletcher's employer wondered if he had been employing an angel unawares these several years and he was giving the matter of this particular gentleman dining at this particular time and place with his particular dinner companion most deliberate concern.

The music came like some dreamy melody across an expanse of lagoon water or so it seemed to Fletcher. Just then Gloria noticed a young man of rugged build and a lean contemplative expression who was sitting alone several tables distant. She and he smiled and nodded to each other. Then to Fletcher:

"That is Edward Brockton. You have no doubt noticed how the press continually speculates on what a wealthy couple we would be if we should marry. We are always a bit amused whenever we meet, because I suppose each of us thinks down in the heart how much more we need than the other's money. He is really worth while, however, and you should know him! I'll have the waiter call him over."

FLETCHER AROSE AS Gloria presented him and they grasped hands. As the men became better acquainted it was evident that a friendship was developing in the nature of a pleasant surprise at the number of things in which they were mutually interested.

The music struck up again and Brockton asked Gloria to dance. This pleased and hurt Fletcher at the same time. He wished to see her dancing to prepare him for the inevitable test which he must go through with her as the cynosure of all eyes. It was logical and as he would have wished it. But, too, he felt a poignant unwillingness to have any one else touching this charming creature. For several days she had seemed all his own!

At last Brockton and Gloria came back to the table and

after they were seated Fletcher glimpsed old Morton, who was leaving the roof, bearing down on him.

Morton had paid his check and ostensibly going to an exit, made his way over in Fletcher's vicinity. As he drew near he attempted to catch Fletcher's eye, but without success. Since he could not stand still very well without drawing attention upon himself, he decided on a bold move and walked directly up to speak to Fletcher. When he was two tables away a diner arose and blocked his path as if by accident.

"Excuse me," asked the politely rude gentleman, "did you wish to speak to some one?"

"Who are you?" complained Mr. Morton, purpling with annoyance at the disruption of his plan.

A lapel of the dinner suit moved slightly, just enough that the rather nettled broker could see the shield of a detective. Fletcher was taking in Morton's discomfiture, much to his own amusement, but he gave no sign of noticing the incident.

Half in fear that he was making an ass of himself, Morton scribbled something on one of his cards, and asked: "Would you kindly hand this to Mr. Van Mortimor?"

The detective beckoned to a waiter, and meantime sat down, virtually forcing Mr. Morton to join him at his table.

Fletcher looked at the bit of pasteboard. It read:

Mr. Van Mortimor:
    May I have the pleasure of speaking to you?

This, the canny broker had figured, would force the issue,

but the human enigma, without so much as glancing at Morton, penciled on the card:

> Sorry. I will have Mr. Fletcher bring you to see me some time.
>
>   S.V.M.

Fletcher then returned the card to the waiter. Morton took it and left, no doubt feeling he had done something foolish. Being so well acquainted with him, Fletcher knew that on the way down from the roof, Morton must have soliloquized, "They talk alike, they look alike," and glancing at the card, "by Jumping Jupiter they write alike!"

It would be beyond him. Yet he could not dare to question openly that the man he had just seen was Sigmond Van Mortimor. No detectives would ever have been hovering around Edmond Fletcher except on his trail, in Morton's estimation.

Brockton had gone after a cordial invitation to Fletcher to visit him. People who had any claim to social recognition were crowding upon them now to meet Sigmond Van Mortimor. Few of these Gloria acknowledged. She was as calculating in bestowing her favors as a merchant in the mart. There was something intoxicating to him in the open adulation from every side. Apparently he was well enough vouched for in high places. Morton and his kind were the ones Fletcher would have to watch.

Edmond asked Gloria to dance, after several more introductions had been made. The gay pretender did not dare put this off longer, much as he both desired and dreaded the privilege.

He was tall and slender, and had determined to dance naturally, come what might. But when he led Gloria Van Mortimor into that smartly sophisticated throng, he felt like Abraham Lincoln at his first ball. With acute apprehension he found his feet moving somehow.

Then Gloria looked up into his eyes as though he had touched some hidden spring in her. He forgot the many things which might have seriously disturbed him in so brilliant a fashionable world. They danced unconsciously as part of the rhythm of the music.

Gloria's eyes soon sought his face and took on a happy dreaminess which he did not believe even she could counterfeit!

IT WAS MUCH later when he bade her good night upon their arrival at the playhouse, and at once retired to his rooms, for he planned a big day on the morrow, his first business day.

Quickly undressing Fletcher stretched himself comfortably between the cool sheets. Looking out westward over the city he could see the sky illuminated by the myriad lights of Broadway. There they were, the millions of hard living denizens of the city and the country, doing their frenzied best to buy what they thought was pleasure and happiness under the bright lights.

He drifted off into slumber, but was shortly awakened by a light in his face. After he was conscious lie caught only a quick flash of it, but from the inclination he felt to rub his eyes, he believed it must have shone full upon him. Since he was soon wide awake, he walked over and looked out the window. It was probable that some searchlight playing over the city had caught him in its radius for he was sleeping at a considerable elevation. Directly across from him he thought he could see the dull glow of a cigarette in a darkened window in the building across the court from his bedroom. Perhaps some one else could not sleep.

Fletcher wandered about over his suite and marveled at the attention to detail and the consideration for his comfort which had been lavished on it. He considered himself rather familiar with the place by this time, but new features to suit his convenience quite frequently surprised him.

At the far corner of his bedroom was a door which was rather intriguing. He didn't think it was a closet, and yet he could not account for its presence. He had been opening closet doors and just curiously looking over his many possessions with which he was unfamiliar.

A key was in the door, but there was nothing unusual in this. He grasped the knob and opened the door. The light from behind him flowed over his shoulders and disclosed where the entrance led.

It was Gloria's bedroom, and there she lay, a vision in pink and cream, her head resting on her elbow among her thick dark tresses, a happy little smile playing over her face while she slept. He started to shut the door gently, but the light awakened the demure little maiden and she saw him. There was not the slightest fear as she drowsily called out:

"Don't run away, Sigmond, dear. Come in and talk to me if you are restless."

"Not for anything," he explained, "would I have disturbed you. I was just exploring my delightful quarters, and little did I guess what a surprise there was behind this door."

She pulled the coverlet slightly about her and turned on

a little night light which cast a soft glow over her pillow. Sitting up she answered:

"Come in. It is no surprise to me. I arranged this all so that you would ever be very near me. Isn't it nice to know that even in the late hours of the night we are so near each other? You are just through that door, my own sweet brother.

"Do you know, several times tonight I was tempted to open it and steal in to kiss you while you slept, simply tuck you in a little bit, or do some little thing for you. I just wanted to see you once more and know that you were perfectly comfortable before I slept. Something held me back. I couldn't say just what it was, for I really wished to come in very much."

He looked yearningly at her, lying there so innocently sweet and so expectantly waiting to be kissed good night. SOME PREMONITION OR instinct caused him to look over his shoulder. The shade and the window in his room, just behind him, were up. For an instant he reflected that he had better draw the curtain before entering Gloria's room, because her bed was directly in line with the window. He half turned to do so when he noticed a slight wave of disappointment creep into her expression, and then he stepped into her room, for he felt to draw the shade would be rather suggestive.

As he crossed the threshold a slight chill ran over him, for ever so faintly he sensed the low, weird cry of the blanched face. Gloria stretched out her arms, with all her impetuous nature, to kiss him, and the nearer he came the more plaintive rang the haunting sound within his ears. He bent over her and soft clinging arms infolded about him.

Such ecstasy to hug close to him the smooth, firm body of this transcendent girl, who colored all his thoughts.

For an instant he forgot everything but the immediately delicious present. What mattered anything on earth if such divine loveliness were within his actual grasp? He kissed her soft warm lips.

The weird notes of the haunting cry beat piercingly on his eardrums, congealing the very blood within his veins so that he stood immobile, unable to kiss her again even if he had dared to do so. She fell back in the bed and sobbed. Between sobs she quavered:

"Did you hear it just as you kissed me? It has followed us here."

Her words brought him partially out of the paralyzing fear which was settling upon him. Turning in the direction from which the warning seemed to come, he dashed for his window. As he faced around it grew fainter, and though he rushed to the window the sound had died out before he reached it.

Everything across the court was dark; nothing stirred in any direction. Retracing his steps to Gloria, the weird noise began as soon as he had reached her doorway. Running back to the window, he could hear or see nothing. Upon his entering her room again it came in a horrid tumult, and Gloria buried her head in the pillows from the dread thing.

"Where is Freeda?" he demanded hoarsely of her.

There came a mumbled reply as she pointed to a door at the end of the room. As he left her bedside, the cry subsided. He pounded on the door indicated, and Freeda loomed up in her nightclothes, hurrying without further instructions to Gloria's side.

When Fletcher hurried out of her bedroom the noise stopped suddenly. Throwing off his dressing gown and slippers he vaulted to the stone ledge outside his window, clad only in his pyjamas. He peered up and down the ledge, above and below it, and across to the other apartment building without discerning anything.

It was only a short distance to the corner of his building and, knowing that their apartment occupied the entire floor so that he would not disturb neighbors, he began stealthily to crawl along the narrow projection to see around the corner. Halfway along, his movement was arrested by a noise at the casement through which he had just emerged. Looking back, he saw the window gradually descending, as though some unseen hand was lowering it!

Returning as rapidly as he could, for he didn't dare be trapped outside, he found the window closed and he knew it was useless to try to raise it, for they locked automatically. In a warm summer night he stood shivering, poised on the dizzy ledge with nothing to grasp for safety; and yet the thing he most desired was one more look at his Nemesis.

A few moments, which seemed hours, he crouched there, fearful of an invisible attack, yet hoping to see something. Then the window was carefully opened and the trembling butler whispered:

"Mr. Sigmond, come in quickly out of that dangerous place, sir."

FLETCHER DID SO with alacrity. Shortly thereafter he received from Gloria a request to join her in a few minutes for coffee, which was being hastily served in the drawing-room of her suite. He shut the door leading to Gloria's bedroom. While he partially dressed and went to her rooms through the mezzanine hallway, he realized, rather nonplused, that he had found no explanation at all of the sinister phenomena.

Some sort of warning had come to him out of the air. Could it have been his conscience? The worst of devils are sometimes right within us.

Gloria had come out of her scare wonderfully. Her freshness was a constant quality, like the waters of a crystal fountain. You might disturb her deeply, but her natural self soon bubbled to the surface.

"I sent Parkins to get you, foolish boy. Do you think I want to lose my brother? Anyhow, what did you find?" Her question was put drearily as though she knew the answer.

"Nothing," he said.

A far-off look came into her eyes, and she spoke gently:

"Many people try to reach the other end of a rainbow because, to them, a pot of gold is there. Even though their pursuit is futile it is worth while, because they have fortune and happiness to seek." She searched his countenance thoughtfully before she spoke again, weighing her words:

"You must not chase rainbows, dear Sigmond, because we have nothing to gain. We start with the pot of gold, the reward is at this end of the lovely arc. Since we must be at the good end of the rainbow, you can guess what is at the other, so do not desire it. You have a hallucination that you can run down this marauder and thus put an end to my fear. That is just a mirage with further horror as its goal. You think you can just reach out and put your hand on this phantom physically, but I know you cannot—for I have seen it." Her voice was choking with emotion.

"Where?" he asked in astonishment, scarcely believing that his apparition had been visible to Gloria.

"Forgive me, my dear brother; it was very near you." She buried her head in her arms so that she would not have to look at him. "Very near—too near you."

He stammered in his confusion. "Gloria, do you not mean that you think this is all in my mind?"

"It can't all be in your mind," she replied, "for I have heard the awful wail too often, but I have seen you quite different from your true good self. There are things we cannot fathom. This thing is intangible, and even though it is closely bound up to you, it is too terrible for you to investigate it.

"Something dreadful may happen to you! You must leave well enough alone. I am so very happy now with you. In time this thing will wear away, but if you try to follow it I just know something horrible will befall you, and then what will I do?"

Fletcher knew not how to answer her words. Suddenly a strange idea broke fully upon her.

"I first heard it tonight when you kissed me and then again when you reentered the room. It subsided as you withdrew each time. Was it wrong for you to kiss me?"

"I don't know, my sweet little Gloria," he stated. "But if it was only the inner voice of our consciences, it certainly had a tremendous echo!"

They both laughed nervously.

"CAN IT BE that some malignant spirit," she continued, "some family skeleton, wishes to keep us apart? We have been separated so long. But let's not talk about it. It makes me shudder."

He would have liked to tell her about himself, but he did not dare in view of his promise and what she had just said. Sometime there would be an opportunity, no doubt, for him to confess the whole thing.

Again he retired. He had never believed in the supernatural, but there were very peculiar circumstances here. He could not doubt his own identity. He knew who he was, Edmond Fletcher. He knew every step that led up to his present status as far as Edmond Fletcher was concerned.

Even if one presumed that Sigmond Van Mortimor had not conspired to put him here, at least there had not been the slightest interference from the real Van Mortimor to Fletcher's assuming his name and place. The press had spread the news of his return and doings at home broadcast, so that wherever Van Mortimor was, he surely must know that some one was taking his place at home. From this Fletcher could only surmise that this much, at least, was agreeable to Van Mortimor.

If he were the steward intrusted with this great fortune he wanted to be a just one, ready to render an accounting at any time. Indeed he would be deeply thankful to his benefactor for this great opportunity and the acquaintance of the marvelous Gloria.

Sigmond Van Mortimor was at least acquiescent in Fletcher's imposture. However, there was one other possibility: the other contingency was that Sigmond Van Mortimor was dead. He really shuddered to think of that, so many ominous things bore it out. If he were dead, of course, Van Mortimor could not denounce Fletcher, and things might very easily have run along as they had.

Could it be that the ghost of Van Mortimor had come

back to haunt the wrong that was being done him, and was hovering over Gloria to protect her in this unique situation? To one who would, for a moment, accept the supernatural, the warnings at the country home, and particularly the distinct challenge tonight, growing louder as he drew near and diminishing as he withdrew from Gloria in her bedroom, would have been sufficient to establish a spiritual message.

Whatever this warning was, Fletcher could not argue with it. It was morally right and he was wrong to be in this innocent girl's room. To Van Mortimor dead or alive, as his benefactor, he would be true; and with this thought in mind he went to sleep.

6

THE ARENA OF BUSINESS

FLETCHER AROSE AT nine o'clock, feeling much better than he had expected after the night's experience. The problem of accidentally encountering his former acquaintances in the city, and particularly in the financial district, had given him some grave uneasiness. But his work was primarily financial, and the only place to establish himself was in the financial district.

He went down to breakfast. Gloria, never withholding her real interest and encouragement, had slipped into the seat opposite him before he had tasted his melon.

As he had come to expect, no mention was made of the previous night's occurrence, and Gloria was elated at the interest her brother was displaying in business. A servant brought the morning papers and handed them to him. Fletcher had laid them aside, Gloria asked petulantly, in the very loveliest of her pouting manners: "Aren't you going to read them while you eat?"

"No, dear," he said, "I'll look them over after I leave your cheering presence."

"But you must read them now," she protested. "In the pictures and fiction all business men read the paper at the breakfast table. They bolt their food and have a difficult time trying to do the two things at once, but they never stop reading the paper!"

"That is only because they don't have you at the table," he replied, as he gently kissed her hair, bade her good morning, and joined his secretary who was then waiting for him in the library.

Fletcher's shoulders were back, and the old spirit of the game was upon him. How great now the stakes! Only time could tell. Something in Fletcher's quick stride brought the secretary out of his chair instantly upon his appearance. Fletcher thought from the way his secretary arose that he would not have been surprised should he have heard Floyd's heels click together and have received a salute from him. Fine—such was the spirit of the employees which he would need.

"Where to?" asked the secretary.

"The Bank of the Western Hemisphere."

"They will not expect us, unless you permit me to phone, sir."

"So much the better. Come along," directed Fletcher.

Colston Floyd, the secretary, was having instilled within him a new respect and admiration for this quiet unassuming young man. This Mr. Van Mortimor had a snap to him like a twenty team whip. They settled back into the car, which turned through a side street, and glided down the avenue.

"FLOYD," FLETCHER SPOKE deliberately, as though he were pronouncing some judicial decision, firmly but after due consideration, "I am taking over today these great business interests, about which frankly I know very little. In the nature of things you may be of very great service to me, since it is necessary that men in my position have others of ability on whom they can absolutely depend to present conditions to them and to carry out their directions.

"My next few words will be on a very delicate subject which will never be mentioned to you again. This is man to man. Give me your absolute, unstinted loyalty in every word and act, which is something that no man can buy, and in return you will receive more than any one else can give you."

His hand went out, and Floyd grasped it.

"Now, Floyd," said Fletcher, "just between you and me, the wise old heads down in the street, I imagine, have me sized up as a soft young hothouse plant, who won't obtrude into the business game very much, a sort of flabby young mollycoddle who can be flattered and cajoled along, and who will leave things for them to run very much as they please. Under all the deference that they will pay me, isn't that so?"

Floyd gasped at this unexpected acumen and frankness. "It would seem probable."

"Well," replied Fletcher, "they may be right, so far as lack of ability is concerned, but they are due to receive the shock of their dear old hearts in other respects. Today I begin to take over the absolute management of everything my estate owns, and you are going to have a very active part in my affairs. How does this appeal to you?"

"Splendid!" enthusiastically exclaimed Floyd. "I think I shall get a great deal of personal satisfaction out of my work."

The Bank of the Western Hemisphere is so large that one does not look for it. He merely finds the block it covers and looks for entrances. If one should happen into this great bank with less than five thousand dollars, and with proper credentials ask to open an account, he would be courteously referred to a remote end of the floor which he would find was the Savings Bank Department. If he should just wander on out at the nearest exit, without depositing at all, nobody would notice it.

Floyd was beginning to feel the leadership of the suave and deliberate young man by his side, and moment by moment was becoming more enthused at being his lieutenant. The secretary led the way proudly through the main arch and across the great banking floor. The private policemen on the entire floor suddenly came to a standstill as if at attention upon the sight of Van Mortimor's bodyguard, which had been following closely.

At Fletcher's suggestion, Floyd led him into the somberly furnished offices of the widely known James Wilkerson, president of the institution.

Mr. Van Mortimor's name opened wide the door of the private office and those inside cut short their business and left.

Mr. Wilkerson sat beyond a great desk, a pale dynamic character. His Celtic features were hardened by steely eyes which bored into you as if he would first drill and explore the subject, even assay the findings, before doing business.

For once, Floyd felt no trepidation in the man's presence. Though he realized it was little known he already believed the stronger man of the two was this quiet young fellow behind him, his chief, to whom alone he was answerable. Half turning, the secretary stated:

"Mr. Van Mortimor, this is Mr. Wilkerson, the president of the bank."

WILKERSON AROSE.

"Mr. Van Mortimor, I am indeed delighted to have you call on me, and to have you visit the financial district."

"So am I," said Fletcher, "but I am afraid you will find this is more than a visit. I should thank you to assign a vacant office here for my use."

"It will be a pleasure to do that," smiled Mr. Wilkerson, and raising his voice slightly, he said: "Mr. Jones."

There entered a sleek man, about forty-five, whose sole business was ever to be present when needed and ever unobtrusively in the background when not of some service.

"Mr. Jones, prepare the private offices in the east wing for Mr. Van Mortimor, who will use them immediately until he can choose rooms which may be more to his personal taste."

Mr. Wilkerson looked quizzically at Fletcher, analyzing him to the best of his ability, dissecting the character of this very rich young man who expatriated himself and then came down here so much like a bolt out of the blue. He might be a little difficult to handle, but his looks read the contrary. "Clay in the molder's hands," his true thoughts ran along, the while he was outward suave and friendly.

"I shall look forward to having you here as much of your time as you can possibly give the institution. It will pleasantly recall to me my associations with your father when he was chairman of the board of this bank, and I know you may grow to be of great service to all of us."

"Mr. Wilkerson," said Fletcher, speaking calmly, and fully realizing the shock his words would convey, "there is an annual meeting of the stockholders for the election of officers next Tuesday, the twelfth.

"On that day I shall become the chairman of the board of directors of this institution, and in the meanwhile, I shall pass upon the merits of the officers who will be continued in office, including yourself. I might say, in justice to your incumbency, that I have no reason up to the present to resist your reelection."

Wilkerson's face went red, and then in a strained effort to be polite, he stammered: "But, Mr. Van Mortimor, you have not had an opportunity to learn the banking business. You cannot understand the purport of what you say are your intentions."

"If you are to remain the nominal head of this institution," calmly stated Fletcher, "your first obligation and loyalty is to the owner of the majority of the stock, which happens to be myself. If I am to have any doubt on this score, I may have to reconsider my original inclinations in your instance. Do you wish to continue? If so, you will, of course, carry out my policies in this bank."

"You took me off my feet, Mr. Van Mortimor," spoke Mr. Wilkerson, thinking hard and fast. "Of course, I have no other desire but to serve your interests."

"I am sorry to have startled you," smiled Fletcher. "I am very grateful to you for the efficient administration of the institution, but we must have no misunderstandings. Please believe that there is no personal ill feeling in my actions.

"I am sorry that I do not even know you. What I do know is that I understand your position, and I am being perfectly frank with you so as to dispel any illusions which you may have about the control of this bank. If you will have your man direct me to those offices you have so kindly put at my disposal, I'll get to work."

The president conducted Fletcher down to the east wing and into several rooms with high ceilings, out of which the files and departmental belongings of the last occupants were being hastily removed.

THEN THE BANKER apologized that several appointments were awaiting him and withdrew, very glad to remove himself for some serious contemplation of the situation. As soon as he could think coherently, he reflected: "Here is the devil to pay! Who could expect that lad to assert himself, and out of a clear sky take over the whole blooming bank. Before I could formulate any personal plans, he frankly and openly challenges any interference."

He sat chagrined and dumfounded. Then the hard, designing look somewhat faded from Wilkerson's face. Reminiscences crowded upon him. Before him swam a vision of the adamant old man, Phelps Van Mortimor, blustering ahead, countenancing absolutely no interference.

"Who says the character dies out? By gad, it's inherited! He's a real chip off the old block. At that, I'd rather follow the true spirit in the boy than have somewhere underfoot a white-livered insult to the grand old man."

Fletcher walked to the end of the suite, which was a large room constituting one of the corners of the building. He noted with pleasure that there were several exits without going through his suite.

Taking a seat at the large rosewood desk in the center of the room, he stated simply:

"This will be my private office. Now, Floyd, the next

one is yours. Step into it and close the door." The secretary did so.

"Mr. Floyd," he spoke, slightly raising his voice.

The door opened instantly and in came Floyd, advancing respectfully.

"Fine," said Fletcher. "It works perfectly. Now we are ready for big business. Funny isn't it?"

Noticing his secretary's strained look of doubt and indecision as to just how he should reply, Fletcher added: "When we are absolutely alone, just feel free to be your natural self." They laughed heartily as the tension was relieved.

"Now, old top, get several undersecretaries for me. Handpick them, and fill the office with help as our needs require. By the way, I am getting in a nice little playmate for you who will be my only other confidential man. His name is Bullard Bland, and if you and I ever run short of nerve he has quite a reserve supply on hand.

"You know, Floyd, I believe a gentleman can get anywhere he wishes in this business game if he has, at certain critical times, a good enough roughneck to help him along. Our little playfellow will be well qualified."

Fletcher looked about him appraisingly. All was well so far. Evidently, the president of the bank had capitulated. No suspicion of his true identity there.

Fletcher knew that to carry out his role, there must be no vacillating. The true Van Mortimor could be procrastination itself and vacillate as much as he wished, but not so with the understudy. He knew he must be a strong man. Wherever interference loomed, he must assert himself. At the slightest sign of opposition to his power, he must

attack—strike fairly, but straight and quickly, right from
the shoulder, and thus inspire fear, that greatest of all levers
in human endeavor, to work in his favor.

GRASPING HIS HAT, Fletcher opened one of the other
exits. It led him into the main hall. Retreating to the rear
of his large private room, he opened another door which,
to his pleasant surprise, led down a private stairway.

Crossing the street and ducking through a building
which he knew very well, he slipped into a telephone
booth, after having ascertained that booths on both sides
were empty.

"Fall 8960," he gave the operator.

As he expected, the operator rang a couple of minutes
before there was an answer.

"Hello?"

"Hello to yourself, Bullard. Here's a little message that
is going to wake you up thoroughly before noon and result
in your coming out of bed every morning."

"Hello, Edmond, what in the devil happened to you?"

"It's important that you forget that. Do exactly as I tell
you. Make yourself as presentable as possible and come
to see Sigmond Van Mortimor at the Bank of the Western Hemisphere at two o'clock. I've fixed it up and you'll
be cordially received. Can't tell you any more—in a hurry.
Good-by."

Another nickel dropped in the telephone, and he called
his office, through the bank. The pleasant, courteous voice
of a young lady answered him.

"Mr. Van Mortimor's office."

"Van Mortimor speaking, put Floyd on, please."

"Yes, sir. Permit me to say I am your phone operator.

Your switchboard and direct lines will be installed by one o'clock, and your number is Beaver 10. Mr. Floyd, sir."

"That is excellent, thank you. Hello, Floyd. Invite Wilkerson to join me for lunch at the Financiers Club. Phone me there if it is really inconvenient for him to come."

Turning into a great building, he shot skyward. The car door opened and he stepped into the Financiers Club. A few times he had dined there with a member incidental to some brokerage service which he was rendering, but he had eaten there more in the nature of conserving the member's time than as a guest. Now he came purely for effect and he did not worry much about being remembered.

Striding into the main dining room, the head waiter approached him.

"A table by a window," he ordered, as the captain started to speak.

The captain led him to a good table, slightly perplexed. This young man evidently belonged in the atmosphere, but he had to be careful. Hopefully he asked:

"Are you dining with some one?"

"Yes, I am expecting Mr. Wilkerson of the Western Hemisphere."

"Yes, indeed, sir. May I be of any further service, sir?"

"No, thank you," and Fletcher noticed that the captain had been called to the foyer.

Two strange, heavy-set gentlemen had just peered into the dining room. The young billionaire recognized them as in his own entourage. Shortly Wilkerson came puffing in, slightly red.

"You know," he said chuckling, "you young rascal, it is decidedly inconvenient for the president of the Western

Hemisphere to lunch on a moment's notice, but I couldn't pass up the opportunity to be the first to introduce you over here. By the way, am I to understand that you are going to take detailed active charge of the bank?"

"Oh, no!" replied Fletcher. "You and the other executives who draw salaries for doing that are going to execute the policies of the bank. I am just going to direct major policies."

As he had planned in advance, Fletcher was introduced in the club by Wilkerson, an undoubted sponsor, and he left with his luncheon companions knowing he was well established in the Financiers Club.

Striding back to the bank, old Wilkerson unconsciously found himself taking considerable pride in his young companion. Several times he detained him to present people they met. The old financier began to feel again the memorable days when the lad's father swayed the district. His step became more sprightly and he felt the more animated. It was really as though twenty years had been stripped from his life.

FLETCHER ENTERED HIS office. Here a magic change had come about. Standing in a pleasant reception room, through a half open door, a battery of stenographers were rhythmically pounding the keys. Through another door he could see an accounting department in full swing. He passed the office boy and stepped into his secretary's office, where several alert men arose and were presented by Floyd as new secretaries. After which his first secretary explained:

"We hope to present you daily summaries and weekly digests on all your enterprises. The system is now in operation."

"Excellent," declared Fletcher, passing into his office and seating himself at the large desk, by which a stock ticker buzzed cheerily for him. "So far, so good," he concluded. Swinging about in his chair, he slightly raised his voice.

"Mr. Floyd." The door opened and silently Floyd came to his side.

"Do you think we do this 'come hither stunt' in just the approved fashion?"

"Perfectly, sir," smiled the secretary.

"Human nature revels, you know, in the symbols of power," he sardonically stated. "Now we are ready for big business. Arrange appointments as quickly as you can for some partner in Alexander, Cromwell & Klaton, Attorneys, to call here; also Morton, of Morton, Keene & Company, brokers. Then in quick succession, have the presidents of all railroads, banks, and other institutions in which I am interested, present themselves here.

"Don't make it too harsh on those who find it inconvenient to come at once, but instantly put an operative on the trail of any one who isn't anxious to see me in these offices, and shadow his every movement, wherever he may be. Of course these measures are precautionary only."

Floyd, the secretary, who had been making notes in shorthand, respectfully withdrew, softly closing the door behind him. He moved reflectively and he was going over minutely everything that he had done since this harmless appearing but gimletlike intelligence had arrived in America. He was concentrating his mind in an attempt to marshal any suspicious circumstances which would indicate that he himself had already been checked up. As he called up one man after another in making the perfunctory

appointments, his mind raced along doubtfully scrutiniz-
ing his own conduct.

Finally Floyd opened up some personal papers which
had been carefully secreted, and in a fit of what he believed
profitable virtue, destroyed two options on advantageously
located real estate which had cost him a pretty penny.
Taking out his wallet he extracted and also destroyed quite
a large check which had come to him in absolute secrecy in
return for merely using a bit of favorable influence.

MEANWHILE IN THE reception room a large heavy set
man with a very bland and innocent face had appeared. It
was obvious that his clothes had been freshly pressed. He
had just hastily partaken of a combination breakfast and
luncheon at a porcelain-topped-table restaurant.

Due, no doubt, to his haste, his breakfast had only
consisted of a half of a melon, some cereal, four fried eggs,
potatoes, various side dishes, and three cups of coffee. This
gentleman had garnished the eggs so heavily with catsup
from a free bottle on the table that they had been scarcely
visible.

When he ate alone he always let his gastronomic tastes
run unchecked. Some of his more sensitive friends objected
so strenuously to this catsup practice that when dining in
company he felt obliged to curtail his natural taste somewhat. He had gulped down these several things rather
hurriedly, due to his curious haste to keep a two-o'clock
appointment, which was rather early for him to begin the
business day. At his leisure he would have had a better
appetite.

What on earth Sigmond Von Mortimor could desire of
him was beyond his horizon. The office boy was out at the

moment. The man sauntered to the window and glanced out. He peered carefully into the adjoining offices. Then, to occupy his mind, he nimbly estimated the floor space covered, and speculated on how he could move the business to another location to the owner's and his own mutual profit.

Returning to the reception room desk, he saw a book in which the boy kept a record of callers and miscellaneous messages. Carefully looking about and listening, he deftly glanced through the book. He had no ulterior motive, merely an uncontrollable curiosity forced him to do so.

His insatiable curiosity had led him into so many embarrassing situations that his experience had made him adept in getting out of them. When caught, such plausible excuses blandly flowed from his tongue that you could not believe your own eyes. Only many repetitions of strange acts could teach you not to discuss them at all with him, for if you did he would surely get the better of the argument. He was watchfully going over the contents of the record book when suddenly, behind him, he heard:

"You are Mr. Bullard Bland."

Though slightly surprised at being identified so readily, he retained presence of mind to drop a newspaper which he was carrying over the record book. As he turned about, with his hand he closed the book under the newspaper. Facing around he encountered the out-thrust hand of a very businesslike young man, who greeted him.

"My name is Floyd. I am Mr. Van Mortimor's secretary. Take Mr. Bland's name into Mr. Van Mortimer," he addressed the boy who had returned to his desk.

Bland, unobserved, pushed the paper with the book

under it into the position where he had found the book, and, not in the least perturbed, picked up his paper while Floyd was addressing the boy.

Floyd was somewhat surprised to see the book where it belonged, and closed. "Maybe Bland wasn't reading it at all," he mused. As soon as the boy could return, they were advancing into the inner office.

"Mr. Van Mortimor, Mr. Bland," announced the secretary as he quietly withdrew.

"Jumping Jehoshaphat," thought Bland, as he looked at Mr. Van Mortimor, who was idly letting the stock tape run through his fingers as he glanced at the quotations. The very image of Edmond Fletcher was before him.

Could this possibly be Edmond Fletcher? If so, he sat near the throne. Many had been the times when a few dollars had been legal tender between them, even quite a favor when passed from one to the other.

Though radically different in personal traits, Edmond Fletcher was the best friend he ever had, and he would trust him implicitly. Edmond Fletcher, thought Bland, always admired an artist whenever he found him in art or business, and openly professed that he, Bland himself, was truly and artistically distinguished for sheer nerve and chicanery.

"WELL," SPOKE THIS Mr. Van Mortimer, as he looked up from his desk and the tape, "I am indeed pleased to know you from the sterling qualities that my friend Mr. Fletcher attributes to you. Kindly sit here by the desk, where I can watch the tape while I talk to you."

Fletcher wanted to get Bland in a position where he could look at the tape part of the time, so as to hide his expressions, when necessary, in conversing.

Mr. Bland was comfortably seated. Turning quietly upon him, Fletcher began:

"As my friend Edmond says, 'Full many a flower is born to blush unseen.' But it is possible that your latent ability may, around here, find very vehement expression!"

Bland was completely perplexed. This young man looked identically like Edmond Fletcher, and had about the same voice. He spoke familiarly of Fletcher. But there was too vast a gap between Edmond Fletcher his friend and Sigmond Van Mortimor, one of the wealthiest men in the world! His mind simply could not bridge it. Anyhow it was more expedient to consider young Sigmond Von Mortimor to be himself as his secretary Floyd had done, and not to try any monkey business.

"My friend Mr. Fletcher phoned me this morning," Bland respectfully stated, "saying that you wished to see me. As I have implicit confidence in him I shall appreciate an opportunity to be of service."

"Mr. Bland," said Fletcher, "from the newspapers you are doubtless aware that I am just taking up the reins of business. I need a few unusually dependable men to help me run my business a little better than the average." He looked full in Bland's face and spoke seriously.

"In Edmund Fletcher I have found nearly all the ability I need to conduct this business in that way. He believes in you, which means that I do. You are offered one thousand dollars a month to start, and if you live up to my expectations there will be advancement for you.

"No further investigation of you is necessary, as I know all about you, even down to the fact that an hour ago you got out of bed and had your suit pressed, which is still warm upon you. You will note that everything is done thoroughly around here. Can you give me your services full-heartedly, and at once?"

Bland felt like answering with the question, "Can a duck swim?" But, realizing that he had better not deal in any merriment where so much was at stake, he simply gasped, "Yes, indeed!"

Fletcher extended his hand.

"You are now one of my confidential secretaries, who will report solely to me." Again he looked seriously with a deep appeal into Bland's countenance.

"Unusual loyalty is necessary. Keep in the strictest confidence what you learn around here, and do not discuss any opinions that you may have with any one but me." Reaching into his wallet, he handed Bland some large bills:

"Just a little advance to relieve you of any financial worry. Even though you may not understand what my plans are, may I always depend upon you? Will you and can you keep the faith?" Bland awkwardly grasped his extended hand.

"You bet I can!" he exclaimed feelingly.

"You are through for your first day," announced Fletcher. "Come in the morning when you feel like it. Just do as you please, but always let me know where I can reach you during business hours."

BLAND AROSE AND walked in a puzzled manner toward the door. Twice he turned and half opened his mouth to speak. Each time the inscrutable Van Mortimor had his eyes fixed on the tape which was flowing through his fingers.

He was absorbed in the prices on the little stream of

paper because he did not dare look at Bland again lest he disclose his true identity.

At the door, Bland turned and declared:

"This fellow Fletcher and I were pretty close to one another. We went through some rather tough places together and he never failed me. We got so that in ordinary conversation with others we could convey messages to one another and answer them without being understood. If he asked me to risk my life for him I could not refuse him. Your confidence in me and your resemblance to him inspires the same loyalty."

The door closed and Fletcher released his eyes from the message of the stock ticker. Good old Bland! With all his faults he stood out alone among a million. This would surely do for one day. Although two news services had flashed over their wires his advent into business, his stocks were closing firm. Bidding the office force good night, he descended to the street. As he stepped into the elevator, two plainclothes men came in and no one else was permitted to ride down in the same car with him. Getting into his motor, he turned his thoughts to home and Gloria.

When he entered the apartment, Gloria begged him to accompany her for tea with some friends at Meirre's. He delighted her by accepting, and as they went along he quickly sketched the day's business.

"You are my partner," he declared, "and everything must be agreeable to you."

She followed his recital, necessarily curtailed in some respects, with breathless interest, and was particularly excited over the forthcoming encounters with some of the railroad presidents whose families she knew personally.

"I forgot to tell you," she exclaimed as the car stopped. "We are having tea with the count about whom I told you, and a charming young lady. I'm sure she will prove interesting to you."

Count Rononotski and Myrtle Marbleton were in earnest conversation as they entered. Under no circumstances would Miss Marbleton have relished the count as a husband, for she was too familiar with the Continental conception of women, but she sincerely liked him and, as his friend, nothing would have pleased her more than to see him married to Gloria Van Mortimor and her millions.

Not that she was in any way sure that this could be effected, for Miss Van Mortimor was very attractive, outside of her wealth; yet Gloria was quite young and, Myrtle guessed, rather susceptible from the guarded and yet orphanlike way in which she had been reared. The dash and gallantry of the count had its appeal, not to mention his old world polish. Moreover, the woman who married the count would grace an authentic title which ran back to Charlemagne.

Myrtle understood the count perfectly, including his impetuous and sensitive nature, for he had proposed to her most ardently very shortly after they became acquainted.

As they came forward the count arose and bowed. Myrtle smiled her pleasure, which was redoubled by meeting Sigmond Van Mortimor under such fortunate circumstances.

After Fletcher was presented they sat down, with Myrtle on his right. In her he found the complete typification of impersonality. She could scarcely be blamed for her excessive artificiality, for she was merely the natural result of her environment.

AT MEIRRE'S YOU found the idle set. That small distracted mob who suffer from ennui. Most of its habitués have become purely impersonal—impersonal in that the family ties and qualities of loyalty and faithfulness which ordinarily distinguish and promote character in the individual have been broken so often that such sentiment is totally lacking. The majority of the young men and women are the offspring of divorced parents, not once discarded but many times.

What ordinary people take as permanent and serious—family ties, marriage, death and even births—are not touched upon seriously in their set. Such things are just incidental, for no attachments are stable. The backwash of all this is that one's social affairs are rather hectic, and Myrtle Marbleton only knew life as she had seen it.

She regarded love as a divine feeling, of course never to be denied because it was so rare. A sort of heavenly will-o'-the-wisp that came, but, according to experience, never lasted. But one could always take that in some way when it arose. In the meantime one must marry so well that she could not possibly lose by it when the inevitable reckoning came.

Though distinguished men appealed to her, wealth was the better balm in the inevitable dark days to come. On account of her own status the eligible men in point of wealth were few in her estimation. Her grandfather had made an enormous fortune in mining out West in the early days, and since the property was willed to her, she had the fortune and its accumulations.

But Sigmond Van Mortimor was truly desirable in this respect, and more than that, he was distinguished by birth.

She now sat intimately conversing with him. Here was a mate worthy of a golden Amazon. The count and Gloria were exchanging some polite inquiries across the other corner of the table.

"I suppose you find America rather stupid?" asked Myrtle, casting a very sympathetic look upon Fletcher.

"Why, no, I rather like it," smiled Fletcher. Her face, breast and arms pallid with powder rather appalled Fletcher at first. Myrtle used no rouge. Only a splash of crimson outlined her mouth. Her hair was drawn tightly against her head and it was a beautiful corn color. Her eyes were blue, deep and wide, made up with heavy mascara.

There was a certain feline beauty about her which first struck him forcibly, then grew upon him. He felt an air about her which said to him plainly: "I make myself up in this way because I like the supernatural. I should feel undressed without it." To accent her exotic voluptuousness, she wore a black silk gown which showed the contour of her body with any little movement.

As though she could almost understand his viewpoint about their native country, she pouted.

"It is so strange how New York grows on one. I always desire to be away until I am ever so far away. Then I wish suddenly to come back here. I have canceled trips in the Orient for no other reason than to hurry to New York. I can understand how you feel now, when you have been away so long. But do you know what I would do when I got here?"

"What would you do?" he asked politely.

"I would go away again somewhere, probably back

where, no doubt, I had just left. That is the trouble with me, I always want to be somewhere else. Like Baudelaire, I seek a blue dahlia or a black poppy. I do not like people who are contented. You, for instance, are discontented, aren't you?"

The sudden question rather startled Fletcher.

"On the contrary, I have every reason to be happy," he replied.

"That is just it: you have every reason to be happy, but you aren't! I thought it might be just America, but it isn't," she languidly affirmed. "Oh! All worthwhile people fight something. I merely fight ennui." She sighed; her hand ever so gently touched his upon the table and a dreamy look came into her melting eyes with a wan little smile. Her lips were slightly pursed up as though she were asking for a kiss. A strange thrill ran through him, and he felt the emotions of those medieval ascetics who had visions of unearthly infernal beauty—succubi and enchantresses.

He quickly glanced at Gloria, and to his horror she was gazing blankly at them.

"Certainly, my dear count," spoke up Gloria so that they both might hear. "You must call on me often in the city. I am sometimes a little lonely, particularly at this season in town."

COUNT RONONOTSKI WAS a handsome young fellow of about thirty, quite a little younger than the average noble-man who comes here. One could not help liking him. He was erect, showed military training in his aristocratic bear-ing, and was yet so pleasant and unassuming that you felt lie was truly descended from those to whom nobility had been unconscious second nature for centuries. He was a

Pole who had lived so long in Paris that he spoke with a French accent.

"Ah, *mademoiselle*," he cried, "you overwhelm me with pleasure! Only tomorrow afternoon will I phone asking your indulgence."

At last they arose to leave.

"Whenever you have the opportunity," languidly purred Myrtle, "I shall be very pleased to receive you, Mr. Van Mortimor. Interesting people are truly so rare!"

He thanked her graciously and they sought the car. As they turned out of sight, Gloria huddled up in the far corner of the seat and appeared engrossed in the scenery. Fletcher could feel her attitude as if by instinct.

"Let me tell you more about business," he parried.

"I do not care to hear it!"

"Why not, Gloria? Have I offended you?"

"That woman flirted with you!"

"I couldn't admit that," replied Fletcher. "But even if she did, would there be any great harm done if your brother paid your friend a little attention?"

There was no answer, but before they arrived home at their play house, he noticed her covertly glancing at him several times.

He went immediately to his rooms to dress. Hardly had he entered them than he received a radiogram:

SS. Levengaria.

Mr. Sigmond Van Mortimor:

—— Park Avenue,

New York City, U.S.A.

Arriving on the Levengaria Wednesday. We are ready to

confer with Dr. Bates.

DR. CARON BENSONHURST,

DR. RANDAU MARTEL,

DR. HENRI LANDEAU,

DR. JOHN MARTIN.

What could these four old world physicians want with him? He felt no little uneasiness. Medical men are most often the kindest of fellow's, but Fletcher had a horror of the profession. A mere physical examination was as far as he had ever voluntarily gone. But this smacked of surgery to him. Why were these specialists crossing the ocean? Had they treated him abroad? Did this, by any ghastly chance, have anything to do with Gloria's terrified and inexplicable remarks about his "queerness" when they had last been visited by the weird unearthly noise?

With many misgivings he showed Gloria the radiogram at dinner.

"Ah!" she cried hopefully. "You will be happy now. They will surely be able to help you."

It was not a comforting reply. Fletcher, who desired neither help nor any change in his status, winced.

"Dr. Bates to speak to you, sir, on the phone," announced Parkins.

Even as he went reluctantly to the phone, he guessed the doctor's purpose.

"Yes, Dr. Bates. Is it about the men on the Levengaria?"

"Quite so," came the physician's voice. "I have made arrangements to spend tomorrow in conference with them, which will give us time to go into the matter thoroughly.

Can you come down to my office to meet them, let us say day after tomorrow, at ten in the morning?"

"That will be—fine," muttered Fletcher. "Thank you." He hung up the receiver, no wiser and very definitely no happier than before.

7

HIS LURID PAST

ASSEMBLED IN THE offices of Dr. Wendell Bates, were four eminent physicians: Lord Caron Bensonhurst of London, Dr. Henri Landeau of Paris, Dr. Randau Martel of Vienna, and Dr. John Martin of Bombay. Dr. Bates had canceled all other engagements, and he greeted them most cordially.

After the usual courtesies of the introductions, Lord Bensonhurst became the speaker for the coterie and began:

"Dr. Bates, as you pointed out in calling this conference, since the age of fourteen, Sigmond Van Mortimor has been attended by one or another of us, so that our services make a complete history of his amazing case."

"Yes, indeed, and it is a pleasure to have you gentlemen here," said Dr. Bates.

"As it is important that we first discuss the unusual history of the case, I shall relate my experiences with the patient. Mr. Van Mortimor was put under my care when he was about fourteen years of age and attending the Dexter Academy at Highhampton. Even at this early age he had a great income at his command. His surviving parent, Phelps Van Mortimor, had just died and his guardian, Thomas Montfort, the eccentric New York clubman, now deceased,

*Van Mortimor's guests had arranged themselves
on cushions around the black marble floor.*

lavished money upon the youth, Sigmond, as America's young prince.

"Strange to say he caused no particular trouble at Dexter. There was one predominating point in his character. He only seemed really interested in those things in which he could excel all others.

"In English, for instance, he composed weird imaginative stories which, without quite offending, shocked and thrilled his masters. This delighted young Mortimor. Having the best of worldly possessions, he was not much concerned about the average thing; he always wished the superlative.

"Sigmond reminded me very strikingly of what I had read of Alexander the Great, for he, too, was an heir to an empire in a way, and somewhat of a prodigy. I often wondered what trend this strange young man's mind would take when he really came into his own.

"Having finished the course at Dexter he matriculated at

Christ College, Oxford. About this time he developed an inclination to be eccentric. Sigmond gave fantastic dinners and entertainments in which his talented friends collaborated with him. Some of them were quite spectacular, as it wasn't necessary to spare expense in producing anything.

"The first concern was occasioned by his attitude toward the World War. Even after America entered it, he was completely indifferent to patriotic sentiment which raged so high during those times. However, he expressed no opinions, did not make himself obnoxious, and in no way interfered with the patriotic activities of the American corporations in which he was such a large stockholder.

"Van Mortimor withdrew from the university about the time he was twenty-two years of age and went to Switzerland. Here in his lodge at St. Remo he lived until the armistice. Dr. Landeau visited him frequently at St. Remo and he will continue with his observations."

DR. LANDEAU BOWED.

"It is to say most *extraordinaire*, the case of this young man," he began.

"I saw Mr. Van Mortimor frequently, and we became very friendly, despite his opinion that physicians were just sublimated sanitary engineers, and that cures were only the result of nature striving to correct itself.

"Probably this was due to the fact that I have always been predominately a psychologist, treating the mind primarily. I think he liked me, too, because I originated the expression, 'A man is as his desire,' and established a school of thought founded on that principle.

"When I first met him at St. Remo he had gathered up the leading cubist artists from Berlin and Vienna. He felt that their mad design and violent splashes of color were a veritable discovery in a world burdened with such a monotony of conversational hue and shape.

"At the beginning he had the rarest of delicacies at his table, but this was not overdone, as he was in no sense a gourmand on mere food. Another cause for his not developing a great appetite was that he became an incessant cigarette smoker. He claimed that the cigarette was the true tobacco choice of a dilettante.

"He soon came to have only a cup of coffee for breakfast and scarcely more than a sandwich and a glass of something or other for lunch. 'I can show any one how to reduce,' he would say. 'Just smoke sixty cigarettes a day and you can't eat much. Consequently you will get thinner.'

"In some unfathomable way he succeeded in getting a powerful airplane in those war days, and late at night, when no one knew about it, he would have his pilot take him to some great height over Swiss territory and then at this dizzy altitude circle out over the warring countries. Needless to say I was very apprehensive of his safety.

"He held long and intimate conversations with me, for he really was profoundly concerned with the working of the mind which is my specialty.

"You see, gentlemen, this young man had had the best of all there is in the world, and anything he had never had was so easily obtainable at his command, that he was fast losing all interest in life. Continually he sought an incentive for interest in living and he had only met with disappointment. We who struggle for our daily bread, the necessities or luxuries of our life, as the case may be, cannot realize the monotony of a highly sensitive nature who had nothing at all for which to exert himself.

"One day, as I was dining with him in St. Remo at the Cliff House, this strange youth informed me that he believed in no reality save that of the senses.

" 'There is no truth or reason in religion,' he told me, 'and so its strongest converts become fanatics—religious fanatics, as they are properly called, and get untold happiness out of it. Religious fanaticism is a form of sensualism. I could never become a silly religious fanatic, a narrow little religious sensualist; but I could become a sensualist; that is a broad word and implies a lot. Life may not be over, and I may be very happy before I die and am lost in oblivion.'

"He beamed, happy as a child with a bright new toy, for ideas were really his playthings; his great wealth quickly translated his thoughts into realities if he wished it. I argued the wantonness of his inclinations, yet little did I guess how far they would carry him. His only answer was to say dramatically:

" 'I think my day has come!' And then he added sardonically: 'How would you like to follow me to Paris?'

"LIKE YOURSELF, LORD Bensonhurst, I could only follow him. I am a physician, not a disciplinarian. The war had been over some time, and Paris was dissipation-mad as France recovered from its grievous wounds. Most of its virile young men lay under the soil.

"Van Mortimor took apartments at the Ritz and a house befitting a prince on the Boulevard Martin. The hotel was used only as a formal address. He lived his remarkable life at the house on the boulevard. How well do I remember the mansion! The floors and woodwork were done in black, and its costly furnishings stood out against this background as jewels in a casket.

"He began to live the gay night life of Paris. He attended the theaters for no other purpose than to pick out interesting women who in some manner appealed to him. After obtaining their names, those were invited to his house; and they invariably came. Of course he had to be introduced to the more important night life favorites, but they soon vied among one another for his favor.

"Van Mortimor was ever a gentleman and the master of the situation. If a woman did not like him, there was no apparent emotion on his part; he did not pursue her, thanks to his theory that every woman could be duplicated in a more desirable person.

"Van Mortimor's cellar was stocked with rare wines and the best caterers in Paris were constantly in his employ. He gave dinners with a few close men friends as guests, and flocks of the most beautiful women in the city as both his guests and entertainers.

"I was often present at these affairs in a dual role. Mr. Van Mortimor wished me there because the services of a physician were likely to be required; and I personally endeavored to be with him as much as possible to guard his health.

"If Mohammed were living he would no doubt have considered some of these evenings a fitting representation of his paradise. In the house was a dancing room with a black marble floor. This had been polished to such smoothness that one could dance upon it without any apparent effort. The walls were hung with black silk and one wall was a perfect representation of that side of the room, but was actually a silk screen behind which the musicians played.

"There was no furniture, just rose velvet cushions scattered about on the floor for the audience. The light came evenly distributed in any color desired through a transparent ceiling. Have you ever seen pink young flesh dance against black marble?"

The other physicians were leaning forward deeply absorbed in this development.

"How do you account for these highly artistic but startling affairs being kept so quiet?" questioned Dr. Bates.

"The price of Mr. Van Mortimor's favor was absolute silence," explained Dr. Landeau. "He followed strict logic in this as in everything else. Men friends of the women were never admitted. The few close personal friends of Mr. Van Mortimor who were present did not wish publicity and the women were always mere playthings and feared to talk because they knew they would be ostracized from the house.

"Epicurean little dinners were served; the appetite was goaded with the most enticing of vintages at each course. Gowns were provided by him for all the women, and costumes for the dancers. And since all would expect to be too stupefied to leave, bedrooms were provided for all guests. The bedrooms for the women invariably had black silk sheets. The beauty which came there was ever seductively displayed. In short, he fast became a libertine. But I suppose this bores you—"

"NO," DR. BATES objected judiciously, "we should know as much as possible about this case. It certainly varies consid-

erably from my rather conventional family practice here,"
he smiled.

"My patients are so phlegmatic," spoke up Lord Bensonhurst. "I can scarcely conceive of an Englishman taking to
vice so delicately."

"A little of the spirit of India was there," ruminated Dr.
Martin with a drowsy look in his eyes.

"Yes, there was," went on Dr. Landeau. "I cautioned Van
Mortimor it might lead to the occult, but he only replied,
'What if it does? I wish thrills and will seek them wher-
ever I can.'

"After dining, all would repair to the *salon de danse* and
arraying themselves about the walls of the dancing room
on the cushions over the polished marble floor, the evening
would begin. Every conceivable liquor and vintage was at
command and passed freely.

"But it was an unwritten law of the establishment that
any one who showed the signs of offensive drunkenness
must withdraw. The penalty of the slightest infraction of
this rule was that they could not come again. But an amia-
ble and quiet drunk was welcome. Some of the agreeable
and gentle souls succeeded in being deep in their cups from
arrival to departure without losing the least of the festival.

"The full voluptuous appeal of nude bodies, the infinitely
more sensual refinements upon female nudity which lies in
semidress, and all the artifices and subtleties of feminine
allurements were brought to play upon this young man
that he might be thrilled."

"Excuse me, gentlemen," interrupted Dr. Martin, "I
suppose we forget our hunger on this case, but can't we eat
while Dr. Landeau talks? It is nearly three o'clock."

Good-naturedly laughing, they went over to a neigh-
boring restaurant, where, securing an isolated table, and
cautioning one another not to mention the young man's
name, Dr. Landeau resumed:

"For a short while he lived a high and joyous life. Since
I had no control over him I trusted that soon he would
become nauseated with all this courtesanship. But he
applied a certain amount of ironical reason to it which
worked wonders in sustaining the spirit of the whole thing.
He never gave a woman valuable gifts, and if one ever
became mercenary he dropped her instantly.

"He did not object in the least to parting with gifts as
he could so easily afford it, but he believed it a poor way
to try to hold a woman. Beautiful women love those who
gently discourage them and even mistreat them but withal
gently. His theory was that you must first interest them in
some way, be very understanding and sympathetic, and
then artfully give them some plausible reason why you do
not want them. Properly handled they would always be at
your beck and call.

"He offered a woman, for a few days or nights as suited
his pleasure, all the luxuries of wealth. Splendid exotic
amusement, the best of dress, food and wine, the utmost
realization of luxury for the time she visited him. It was
something rare to these women to know that they could
drop in for a little of this sort of thing.

"ABLY GENERATED, THIS life continued under its own
momentum for a couple of years. The affairs which he gave
well rivaled the debauches of Alexander that you suggested,
Lord Bensonhurst. But along with our culture, since that
time, we have developed refinements in our vices which

the ancients did not know. All these were added to Van Mortimor's entertainments.

"Cocaine and morphine were at first surreptitiously slipped into these repasts to stir their jaded emotions after their appetites for food, wine, and voluptuousness had become dulled. As I protested violently, I simply found myself excluded from these gatherings, and as I scarcely wished to call in the police I could only hope to do something for him if the opportunity presented itself.

"Rapidly becoming a connoisseur of everything that interested him, Van Mortimor quickly ran through the use of morphine, opium, and had his fling at practically all drugs in domestic use. But ever he sought the thrill which was unattainable.

"Soon he became a confirmed drug addict, much as I strove to prevent it. During this period of his residence in Paris, he seemed to get the greatest happiness out of the eating of opium. Although as a matter of fact he usually took it in the form of laudanum mixed with wine. Often in talking with me—his remarks growing rather disjointed— he would sit sipping from a tall wine glass. An analysis of the dregs showed that he had his system sufficiently saturated to take a thousand drops of laudanum at a sitting, without death overtaking him—"

"Amazing," murmured one of the others. "Pardon— proceed, doctor."

"As he had often stated before about his earlier exploits, he would now claim that he found absolute happiness in the fruit of the poppy.

" 'Everything you know or do, or that I have experienced, is trivial, doctor,' he would say, 'compared with the delights

I experience in this potion. After I have just gradually and properly sipped this mixture of the divine poppy, care slips from me as a cloak.

"There are infolded vast cities of crystals through which I wander with a continually expanding ego. Exquisitely beautiful buildings so translucent that you may look into them, out of them, or through them, so unreal and yet so delicately perfect they are.

" 'Legs, arms and body vanish from me as impeding baggage. My inner self expands until I throb with the universe and am wafted here and there as I wish, all-perceiving and omnipotent.

" 'At other times I float tranquilly on a placid silvery stream at perfect content, at absolute peace, until I am rested in body and soul while celestial music is wafted to me from some bourne beyond. Then I wish to attain that bourne, and, as in this delectable state, the wish is father to the act, I feel myself beginning to float down this ethereal stream. Ah, the sublime ecstasy of it!

" 'As the music grows louder, bringing me nearer, and the glittering sheen on the stream ever changes, I pass vast primordial forests on either bank in which little white monkeys and blue parrakeets play, while gorgeous huge parrots strut and gently fly on their yellow wings.

" 'Then ahead, where I cannot see, I hear great volumes of water falling, falling, falling, and I realize with pleasant anticipation that I am soon going over a prodigious waterfall, to shoot to great depths in worlds of rushing water and frothy spray. Exultantly I await the plunge while my way cannot but lead to the dulcet music which floats from this Utopian beyond.

" 'ᴀʜ! ᴀᴛ last I poise on the brink of this great waterfall; the soft green boughs, the monkeys and the bizarre parrots fade out, and I plunge onward to my goal. Miles and miles I shoot downward, head first, accompanied by tons of gray and white spray, mid roar, and silvery tintinnabulating glamour keeping time to my pulsating thoughts.

" 'I am dropped downward, breathlessly at times, for hours and hours, and after an indeterminable period of time shoot upward in a vast expanse of cascades. Great multicolored jagged rocks are all about me, and the waters storm them and churn me about to my unutterable delight. To my excruciating pleasure, I am dashed against a great pinnacle here and some sharp rock there, but I am not injured and feel no pain, for I am invulnerable.

" 'Above it all I hear the sweet chorus of sirens ever calling and am washed out on a broad gentle stream which, after my floodlike baptism, takes me as a fresh clean spirit on its broad bosom—onward toward the sweet notes from the paradise which beckons. On and on I float in a happy but melancholy and deferred hope. Years and years I seem to go, until I am emptied into mighty oceans.

" 'But, oh, my dear doctor, I do not reach the heaven of desire which calls so plaintively. I have gradually increased my laudanum until I am taking as much as I believe any human has ever drunk and lived, but, doctor, though I travel farther and farther I cannot reach the music which ever floats so sweetly to me.'

"A look of abject sadness passed over his face. I moved over and wiped from his brow the large drops of sweat which always accompany such deep opiate intoxication.

"Van Mortimor usually took cocaine when traveling,

because he found it convenient to carry in powdered form. This I most dreaded, as it kills the finest instincts quickly, and dreadful crimes often follow its use for the reason that it absolutely deadens the conscience.

"He never was able to attain the other shore in his poppy dreams. However, he took so much opium in an effort to reach the seductive strains that he got so there was a sound of a torrent of waters rushing at all times in his ears, whether he took the drug or not. To get rid of this, and also to ward off the intense sufferings which had begun to fasten on him in the relapses after intoxication, he resorted to strange stimulations.

"Once I called upon him and found a tank of ether sitting by his bedside, and each time he came out from under its influence he would reach for the tube and administer some more of it to himself. I was informed that he had taken a fancy for this while visiting a dentist. By this time women were completely forgotten. He was well on the way to what he termed the superlative thrill, and mere humans had lost their charm.

"One night I came in to call as usual and found him gone. On the library table were many books on narcotics opened usually at some reference to the drug hashish. I was informed that he had left for India. I asked the American Consular Service in India to look him up. Dr. Martin can tell you what happened in Bombay."

They arose from the table and repaired to the office of Dr. Bates, where the conference went on. Dr. Martin reported a weird tale:

"**THE FIRST THING** that I knew of this case was when the American consul asked me to call upon Mr. Van Mortimor at the Taj Maraj, a hotel in Bombay. Upon presenting myself at his suite I was received by a princely Hindu, who courteously asked the nature of my call. I explained and while I waited I noticed that everything was Oriental. All European furniture and small evidences of English habitation, even such things as the little personal effects of an Anglo-Saxon traveler, had been removed and substituted therefor were all the evidences of a high cast Indian residence. The object of my call had, I feared, succumbed to the subtle influences of occult India.

"Mr. Van Mortimor received me in an adjoining room. He reclined on a couch, dressed in the robe of a high caste Brahman; and the only respect he paid my greeting was to raise himself slightly on his elbow. He was partially under the influence of some drug, which one, of course, I could not just then determine. He moved his eyebrows superciliously and languidly spoke:

" 'To me the most pertinent thing about you is that you are a white man. What could any white man require of me?'

" 'Mr. Van Mortimor,' I hastened to explain, 'the American consul here, at the urgent request of your people, has asked that I see that you have every attention.'

" 'Ah,' he drawled. 'Every attention. What a word! Of what aid could any white man be to me? I tell you that I have drunk the cup of the white man's civilization dry, that it is all a monotonous routine of viciousness, disguised as virtue, law and order. Everything your kind can offer I have exhausted, and there is no thrill left for me in your vaunted culture.'

"I looked around very carefully and, believing that I would not be overheard, I declared quietly:

" 'I think I understand. The spell of India is upon you. I know these people. The occult, the magic, the philosophy, and the whole insidious atmosphere has been my work-ground for years. Be careful. No white man can ever really penetrate and understand all these mystic things, and it all may end very disastrously for you. Just take my friend-ship on trial; it may prove very helpful at times, especially should you wish to avail yourself of a possible exit through me if you wish to retrace your steps.'

"He acquiesced to a very limited degree in my request. On condition that I never try to deter him from his deter-mination, except on his specific command, he admitted me quite freely to see him at nearly all times.

"He fraternized with the leaders of the various esoteric religions and philosophies in which India abounds; and, to my surprise, he was received on unusually intimate terms by these men. Of course this was in his lucid intervals, as a large part of the time he was so abjectly under the influence of drugs as to be lost to any intelligent communication. As you know a great number of these men are very worthy, and, strangely enough, he associated with the highest as well as the lowest caste, the best as well as the most weird sects. Nobly born princes and philosophers met such lowly and outcast characters in Van Mortimor's rooms that they could not deign to touch what they had touched, but each had his appeal and in return were attracted to their host.

"In pursuit of his drug mania, he soon became a slave to hashish. He smoked it, chewed it, and drank it in all its various forms. At first it was highly pleasurable to him, and then its various inevitable effects began to work upon him.

"There were subjective sensations of mental brilliance

which greatly delighted him. The dark brownish-green color of the various concoctions of hashish and its faint peculiar odor were now ever about him. As I so often warned him, the pace he was setting could only lead to such a torment that nothing known could ease his pain and raw senses.

"In association with the morbid element from which he procured his drugs he became intrigued with the marvelous tricks which the fakirs perpetrate. With an uncanny instinct for these unexplainable things he delved into their mysteries, mastered many of them and created several of his own for their edification.

"**ONE DAY, I** think to shock my Anglo-Saxon ideas, he arranged a most astounding reception for me. When I called upon him, he was lying on the couch in his bedroom where I was accustomed to find him. I noticed that the surface of the couch was higher than it had previously been, and that he had a silken spread drawn over himself. He asked me to remove the spread, and, to my horror, I found him peacefully reclining on a bed of sharp spikes.

" 'Mr. Van Mortimor, get up,' I expostulated. 'Don't you know that even if you can stand the pain, you may become poisoned from that sort of thing?'

"Quickly coming to the center of the floor, he asked me to examine him for injuries that could cause pain. There was not a blemish on him. I examined the bed of spikes for some support but could find none, even pricking my finger on one of the needle sharp points. How he did it I don't know.

" 'There, doctor,' he gloated. 'You are certainly egotistical to think you can help me when you do not understand a little thing like that. Now leave me while I take repose,' and he crawled back on the spikes.

"One day when I called he had the large central room darkened, and a Hindu appeared with a rope.

" 'Observe closely, doctor,' Van Mortimor remarked. The Hindu threw the rope into the air and, hand over hand, ascended it, passing through the place where once there had been a ceiling. Gentlemen, as far as I could make out, he disappeared into thin air. Although Van Mortimor permitted me to flood the room with light I could not explain it. 'Now, doctor,' he asserted, 'if you think that was a mere trick, I shall do it myself,' and he threw a rope upward. It stiffened like a pole. Hastily I assured him that it wasn't a trick—not because I believed what I was saying, but because in his enervated condition I knew he would try it, and I didn't want the results on my hands.

" 'Doctor,' he would say, 'I could tell you things which I know, things I can do which would be so incomprehensible to you that it is foolish to discuss them. So much for the physical side. But, doctor, far greater things can I do through the mind.'

"About him always were vast piles of books. He was ever a prodigious reader, and now his mind ran to the occult. Always under the influence of drugs, I did not doubt that these sayings were the outcroppings of his vaporous dreams.

" 'I can murder with fear alone,' he would exclaim, and then, his face softening, he would say, 'and I can build paradises with love alone.'

"I would let him ramble along, the poor fellow. Hashish was his besetting sin. In his deliriums from this drug, he emitted a curious weird noise or song. He called it the cry of ultimate desire, a yearning cry for that superlative thrill which he could never find. Finally this sound became so unendurable that the management of the hotel requested his rooms. Though he had taken much empty space in every direction to keep from disturbing other guests, the weird blood-congealing air became so harrowing and penetrating, in the small hours of the night, that many guests departed from the hotel at most inconvenient hours and would accept no excuses.

"Van Mortimor suddenly left for the wilds of Africa, where he hoped to find that the heart of nature still beat undisturbed by the mechanisms and customs of mankind. It was erroneously supposed, and we were practically compelled to announce, that he went there to hunt big game, but, as you know, I accompanied him and I tell you he made this expedition to study wild animal life. Days without end he stalked animals to study their habits, to learn from them, he said, the springs of fundamental emotion.

"Wild men would come from miles to hear his weird cry at night when he occasionally gave vent to it. The surrounding jungle was infested with a rapt audience of head hunters and wild beasts drawn in from all directions by the inhuman incantations. Van Mortimor's soul-rending notes struck a responsive feeling in the breast of the savage.

"As his interest in Africa faded after a year or so, he drifted back to civilization with an English crony he had met, Sir Archibald Cleavington, and you gentlemen, with the exception of Dr. Bates, recall all the incidents of our Paris conference.

"In my estimation, though, the rough life of Africa has strengthened his body. I think almost any measures are warranted to save this brilliant though strange young man, for with the amount of drugs taken and dissipation which lies behind him, I do not believe he will live much longer, and if he does it may be in abject pain and misery. Dr. Martel, in my estimation, can alone permanently remedy his condition, if it is possible to do so. What do you think of his heart, Dr. Landeau?"

"In a very weak condition naturally. It requires now extreme stimulation to function properly. I would not be surprised to see him drop over dead at any time. You know how it is in these desperate cases. This quick glow of very apparent health usually signals the end.

"I warned him, in Paris, and he replied that it did not matter in the least whether he lived or died. As he enjoys having you banter with him, I said, 'Come, don't say that. Why not emulate a cat and have the full nine lives?'

"With the supreme ego of a hashish eater, he took me very seriously and confided, 'Perhaps I shall.'" Dr. Landeau sighed.

These physicians then went into a deep scientific analysis of the physical and mental manifestations of this tremendously grave case. The continental contingent as a unit insisted on a drastic course of action. Dr. Bates alone had divergent views, and the gallant old practitioner stood out against them like an obstinate juror. At last they adjourned to snatch a little rest before the consultation with Van Mortimor himself tomorrow.

8

THE INQUISITION

AT TEN O'CLOCK Edmond Fletcher presented himself at the offices of Dr. Wendell Bates. The visiting physicians, Lord Bensonhurst, Dr. Landeau, Dr. Martin and Dr. Martel, were awaiting him grouped around the consultation table.

He thanked his lucky stars that Gloria was not with him. The exposure would very probably occur here: this was the crisis. Instead of welcoming it as his honest self prompted him that he should, he sincerely hoped he could avoid denunciation, for he felt chagrined that fate had not permitted him to explain the matter in a more gentlemanly manner to the lovely Gloria. Now he was so far committed to his role that exposure in any abrupt way would prove utterly embarrassing.

A wave of surprise ran over the assembled group as they first saw him standing in the doorway, his cheeks aglow and the very picture of health.

Lord Bensonhurst arose and extended his hand which Fletcher grasped in a hearty fashion. He sensed that he should appear happy to see them.

"You are looking well," said Bensonhurst.

"It is particularly to say so," gasped Dr. Landeau as

he grasped both of his hands and leaning far back jocularly peered into his face. "What is it you are taking now? Strychnine?"

Fletcher grinned sheepishly. Was he a dope fiend? Well, they might have any opinion of him they wished, as long as they thought him Van Mortimor.

Dr. Martin insisted on taking him into the full light of the window where he called to their attention:

"We can all see the changes which are wrought in the countenance of a man who has pulled himself out of the occult."

"The facial changes are quite considerable, I imagine. My mind now seems quite clarified," interjected Fletcher thinking the doctor's remark quite an opportunity for him to get in a favorable word.

"One thing I would ask of you," cried Dr. Martel. "Were the snakes in Africa so big as those in your dreams?"

Fencing shrewdly, he replied:

"It is hard to improve on nature." Evidently among these physicians he was passing as Van Mortimor. What a farce! If these great men could not distinguish between two human beings, what havoc might not their decisions easily create?

After their smiles at his last remark had vanished, a look of solemnity came over them.

"Shall I state the result of our deliberations and go ahead?" asked Lord Bensonhurst, looking about.

They all nodded, and Dr. Randau Martel added:

"This apparent ruddy good health and the flash of a normal mind only precedes that which you can readily guess. I believe now that action is imperative."

They all looked at Dr. Bates, who shook "his head in the negative; but he qualified his action with:

"I am the only one who dissents. We must be guided by what you say."

LORD BENSONHURST REACHED among some photographs laying face downward and selected one which he turned over.

"Here you see an X-ray of your head taken two years ago—you will recall, in Paris."

Pointing with a pencil:

"This is the cerebrum of the brain which controls human thought. You see just above the center of it a small speck or spot. This was not of sufficient purport to alarm us at the time the picture was taken, as nearly every such photograph shows these without serious consequences."

Bensonhurst reached for another photograph.

"This is the X-ray which we took in Paris before you sailed for this country. You will notice that the speck has now grown as large as a small pea." The physician reached over for quite a large photograph.

"This is the last photograph, magnified ten times. You see it virtually becomes to us a map of that part of your thinking apparatus, and on this picture you see a large dark spot with telltale darkness radiating from it along all the little veins. It is spreading farther."

Fletcher was mildly elated that they were letting the talk run along medical lines. It was also very interesting and uncanny the way they read maps of people's anatomy. He trusted he would not have to take any treatments for the other fellow's blemishes. The next words shocked him to the core.

"That is unquestionably a blood clot on your brain," the doctor was saying kindly, "and you must know the only effective treatment for it."

Fletcher was stupefied. Surely they would not resort to any desperate measures upon a man as well as himself. Yet how could he show it without disclosing his identity? Bensonhurst read his blank expression as a doubt of their conclusions.

"These enlarged sections of the brain are an open book from which your very thoughts, inclinations, and future can be easily read. Let Dr. Martel, whose reputation as a surgeon you well know, give you a surprise about your own thoughts and tell you what will happen if this isn't taken in hand."

Dr. Randau Martel the noted Austrian surgeon, leaned on his elbows and began:

"I can only discuss this frankly. The clot is unmistakable, and in time leads to a hemorrhage and death unless it is arrested in its growth. But in this case, far worse results than the mere death of the subject may ensue. The subject in an attempt to satiate his mind with all known thrills as this clot has grown, has practically run the whole gantlet of human emotions except one kind."

He paused impressively.

"IN MY STUDY of many similar cases, the most atrocious criminal tendencies have invariably cropped up before the actual breaking of the clot. In the ignorant and poor, it takes the form of brutal crimes, robbery and lust for that which has been denied them. In the highly cultured and rich where practically nothing desired has been denied, atrocious criminal acts are committed merely for the thrill in itself.

"The subject has run nearly all the gantlet of human sensations and thrills except this last kind. He would probably at about this stage begin a study of human emotions—as he has. His mind, previously concentrated on his own thrills, would now delight in playing upon the emotions of others.

"He might become a force for good in studying, arranging, and classifying his knowledge of the working of the human mind—in short, he might become a psychologist or criminologist. More likely, however, he would wish to experience crime rather than to study the acts of others.

"I would say that as soon as he got into this, at any cost he would put some human being in deadly fear of him and enjoy it in the same way that a snake charms a bird, or a cat toys with a trembling mouse. This form of thrill intoxication invariably leads to one result, the supreme thrill of killing the victim after he has sufficiently tortured him, just as the snake finally kills the bird, and that is where the dreadful crimes come in."

Fletcher was grasping the table, cold beads of perspiration were forming on his forehead, but the emotions which were sweeping him at the moment were not actuated by worry about anything of that nature which he might do. He was beginning to fully understand some things which had previously occurred.

Lord Bensonhurst spoke gently: "It is our consensus of opinion that the clot must be removed from your brain in the hope of restoring your health and—er—saving your mind!"

Dr. Bates leaned over to speak, but before he could do so Fletcher, calmly weighing his words, asked Dr. Martel: "This is a capital operation?"

"You cannot touch the brain with impunity. But the continuance of your condition forebodes far worse results than what I must admit are the grave risks of the operation."

Fletcher felt himself in the position of a patriot who must charge the full blast of a cannon. He had assumed the role, had already accepted its rewards. A beautiful little girl believed in him, and whatever happened, he must avoid exposing *her* to ridicule, shame, and disgrace.

But could he by any chance avoid exposure? If he protested about this operation, they would probably take new X-ray photographs of his brain; and Fletcher was too shrewd to hope that the enlarged map of his brain would bear enough resemblance to Van Mortimor's, when placed side by side, to fool these trained physicians.

If no possible means of escape offered, he would be confronted with the choice of undergoing this operation, or confessing outright. He didn't know much about medical matters, of course, but he guessed there was a chance that the surgeon, finding the blood clot gone and his brain apparently healthy, might not be able to identify it as an impostor's. There was also the very good chance that he would die on the operating table. Here was a colossal gamble with destiny, one to appall even as sporting a spirit as Fletcher's.

Dr. Bates had been whispering to Dr. Martel, who only shook his head.

GLORIA'S SWEET LITTLE face came to Fletcher's mind.

He probably could never have her anyhow, but she alone was worth the risk of his life. He would play the game to the very end!

Fletcher looked straight at the great surgeon, Martel, his eyes challenging him.

"Gentlemen," he said, "make your arrangements. I am ready at your convenience."

Tears sprang into the famous surgeon's eyes, and in an outburst of eccentric emotion, which was characteristic of him, he wheeled upon his associates with a burst of passion:

"Mein Gott, haven't you *dummkopfs* any intuition? Such a history you give me of this case! Your stories suggest an enormously selfish cad, a narrow degenerate, a licentious hog." He glared at them. "If he were such, this man would protest arrogantly at our decision."

Turning to Dr. Bates, he shouted. "I didn't expect such heroism! There's very fine stuff here!"

A smile of gratification was enveloping Dr. Bates's features, which had been so tense the moment before; and in his eyes was the light of unmistakable pride about something. More than ever Fletcher was convinced that this man was his ally in some definite yet mysterious way.

"Gentlemen," Dr. Martel was saying, "please forgive my rudeness. I am an old man, and great heroism touches me deeply."

They smiled in their bewilderment, and made no attempt to answer him, for they were accustomed to his behavior. Often it even proved to have good reason, but they did not quite grasp his full meaning this time.

Lord Bensonhurst arose.

"Dr. Martel, we shall now leave the case in your hands.

Sigmond, your complete surrender to Dr. Martel's skill is going to be the turning point in your life."

Adieus were said, and the old surgeon Martel alone faced Fletcher and Dr. Bates across the table. No words were passed for a few minutes. Each man had his own thoughts, and no two were alike. Each one was about to begin fencing with words, and each wondered how to start.

To Fletcher, and well he knew to the departing physicians, this operation was a certainty. Truly he was in high favor with all in the conference, but in attaining their high esteem he had committed himself to a dire risk.

"No wonder you are a great surgeon," spoke Dr. Bates abruptly. "I can see how your seeming miracles are often due to a prescience just a little above surgery. Dr. Martel, I am a bit old-fashioned, and I have some set ideas on this case. I believe by using only some sensible, ordinary treatments I can bring Sigmond around.

"Each one of these physicians," logically argued Dr. Bates, "has had Sigmond in charge for a long period, and according to their own stories he has steadily grown worse. I have had him a very little while, yet look at the remarkable improvement. Do you think that within your professional discretion you could see your way clear to back me in a request, which I could make at our dinner with them tonight—a suggestion that in all fairness I be allowed some time to see what change I can effect in Sigmond before this desperate operation should be attempted? I might even further say that if I am allowed this privilege I am confident Mr. Van Mortimor's recovery will be so rapid that the operation will not be considered again."

THE EMINENT SURGEON raised his eyes from Fletcher's face till they paused above the door of the room, and suddenly he burst out laughing. Such were his traits, it seemed, tears and laughter on the same subject matter. He looked at Fletcher quickly and back at Bates. Again he laughed heartily.

"Frankly, Bates," he chuckled, "I think you are somewhat of an old fox. I do not care to go into this deeper, and I don't think you wish me to. I believe you have Sigmond Van Mortimor's welfare at heart."

He drew the X-ray maps to him and spread them out contemplatively.

"Here is irrefutable evidence of the necessity of a capital operation, and yet to act upon it, backed by my profession and protected by every law, would be little short of murder. On what a thin thread often hangs momentous consequences!"

His keen eyes focused the two of them.

"Bates, tonight I shall recommend a postponement of the operation, to give you your chance; and tenderly I bury in my memory a rare act of heroism. Further, the extreme delicacy of this situation, and the very warmth of my feeling for this young man, will ever prohibit me from divulging certain opinions I may have formed."

With a sweep of his hand he pushed the photographs and data toward Dr. Bates. A shake of Fletcher's hand and he was gone.

Fletcher and Dr. Bates were now alone. Something of comradeship had grown up between them, and both experienced a sense of great relief.

"Let's lunch," smiled the doctor wearily.

They passed out into the warm sunlight which seemed

to soothe and caress Fletcher's distracted nerves. He felt a profound sense of gratitude to Dr. Bates. Across the luncheon table he tried to express it. Why withhold anything from his obvious ally?

"Doctor," he confided in a low tone, "I wish to be honest with you. You know I am not Van Mortimor, and—"

A look of chagrined surprise came across Dr. Bates's face as he stopped Fletcher's words with an upraised hand.

"I have just staked my reputation," Bates glared at him, "to save you from a dangerous operation. You, Van Mortimor, have just risked your life to remedy the results of your past. Do you want me to change my mind and think you are crazy?"

Fletcher reddened and remained silent, his bewilderment overpowering him. Dr. Bates fumbled uncertainly with a package which he had been carrying.

"I have been pondering whether I should give you this to read. Your remarks have decided it!" Now he nervously unwrapped the parcel and handed Fletcher a great sheaf of typewritten pages, which were bound together into a book with heavy covers.

"This is a stenographic copy of the history of your case as your physicians reported it. Read it over and try to get your worst hallucination out of your mind."

Fletcher took the medical transcript mutely and tried no further confidences on the rather delicate subject of his identity. What was, what could be the doctor's motive and position in all this?

Bidding the doctor good day, he called up Gloria. Her sweet voice over the wire put the warmth fully back into his veins. Stepping into his car, he directed that he be driven to his offices.

SINKING INTO THE cushions of the car bearing him down town, Fletcher reviewed the day. He had escaped a terrorizing operation, but he had added to his fears; for just as surely as he was not Van Mortimor, the true Van Mortimor was a horrible fiend, if alive. The thinking that emanated from that spot on the brain which he had seen might result in almost any horrible tragedy for Fletcher. He shuddered to recall Dr. Martel's analysis of what these degenerates do. That Martel was a genius, who knew what he was talking about.

All along, Van Mortimor had been running true to form. The price which Fletcher must pay for all that he was getting, was beginning to loom up. He looked out at the warm, sunny streets. Soon the night would come and somewhere this arch fiend would be lurking, waiting to pounce upon him; for from what Martel had said, things would culminate rather quickly now. Martel had stated at all costs Van Mortimor would play upon the emotions of his victim, charming and terrorizing him. Had he not already begun it?

The car door opened with a click. He peered out as if he were driving an old, ramshackle car and had just thought he heard a puncture.

"Ah, yes," he reflected hastily, "the Bank of the Western Hemisphere. I have some little national affairs to look after here. Very well, I'll attend to the business in hand."

9

THE FORGING OF A CHARACTER

BRISKLY FLETCHER WALKED through the main floor of the great bank as innumerable customers and employees craned their necks at him. News about the young man was spreading like wildfire and he promised to be somewhat of a sensation.

The previous day Fletcher had disposed of engagements with many railroad officials and corporation presidents. His demeanor and message had been about the same in each instance, courteous but formal. To each one whom he interviewed, he explained that at the next regular meeting of the board of directors of that particular corporation, he would become the chairman of the board and absolutely dominate the policies of it. As they went out, each was impressed by the fact that he was dealing with a strong if inexperienced character in Van Mortimor.

The interviews with the attorneys and his new stockbrokers, Morton, Keene & Co., had been deferred until after the conference with the physicians, which he feared might obviate the necessity of ever seeing him.

Floyd now informed him that he might expect Mr. Morton over at any time. He glanced idly at the stock tape. The market had not changed perceptibly since he left the Street on that auspicious day. Just a trading affair, was all he could make out of it.

"Mr. Morton," announced the secretary.

"Mr. Floyd, have twenty-five thousand shares of G.T. and X. out of the safe-deposit vaults for delivery today," answered Fletcher, so that Morton would have the full effect of it.

"Mr. Van Mortimor," greeted Mr. Morton as he observed Fletcher like a hawk. "I am very sorry I intruded with my request to see you on the roof of the hotel the other evening. I am indeed pleased to know you, and I can see how much more businesslike it is that you wish to receive stockbrokers at your office." He extended his hand.

Fine old Morton. Fletcher would very much have liked to shake hands, but there were certain necessary formalities that he knew he must observe to impress this well-seasoned broker. Not that he cared in the least, but he noticed that the men he had been meeting, in deference to his exalted position, did not offer to shake hands unless he did so first.

"Just sit here," kindly motioned Fletcher in a matter of fact tone. "I am very sorry I do not shake hands. There is nothing personal in my refusal, just a rule I follow for obvious reasons."

Then in a businesslike manner he shot at the canny broker:

"Can you unqualifiedly recommend Edmond Fletcher, so far as his honesty is concerned?"

"Certainly." Morton stared at him in patent bewilderment.

"Well, I have some need for him that will take him away

from you indefinitely. I shall give you a lot of stock business in return which you can credit to him, if the arrangement is agreeable. This to be strictly confidential, of course."

"**ALL THE MEMBERS** of our organization are at your service on your own conditions," answered Morton, who was already impressed by the tremendous authority which this young financier wielded.

This cold-blooded youngster certainly could not be Fletcher. There was no human way that he could fit into Van Mortimor's boots. Any doubt in Morton's mind was soon dispelled absolutely.

"I am sending over to you today twenty-five thousand shares of G.T. and X. Sell it until," the young financier's eyes sought the tape, "the price reaches two points under the present market, forty-one and one-half. That is in the strictest confidence, which I will see how well you can keep. There are, Mr. Morton, no blind spots in the eyes of my organization. I trust you will excuse me now," he ended. "Please pass out," he indicated the door into the hall, "through this exit."

Morton quietly moved to the door, his manner hushed by the spell of the great commissions impending.

"One minute," called Fletcher, getting up from his seat. "You know I must have very great confidence in your good faith, to make you my broker on what little I know about you. I sometimes break a rule and indulge in what is otherwise a time-wasting formality, when it really means something. May I depend on your strict loyalty to my personal interests?" He offered his hand.

Morton grasped it. Morton would keep his word

through great personal hardships, Fletcher knew positively. Ah! What an organization he was building!

The most that could be said of Fletcher was that he was
excellent material.

Ordinarily he would have stood out only a little from
the crowd as an idealist. That is all. Now he found himself
in a boiling cauldron of opportunities, and the tremendous forces being brought to bear upon him were forging
a noteworthy character, just as with poor material and its
low ideals in the same potent surroundings, the great forces
at work would have produced a weakling, or more likely
an explosion of him.

Fletcher was unifying this great fortune into an absolute
one-man control, and very soon he would have it working
like a vast orchestra with him wielding the baton.

He had decided that he would own nothing short of
control in anything in which his money was invested.

He was checking up the prospects of each such investment, whether to buy additional stock at a fair price to
obtain control or to sell his holdings in such a company
without sacrifice. This G.T. and X. was an investment
which he wished to sell.

After looking over the day's correspondence, he was
surprised to find it getting late. He grasped his hat and the
book of papers which Dr. Bates had given him.

GLORIA WAS WAITING in the library of the "playhouse."
How delightful it was to have this lovely young creature
so solicitous of his coming and going. She was jubilant,
radiant with smiles about something as she threw her arms
about him and kissed his cheek impetuously.

She seemed relieved from some great nervous anxiety

and strain, and he wondered if she were familiar with the happenings at Dr. Bates's office, as he had been very careful not to alarm her with these developments.

"Gloria! You little minx," he asked, "with whom have you been talking today?"

"No one would tell me much," she explained. "When you slipped out this morning, without seeing me, I knew you were eluding me for some purpose, probably to spare my feelings. But, Sigmond," she cried, "I couldn't let you go like that. Those doctors might hurt you. They couldn't love you as I do." She hugged him tightly.

"I gave you time to get there and then I went directly to Dr. Bates's offices. You were in conference in an adjoining room." She looked up defiantly. "I listened at the keyhole, not a nice thing to do, but you are mine and I don't care. I only heard snatches of the conversation and I could not quite understand it all except that they wanted to operate on you, and only Dr. Bates took up for you.

"If they had dared touch you," she exclaimed, "I would have been right on top of them and put a stop to it instantly.

"I did some good though, I think. When Dr. Bates was begging the surgeon to let him have you for awhile, with just you three left in the room, I got on a chair, climbed up, and peered through the transom. I had such a hard time doing it that I bumped my head on the glass and looked directly into the face of that old foreign doctor across the table. I jumped down as quickly as I could, but I heard him laughing and then I listened at the keyhole and it was all right. He must have seen me and known I meant trouble."

"Anyhow, it is all over now, little sweetheart," he laughed, not wishing to alarm her. "I'll be all right, I know."

GLORIA HAD MENTIONED that Myrtle Marbleton and probably the count would be over that evening. Fletcher dressed, and seemed very absent-minded until the arrival of the count and Myrtle recalled him to his duties as host.

Shortly thereafter, the four of them drove out to a very exclusive country club to dance. Fletcher met a few people, but Myrtle contrived to occupy most of his attention which suited him just as well. He would have much preferred to have retired early, but he was—he could not deny it—jealously unwilling to leave Gloria to the count.

Myrtle, whenever she was alone with Fletcher, expanded her allurements more than slightly. If you were interested in the amorous charms of a seductive feminine body, Myrtle certainly displayed them in ample measure. She believed that the best and most potent appeal in woman was purely physical.

If the mind could lend an air, create an atmosphere for her polite courtesanship, so much the better; but the major appeal lay in the body itself and of this she was ever cognizant. To her a woman was only as great as her allurements. Certainly the army of men who marry and otherwise go to perdition over women's bodies, without any other appeal, would fortify her claim.

She knew the alluring value of perfume and one could always detect the faint odor of a mixture of amber and jasmine about her. She was a well-bred, gentle and sophisticated siren who under the guise of conventional manners held forth the promise of the utmost of human passion to a favored one.

All this Fletcher recognized, as the types run the same in every walk of life.

She nevertheless was resplendent, so resplendent that you felt so much was in her brocaded, that the product, Myrtle, justified her tinsel. Myrtle maddened the senses to look at her, intoxicated the gaze. Fletcher preferred to do this—just look at her; she interested him and was a magnetic creature.

But unfortunately she insisted on talking, which greatly interfered with his enjoyment of her, for he had small sympathy with the fierce, ruthless love of power, and domineering force, which she unashamedly avowed. A certain hardness came into her face as it broke into a cynical smile.

"A little poodle dog comes along and the men in the street kick it, but let a bulldog approach and every one gets off the pavement. If I were a man I would be a bulldog," she laughed.

Fletcher wondered at her utter sophistication, and the very practical philosophy of ruthless wealth which he knew gleamed through it.

His mind wandered to Gloria dancing with the elegant Frenchman. Her happiness was worth more to him than all Myrtle could conjure up. This beautiful little wisp of a girl pirouetting out there with so charming a partner. He could understand how mothers of heiresses would buy such men.

"I like that darned count," reflected Fletcher, "he has caught something that I can't have, in his absolute detachment from the struggles of life, and if his charm can bring happiness to Gloria, maybe it would be the better for her."

What could Fletcher give her, in comparison? Actually the count could not be poorer than Edmond Fletcher, and Edmond lacked even the qualifications for congenial companionship in which the polished gentleman excelled.

Shortly they moved homeward, and as Fletcher left
Gloria in the apartment, she made a little wry face and
exclaimed:

"Ugh! You smell of amber perfume!"

"Good night, countess," he rejoined, as he dived for his
rooms.

10

A STRANGE MISSION

IT HAD INDEED been a strenuous day. Entering his rooms Fletcher sought the comfort of a big chair in the living room.

Idly the well-meaning usurper picked up the volume of papers which Dr. Bates had given him: the history of the case of Sigmond Van Mortimor. Edmond Fletcher felt that he might just as well familiarize himself thoroughly with all the details of this elusive antagonist. Maybe then he could better understand some of the strange things in the past and defend himself against the ones to come.

Deeply absorbed he ran over the first part of the history. This Sigmond Van Mortimor had intelligence, and Fletcher surmised that he himself was only the pawn in some great though probably criminal scheme.

Only confinement or death would stop this fellow's sinister activities; and even then the occult, in which he had become an adept, might be brought into play.

Narcotic drugs and the magic of India—what was there that he might not expect from this monstrous libertine, who was playing with him as a conscienceless cat with an interesting, quivering mouse?

Especially was this true if Van Mortimor was wandering around somewhere near. Even if he were dead, which would seem to end any fear of him, had he not said Dr. Landeau, "Nine lives? Perhaps I shall."

AT FIVE MINUTES of eleven a silent, serious young financier accompanied by his first secretary, Colston Floyd, left his offices and repaired to an impressive board room. Ten minutes later after adjourning this meeting on his own motion, it was a new chairman of the board of the great bank who returned to his private offices.

He had scarcely spoken a dozen words. A few formal introductions and a few crisp remarks. That was all. A man in his position could not permit familiarity on short acquaintance. The air was getting chillier as he ascended the frigid heights, and Fletcher was beginning to get the "feel" of great power.

Sitting at his large desk, with the doors of his room tightly closed, he looked over endless summaries and digests privately prepared. Scarcely any communication or business report came to him directly. Secretaries waded through all matters and submitted just the kernels of things.

From time to time a resolution of his election to the chairmanship of another board of directors was laid before him. Other meetings that day he didn't even attend, merely sent his proxies with directions how they should be voted.

Bullard Bland, dutyless and puzzled confidential secretary, had meantime set himself one duty. Just before he was so abruptly engaged Bland had made a deposit of five dollars on a great bargain in the way of a suit of clothes at twenty-two dollars and a half.

This order he precipitately canceled, and took, in lieu

of the complete loss of the five dollars deposit—which seemed to him akin to sacrilege—a pair of five-dollar socks, as there was really nothing else that he could now possibly use in that cheap store.

He gave orders to some sartorial experts of the Avenue, who promised to make his bay window appear merely as an attic semi-sash. But he felt an immediate crying need of getting this personal atmosphere to invigorate him and his surroundings, and he appeared at the most exclusive ready-to-wear establishment in the same locality.

Here he displayed some of his precocious ability for handling a delicate matter most admirably. He asked for the manager of the store by name, having first ascertained that before entering the store, and introduced himself. Naturally he was very favorably received.

"Mr. Chiltonwaggle," he stated, "my business affairs take me all over the world, and it puts me a little out of touch with the latest correct thing in dress. I would very much appreciate the favor of having a clerk assigned to serve me who can be depended upon to supplement my taste correctly."

Mr. Chiltonwaggle fairly gushed his delight at receiving *carte blanche,* and did nobly.

Various colored topped shoes with pearl buttons struck deep and responsive chords in Bland's heart; but he accepted spats without a murmur.

ON THIS TUESDAY, while the great Sigmond Van Mortimor sat at the big desk and took over the complete responsibilities of vast corporations, a new Bullard Bland had come into the secretary's private office.

For this new man wore a suit of some wonderful dark-

blue cloth which blended with the color of his Copenha-
gen blue eyes as though a genius had experimented with
all blues and then triumphantly pointed out this harmony.
If his two hundred and twenty pounds of avoirdupois had
been melted and poured into his clothing the fit would not
have been more perfect, nor would the weight have been
half so well concealed. A gray tie of just the right shade
and light gray spats completed the picture.

Much earlier than Van Mortimor's arrival Bland had
tossed his cane into the corner of his office and adjusted
the flower in his buttonhole. For once he had forsworn the
tempting couch, early as it was. He simply hadn't the nerve
to muss the clothes. At times he could not help but harbor
secretly the idea that this Sigmond Van Mortimor was in
some inexplicable fashion his old friend Edmond Fletcher.

When this Mr. Van Mortimor came in he diffidently
presented himself the first time at the door. Without any
change of expression Fletcher, with his mind engrossed,
only shook his head.

Several other times during the day, at various intervals
in Fletcher's strenuous efforts, Bland tried to attract the
young magnate's attention. Each time, however, Fletcher
had only looked at him kindly but absently, with a shake of
the head. With a firm conviction settling upon him, Bland
at last sank into his chair at his desk. There he soliloquized:
"I know positively now that not in any way on earth could
this fellow be Edmond Fletcher. He would have fainted if
he had ever seen me dressed like this."

It was getting after two o'clock. Fletcher notified Floyd
that he would not take up any further business that day.

Edmond's face gradually softened. "I'll give Van Mortimor all there is in me," he mused, "but I'll not work-long hours. Lots of relaxation, that's the thing that makes you hit hard when you do work."

As he slackened up he felt a vague loneliness in his high position, a yearning for friendship, for real companionship, for some one he could talk to without his thoughts being betrayed. Such warm and true hearts would be hard to find up here in the land of the frigid financial heights. Then his thoughts turned to Bland, good old Bland, with all of his faults, yet one in a million.

"Mr. Bland!" He slightly raised his voice.

Mr. Bland was nodding at his desk. He could not sleep in those clothes without the fear of disarraying them. The best he could do was to indulge in a very deep reverie. Quickly Bland looked about him. Could it be possible that at last he was wanted? That there might be even the faint semblance of a hope that he be given some little service to perform? He peeped into the great financier's room, only half believing. Yes, indeed, there he sat, his desk cleared and awaiting him. What a pleasure to serve if he would only tell him something to do! He eagerly started into the room.

As the full sartorial splendor of Bland, from the imported linen collar to the pearl gray spats, dawned upon Fletcher, he was seized with an abnormal interest in the market and grabbed the tape wildly.

"Quick!" Fletcher gasped. "Get me a *Wall Street Journal!*" BLAND WAS OFF like a shot searching through the bank for one, and Fletcher, as his steps faded away, gave vent to an uncontrollable burst of laughter. When his merriment subsided it occurred to him that Bland's dramatic entrance had been worth a million to him. The hearty laughter had cleared his mind of the day's strain, relieved the drastic tension he was under, and made him normal again.

By George, though, the fellow was a wonder. Fletcher thoroughly appreciated that he was a suave wizard in his speech and actions at ferreting out anything or at any scheming whatsoever, but he never before had believed him capable of any sort of taste in dress. Really, Bland was a human chameleon. The way he had so readily blended into the environment pleased Fletcher exceedingly, and he realized that he had a very exceptional confidential secretary.

It just happened that the new office had not subscribed for the paper, but we won't go into the details of how Bland got a copy. Probably some vice president missed the sheet which he had laid aside for an instant, or some files sacredly complete for a decade suffered this day; but it was Bland's first assignment to duty, and, needless to say, very shortly he appeared, paper in hand. If the order had been to bring the president of the bank in by the nape of the neck he would have produced him just as promptly.

By this time Fletcher was completely himself. He thanked Bland and looked over the paper, while out of the corner of his eye he accustomed himself to the transformation of his friend.

Finally laying down the paper when he was fully confident of himself, Fletcher addressed him:

"Mr. Bland, you are looking surprisingly well. Allow me to compliment you upon the very good taste in your dress."

Bland did not answer. His clothes were very much a delicate matter conversationally, since another mind had dressed him; such a delicate matter indeed that he had not been able to lie down the whole day!

For a time Fletcher and Bland chatted. They just drifted along, their conversation getting friendlier. Here was a fellow with whom Fletcher could let down the bars in a way, so long as he did not disclose his identity. He had great work to do, and Bland could help him, because no matter how bad his faults, he was a brilliant thinker, an unconventional genius.

He knew that the obvious faults in Bland under his direction would become great virtues for helping him in the vicious game of business. Gall, unbounded nerve, and clever chicanery were powerful assets when carefully directed by another; and they would counterbalance Edmond's weaknesses. The fact that he had never deigned to use such qualities personally, Fletcher realized, had accounted to a great extent for his previous comparative failure in business.

When absolutely necessary now to fight fire with fire, he meant to rely on Bland in these noxious particulars.

FLETCHER GLANCED AT his watch. "By the way, Bland, come and ride as far as your home with me."

When they entered the car many wondered who was the debonair heavy-set young gentleman who accompanied Mr. Van Mortimor. Evidently some European friend.

"What a wonderful country!" mused Fletcher. "Just a little brushing up is all the difference often between the humblest and the most exalted."

Home and Gloria, so the thoughts of the serious young pretender ran always at about this hour. That incredibly delightful little creature, so beautiful and so unacquainted with reality.

Situated as he was, he knew in time he might by some

quick coup win her. He knew, if their present relations continued and he used his best endeavors, she might impulsively marry him, but this young Edmond Fletcher had rather a keen insight into human emotions. He knew that just to marry her might be of little avail!

His reason for such a conclusion was that their minds necessarily thought in different languages, and, as at present constituted, could no more mix permanently than oil and water.

Mated happiness seemed to Edmond Fletcher dependent upon absorbing interests much greater than any mere physical thrill could inspire. He could never enter upon Gloria's formal, sophisticated plane of thought, and therefore the question was, could he ever bring her down or up to his own, whichever it really was?

More than her body, he wanted her whole soul, and if he ever had Gloria Van Mortimor that completely, he intended to have more than the mere modern formal lie of marriage for her promise.

Such idealism, he admitted, verged upon the ridiculous in the minds of many today. But then, nothing is impossible in the eyes of youth, and so he did think anyway!

Now the problem that confronted him was how to change Gloria, remake her to his own liking, and thus his very own! His was the dominant role or nothing!

"Surely," he pondered as he rode at Bland's side, "if one could once impress her with the seriousness of life, her true sweet heart would respond to more worthy things than the social fripperies that now engross her."

She must see his viewpoint if she were ever to become his true wife. In a flash he thought of a scheme by which he could change and develop Gloria, if it worked. Instantly, he was again the great gambler, staking everything on a desperate chance, but to him an infinitely worthwhile one, for the prize was the life and soul of Gloria Van Mortimor herself!

FLETCHER WAS SITTING erect in his seat now and was staring straight ahead with a distant look in his eyes as the idea formed in his mind. Bland was alert to the situation. Something of momentous importance had dawned upon his amazing chief.

Bland dared not move lest he disturb the young financier. As the hope leaped into his breast that out of this he might get something to do, he watched with avidity the roll of the mental dice.

Slowly Fletcher's gaze fell on Bland, who strained himself to clear his mind for quick action on some of this highly mysterious work which might be forming in the financier's brain.

Bland," he directed, "go at once to the East Side and find three or more appalling cases of destitution, in just as miserable and abominable surroundings as you can. Try to find a very old person or couple literally starving to death. Let's see, find also a very poor person who is desperately ill; and—though this is rather more difficult—find some one who has just died, alone in squalor!

"As quickly as you have located these cases, bad enough to horrify you, telephone me the information. Then you are through. I'll personally take charge. These people are to be dramatically pitiful! Show your genius, Mr. Bland."

Bland dropped off hurriedly.

"Better bring along a lot of handkerchiefs," he flung back quietly. "You will need them!"

As Fletcher came in Gloria ran to greet him.

"You are filling up the newspapers, Sigmond. All day I read about you. They say you are a strong man, just like dad, and that it is going to be just the same as if he had come back."

"Don't believe everything, Gloria," he laughed. "What do you say to forgetting it all, and let us go shimming?"

"How lovely!" she exclaimed. "Must I act 'tough'?"

"As 'tough' as you wish. We'll have an early dinner and then go out to forget who we are."

So Gloria came down to dinner in a little street suit. Her mind was full of romancing through Chinese dens and charmingly villainous places with her big brother. Fletcher looked at her pityingly. He disliked to shock this lovely doll-girl and break up her beautiful crystal world. He was called to the phone. It was Bland. A notebook soon contained some addresses and further information.

11

GLORIA GOES EXPLORING

THEY STARTED FORTH as on a holiday excursion. Gloria clung to Fletcher's arm in the car as if they were about to explore a strange and dangerous country. Never in all her experience had she been beyond Third Avenue, the beginning of the tenement house district, although she had lived most of her life within a few blocks of it.

By some strange irony of fate, in great cities the tenements and poverty always lurk only a few squares away from the exclusive residential sections. All Gloria's knowledge of the slums was pleasantly modified, amusing melodrama with the shock extracted.

Four hours passed in that strange and extensive brick world of grinding poverty; four hours of shock, disillusionment, awakening to reality for Gloria; four hours of equal torment for Fletcher, who understood only too well the agony and horror of spiritual rebirth that was racking the slight form which so bravely stayed by his side as long as her beloved brother wished.

At last they left the dismal room which had just been the scene of a squalid and horrible death. Their unseen stage hand and *deus ex machina*, Bland, had found one for his employer with ease—with tragic ease.

Gloria was shuddering as they sank back against the car's soft cushions. She had always been so carefully shielded from all knowledge, let alone sight, of human sorrow and suffering.

Fletcher's emotions were rather mixed. The plan had worked, thanks to Bland's masterful and truthful dramatics. He himself had been grieved—though not startled—to witness these scenes in the Van Mortimor tenement property. But Gloria was awakening, he knew, into a truly glorious creature. About this he could not help but be elated. Misery did not long oppress him. He had seen and even experienced not a little of it.

But now he wondered whether he had not perhaps gone a little too far within the bounds of his trust. What would the cold, calculating Van Mortimor think of Fletcher's playing on the sensitive sister's feelings? Van Mortimor would scarcely be in sympathy with the impulses toward social justice that would probably follow Gloria's excursion.

From the history of his case, it appeared that Van Mortimor had elected himself alone to the office of dealing high-handedly and ruthlessly with the human emotions involved. Surely he would not relish the idea of his pawn and victim entering this field even in a small way, particularly when it concerned Van Mortimor's own sister. Under his obvious calm, Fletcher was really a little nervous and excited.

AS THEY NEARED the edge of the better part of town, an undertaker's motor hearse shot out of a street ahead of them and blocked their path. To be sure, it was nothing unusual to see one of these death cars on parade, but

"Well," snarled Skyles, "I see from your
looks that it's all up with me."

it struck him that it was very strange at this hour of night. Normal people don't bury their dead after dark!

When he and Gloria finally got past it, the funeral car dropped in behind their motor, cutting in ahead of the plainclothes men in the other car which trailed them.

Fletcher looked back, quite casually—to discover that the haunting thing was following him! Of course it might just be going their way on some casual errand. But the possibilities of that "errand" made him uncomfortable.

Very faintly, as they passed through a dark tunnel of a street, Fletcher heard a sinister sound, the low shrill notes of the blanched face!

The damned thing was with him again! Terror-stricken, he glanced back once more. It was rather dark, but the hearse loomed up, obliterating everything else. The ghastly vehicle was so close behind him that its mudguards must be touching the rear of his machine.

Why did it have its lights turned off? Why didn't Fletcher's detectives keep that infernal thing away from him?

Fletcher felt suddenly alone and helpless. He drew the curtain in the rear of the car to shut out the maddening sight, in case Gloria's eyes had followed his strained gaze. She had not said a word. He hoped she hadn't heard the weird cry.

The car turned quickly into a broad, lighted avenue. What a boon to mankind was light, floods of light! Edmond Fletcher boldly raised the rear curtain. As he had suspected, the hearse was gone.

"I must have light at all times hereafter—lots of light," he meditated solemnly.

What an arrant fool he had been! So many big things he was confident he could do, and yet he could not conquer his own ridiculous fears. He realized that in fact he had been as frightened as a child in the dark!

12

A HUMAN DYNAMO

THE NEXT MORNING Edmond Fletcher arose early. His personal desires must be subordinated for the time being. First, he must get into the harness; set his house in order. Such excursions as that of yesterday were a trifle premature. He must get his great business machine running smoothly at once, hitting on all cylinders; and it certainly had as many cylinders as a centipede has legs. Then if he wished to win Gloria or delve into philanthropy, he would have a clear mind with which to fight the occult influences that surrounded such attempts.

Fletcher sat down before his clean desk and chuckled gleefully. Let Floyd, his front secretary, and the willing gang of underlings dig the stuff up, wade through it, sort it out, and bring him its essentials. He would pass them on to his other secretary, Bland, for an acid test, and then he himself could make quick decisions on policy. He glanced at the opening prices. Everything was rolling along merrily!

Two weeks of incessant business activity followed. Through the days Edmond Fletcher interviewed important executives, took over control of enormous corporations, visited his banks, and displayed generally the qualities of a human dynamo, plus the startling ability to strike like forked lightning.

He might have been seen just dropping in wherever he had interests at any time, without notice, looking through the vaults, and delving into the actions of all his institutions for any signs of favoritism or fraud among their officers. Many a man broke into a cold sweat at his mere appearance. Others by herculean efforts made quick restitution when the news of what he was doing spread through the ranks.

THE FEW WHO were caught red-handed were handled without much mercy. After a scathing denunciation before his fellow officers, the guilty party was told to report the next morning at Mr. Sigmond Van Mortimor's office and warned that if he tried to escape he would be relentlessly hounded down wherever he might go.

One famous bank president and several men of impeccable reputation answered this stinging summons. This avenging angel dealt with all of them alike in private, although not one of them ever knew exactly what happened to any other than himself.

As soon as this Sigmond Van Mortimor felt he had the last penny of restitution which he could possibly get, he ordered the guilty party to settle up his affairs quietly, and just as silently leave the country with his family. The price of every parole was utter secrecy; each one was warned that if he divulged anything about his disposal he would be arrested, brought back and summarily tried in the courts. If they were penniless he gave them funds.

These complete and unexplained disappearances served Fletcher much more effectually than any public punishment. In each instance Fletcher's parting words had been that he bore the man in question no personal ill-feeling. It was simply that he and his institutions could no longer afford to associate with the fellow, nor would he permit him under any conditions to pollute the atmosphere of his companies by a "rotten apple" presence in the country. Edmond Fletcher always said these things with a secret smile, for actually he was taking a tip from the real Van Mortimor, utilizing the tremendous potency of the unseen.

Gradually this determined "understudy" covered all his interests in New York, and in a few more weeks his influence crept out through the country over the railroad systems he controlled. As time wore on, he was learning at first hand the integral parts of his vast machine. Clerks looked up from their ledgers, great lawyers came out of private offices, railroad officials turned about sharply, office boys stuck cheap literature in their desks; cashiers heard a new key turn in the locks of their cages, to find a solemn but kind-spoken young man at their shoulder.

The humblest to the mightiest under him never knew but what this firm youth of avenging fire might appear like a flash from the blue. Strange to say, he was admired for these very qualities. Wherever anything was wrong in the entire Van Mortimor regime, he grew to be expected— and he came!

Steadily, through shrewd orders to Morton, Keene & Co., the adamant young leader was getting rid of all the minority interests in various stocks which he did not want, and acquiring majority stock interests in useful companies.

"Edmond Fletcher's commission account should show big earnings in Morton, Keene & Co.," he reflected sagely.

That, he felt, was permissible pay for his services, inasmuch as his deals would have cost the same commissions
anywhere else. In painstaking fashion he was now welding
his mighty business machine into its maximum working
power.

For a month he had been so busy that his only relaxation
had consisted of a few hours with Gloria in the evening.
They would go to some affair, meet some of Gloria's friends.

Fletcher's terrific activity, as reported in the papers,
was an ever-recurring wonder to Gloria, who had been a
pampered, idle orchid in a field of perfect leisure, and she
found considerable pleasure in just having with her this
striving young Hercules. It was a joy to her to domineer
playfully over him in their home.

The rude view of life which Fletcher had given her was
instilling within her a healthy new curiosity about humanity in general. As a result of that memorable excursion
into the slums, Gloria bombarded him with questions
about the poor, and about the tenement properties which
the Van Mortimors owned. Edmond could see that as
soon as he found time for it, he could direct-Gloria's new
and genuine interest into valuable work in permanently
bettering conditions. In time, the Van Mortimor properties
would prove, not an "obstacle to progress," as city officials
had termed them, but a great force for good. But Fletcher
dared not think of philanthropy for the time being. He
explained that he must get the Van Mortimor business
firmly in hand, and then they would work, hand in hand,
along other lines.

STRICT ATTENTION TO work and abnegation of his
generous nature was showing splendid effects in clearing

Fletcher's mind of his greatest enemy and weakness, fear of the incorrigible Van Mortimor.

Evidently he was pleasing the occult roaming spirit, if such there was, for the moment, and his derelictions had been overlooked, for not once since the incident of the mysterious hearse had he been disturbed in the least. He realized that it was paramount now that his mind be as free as possible while he completed the organization of his huge affairs. As an extra precaution he even began keeping distant from Gloria herself. But she didn't exactly approve of this tendency.

Her "brother" had opened up flood gates of new emotions in the dazzling little beauty, and although she admitted his superior judgment in most things, she wanted more of him now than his time afforded. Gloria Van Mortimor had deferred many of her plans for the social season merely to be as near him as possible, and she believed that she was getting cheated! Sunday afternoons afforded no business excuse for an absence, and on one of these Fletcher sat quietly smoking by the pensive Gloria. This Park Avenue scene was singularly domestic. A very dreamy look came into the girl's eyes—and Fletcher started to call Parkins for his hat.

"Sigmond, dearest!" she asked very contritely, "can a sister love a brother as I love you?"

"No!" he answered emphatically.

"But, Sigmond!" she exclaimed, "I know positively that you are my brother, and I am very much ashamed of myself at times!"

She became so distressed that he simply kissed her and told her to forget about the matter.

BY DINNER TIME Gloria was her natural self. Fletcher had already learned that when she was in the mood of the afternoon it was better not to argue. He well knew that the affection of a beautiful woman is as uncontrollable as the ocean wave. One has it or one hasn't. To attempt to control it directly is futile. He believed that the love of woman must come voluntarily of its own accord, and if, as it so often seemed, it thrived to some extent on discouragement, Fletcher hoped that element too would break in his favor! He waited for Gloria to raise the subject again.

"We shall forget," she soon began, "what I said. You are my brother, and that settles it! However, if there should be anything to your queer fancies, which I just won't permit you to discuss, it surely will all be decided conclusively in a few months. Suppose we just forget about it for that time and be happy, since we have each other anyhow."

Fletcher readily agreed. He himself badly needed time to get his bearings in the Van Mortimor mystery and to work as only a very few mortals had ever had the opportunity to work in this world.

But though Gloria had arbitrarily settled their personal relationship for a trial period, it was too big a matter to remain definitely in suspense. One morning at breakfast Fletcher sensed heavy tragedy hanging in the air the moment Gloria greeted him. Her face was pinched with anxiety, and all that he could draw from her was that she "didn't feel very well." He realized that this answer unsupported from any woman was just a little worse than none.

The truth came out when Fletcher attempted to leave the table. Gloria did not want him to go to the office that day, and she became frantic about keeping him at home as he insisted upon going. Finally, when she could keep him no longer by her pleas and even tears, she produced a tabloid, the *Morning Star,* which had evidently been brought to her attention by one of her maids. Gloria handed him the newspaper with the words:

"You will find out anyway, Sigmond, as soon as you leave—so I might as well show you!"

Before his eyes danced big headlines:

SIGMOND VAN MORTIMOR
IS NOT HIMSELF!
In His Strength Is His Weakness!

This paper will expose one of the most daring and amazing frauds ever perpetrated anywhere, involving Sigmond Van Mortimor, our leading young American financier, in a series of authentic articles which will begin in tomorrow's issue.

This paper renders a great service to the whole nation with our astounding information. It will present simply enough of Mr. Van Mortimor's real character for the people at large to know him and then compare that knowledge with Sigmond Van Mortimor's present life.

Strange to say, in the surprising strength of the pseudo Sigmond Van Mortimor lies his greatest weakness, for this alone, when we are through presenting the matter, will be ample to prove that everything done by Mr. Sigmond Van Mortimor since he started his business career in this country has been either the work of an insane man or a substitute!

This "great" man and all he has done will topple over like a house of cards when the real facts of the case are laid before the public!

Imagine the situation in the financial district when it is

conclusively proved that every recent business act of Sigmond
Van Mortimor has been the work of a lunatic! That every
recent signature of his has been a forgery! Imagine the
consternation which will prevail among the thousands of
railroad employees and officials throughout the country who
get their bread and butter from this man's shifty hands—not
to mention the plight of those who draw their pay from the
interests which he has in banking and realty circles right
here in New York.

Imagine the dishonesty, legal complications, and snarled
financial dealing already perpetrated by this man, if he is not
himself!

The *Morning Star* is safeguarding the rights of the American public with this startling disclosure as no other paper ever
has done! For your own personal sake begin these articles in
tomorrow morning's issue of the New York *Morning Star!*

THERE FOLLOWED LONG columns about Sigmond Van
Mortimor and his enormous fortune. Through it all, carefully written in, was a thinly veiled hint of the true situation.

Somebody knew what he was talking about; had either
pieced all of this together, or could guess enough to take a
chance on opening up a broadside fire upon him!

Fletcher was struck dumb with amazement, for what
confronted him was the literal truth! How could he deny
it? Somehow his imposture had never seemed quite so
bad as all this. But on even a momentary reflection he was
bound to admit that everything was as the paper said.

All Fletcher could do was stare stupidly at Gloria Van
Mortimor, now miserably huddled in a chair. Her head was

down in her arms sobbing as if her heart would break. Then as if he were in a daze Fletcher began wondering vaguely why she should take the very truth itself so hard!

Of course, the world had stepped on him now—but then, he had stepped on the world! The truth about him had to come out some time. Awful as this was, it came as somewhat of a relief from the great strain he had been under for a long time! Maybe the big conspirator behind it all, and any others involved in this tremendous affair would be forced into the open now, and Fletcher could patch things up decently. But Gloria's terrific disappointment presented a real problem.

Fletcher went over to her and touched her gently.

"Gloria," he said sadly, "it seems that the game is up! Will you remember me long?"

She looked up at him in stupid bewilderment and as he continued to stare at her, her expression changed into one of deepest anguish.

"Sigmond," she answered, "are you going to let them say these horrid things about you—that you are!"

"Do you still believe I am your brother?" he asked, incredulously.

"Before everybody in the world," she declared, "you are my brother!" And there could be no doubt of her sincerity in that answer.

"Then," he said, "I am!"

His words had come painfully, sharply, as though many things which had escaped his attention were suddenly flashing before his eyes now. Simultaneously, his face hardened. "Parkins!" he called through the door. "Plug me in a phone here at the table!" He pounced down in a chair as the butler hastily obeyed.

"Oh!" exclaimed Gloria, a smile dawning in her tears, "you are going to fight them!"

"Hell, yes! Pardon me," he barked, grabbing the instrument away from Parkins. "Good thing you delayed me, Gloria—office is open now.

"Come on, operator! Beaver 10—Bland, please—glad you're on the job! But keep awake! Have you seen the *Morning Star?* They've been trying to get me, eh? Fine! Some dirty work at the crossroad there! Hold the line! Gloria, dress for the street quickly! Don't ask me questions, just hurry!"

As soon as Gloria had run out of the room, he resumed:

"Bland! Listen closely. The *Morning Star* is due for an eclipse! Dig out this libel and get hold of all the parties responsible. Call in all my secretaries and split these duties up among them quickly. Find out who owns the *Morning Star* and find out who holds its obligations! Get name of the landlord of its building! Have every man connected with it shadowed for all outside contacts! Notify press associations and wire all major papers labeling the story a canard, but give out no other statement—I'll do that! Now get the screws ready for this gang and wait at the office for me!"

THE RECEIVER SMASHED in place, and there stood Gloria before him, perilously balanced on one heel, but ready for the street.

"You do love me, don't you?" she asked excitedly.

"Well—if what I do to that paper is any evidence of it, just wait and see!"

"Where am I going?" anxiously inquired Gloria.

"Come on!" he ordered, and then a little more kindly: "You're coming along with me. I may need a lot of your sort of faith in me today!"

They rushed down to the car and Fletcher slammed the door so hard that the servants nearly fell over.

"I believe you are mad!" exclaimed Gloria, jerkily. "And goodness, you didn't eat any breakfast!"

"This is horrible!" declared Fletcher, giving away to his feelings. "I should be ashamed of myself getting you into this awful mess."

"I can stand it all right! But what about yourself?" hazarded Gloria.

Gloria was watching intently the present actions of her new brother, and well she might. Fletcher was undergoing a terrific mental readjustment. His folly of grasping at any straw whatsoever to humanize Gloria, even to the extent of parading her around in the slums, had probably suggested this scandalous exposure.

In short his infernal and impractical idealism was showing its usual results, much as might be expected. He was falling down on his great job and hurting Gloria, the dearest thing in the world to him, even while he was trying to help her.

How differently would the real Sigmond Van Mortimor have acted in these late circumstances! Never would he have embarrassed the family unintentionally—at least anything that sinister personality might have done would have been done purposefully. At worst Sigmond Van Mortimor was not a blundering fool!

Nothing hurts a man so much as to be made to appear

ridiculous. This rag of a paper was undertaking to make a fool of "Sigmond Van Mortimor"; and nothing can hurt so much or make one quite so mad in such a situation as to know that he has been acting the part. A very little more of this kind of thing and Fletcher knew that he was through! He was human, very, very human, and the madder he got at the ridicule which the newspaper was heaping upon him, the more he realized that this sort of thing must be stamped upon.

In a flash of anger, there occurred to him the thought of what the old man, Phelps Van Mortimor, Gloria's and Sigmond's father, blustering along and brooking no interference, would have done if some one dared to take advantage of him in such a meddlesome manner!

He must root this rotten thing out at once, and the more he thought about it the angrier he got at this yellow sheet. He would show them in very quick order how he could obliterate his enemies! Any one who trifled with him and, which was much more serious, the great name he bore, would shortly realize his error and retract his words!

Gloria was deeply concerned with this entirely new development in her brother. Such violent resentment was decidedly alarming in one whose past was rather noted for excesses. She had never seen him angry before, and now her calm, easy-mannered brother was burning with rage, a quiet white heat that penetrated the atmosphere about him, and she, did not like it.

He banged on the chauffeur's pane.

"Break through that traffic!" he said sternly. "I'll handle the police!"

They were moving at a frightful pace now and though

Gloria expected some dreadful smash at any moment, she was much more disturbed over what was going on inside her brother's head.

She did not like this overmastering rage. For some deep reason which she could not fathom she even partially feared this singular relative, not for anything which he might do to her, but for other things. There were always to be considered those horrible rumors about him in Europe, and at times even with her his conduct had been so queer. **"WHAT ARE YOU** going to do to these people?" she gently asked, half afraid of his burning temper.

Fletcher's face had become long and set and his upper lip was just a thin white line as his anger mounted higher and higher, and he decided upon the punishment, which not for one moment did he doubt that he could put into execution.

"Wipe the country clean of them," was the verdict, uttered through set teeth; then, as he saw a wave of fright sweep over Gloria, he added:

"No personal violence. I wouldn't so much as leave the bodies of these curs around."

"I don't know how to understand you," soothed Gloria, "you are so kind and good, with such admirable qualities, that I never suspected you had such a terrific temper. You know, dear, there are some very strange things about you. Please don't get too excited!"

Fletcher subsided into a better outward demeanor lest he unnecessarily scare his precious ward.

With one long and undulating shrill blast of the horn, they had come flying through the financial district of the metropolis. Could all of those crooked little streets have been cleared for him? Traffic backed and filled as if making way for the fire department. No one else would have dared to thread the narrow needle of Nassau Street as he did at high speed. But he did it, not knowing that it could not be done.

When the car came to a standstill before the bank, his information was before him at his desk. William Thomas, majority stockholder of the *Morning Star*, banked at the Tremont National Bank. William Skyles was the managing editor and a large stockholder, and there were other sundry and pertinent data. Through his banks, Fletcher knew an effective lever to use on the Tremont National Bank if it should be necessary.

A few minutes at the telephone and he had several persons in quiet conversation. Little do most people realize what power bankers hold, but Edmond Fletcher did. They literally can decree the life or death of industry. The grim words "no money" are uttered, and industrial death ensues; on the other hand easy credit is allowed some favored endeavor, and it flourishes like the proverbial green bay tree.

"I have taken the liberty," reported Bland, "of buying the building which houses the *Morning Star*, and everything else about them that was purchasable on the instant from the third parties. The press manufacturers still have some liens on their printing presses, and already feel that they might get rusty where they are!"

"Thanks!" said Fletcher. "We can just wait right here for these meddlesome people to drop in as we turn out the light of this morning star! But say, Bland! Better go out and drive in forcibly any of this crew that are slow in coming!"

"Yes, sir!" replied Bland instantly departing.

SOON THE ANTEROOM of the private office began filling up with strangers. Prominent among them were a fat gouty man and a tall, cadaverous-appearing individual. They seemed to be the ringleaders of the aggregation.

Through an open door Fletcher sat silently, studying each one as he entered his outer office. They had been informed that Mr. Van Mortimor would see them a little later, and soon they were pacing up and down in full view of him exercising their pent-up energies and glowering at one another.

"Go outside," whispered Fletcher to Floyd, who was hovering at his elbow, "and use your own judgment in admitting them; and, Gloria," he said as his first secretary went out, "step in Bland's office and leave the door open! You may be my very best weapon and safeguard yet. Keep unobtrusively but plainly in sight in that other room all the time!"

"Sigmond! You certainly do act peculiarly," she whispered over her shoulder but with all the confidence in him that could possibly be crowded into those big eyes.

"And you, Gloria," he answered, "can scarcely guess how much you are helping today!"

A portly banker, neatly dressed, spoke a cold good morning to those outside and passed through the anteroom. These bankers had to be so very careful—one could never tell what change in standing might come over a good depositor in a night! The sleek president of the Tremont Bank was instantly admitted into the inner sanctum. He took some papers from his pocket just as a door closed shutting out a view of him to those who waited. Shortly the banker left the inside office—rather hastily, it was, too, as though now he feared some one of the men outside might in some way try to presume upon his acquaintance.

William Thomas, the owner of the paper, was the fleshy man; and he was let in next.

"I am the owner of your personal notes and all the obligations of your newspaper," stated Fletcher in very evenly spaced words. "Some large items will come up for renewal soon. You look to me like a poor banking risk from the rotten way you conduct your sheet. Let me have the truth about this libelous attack!"

"Mr. Van Mortimor," sputtered the gouty gentleman, who was out of breath from all the clamor about the story, and fully realized the purport of what he had just heard, "I only run what I think is true. I try to make an honest but sensational newspaper. My editor must have gone crazy. He said he had a big surprise for me! And so he did! But I never thought it would be one like this. I have brought this lunatic to you and I wash my hands of him!"

"Are you willing to print a full retraction in the same space and headings, and to handle this rat as I direct?" shot from between set jaws.

"Yes, sir!" Thomas quavered.

"What's your editor's name?"

"Skyles."

"Have a seat!" snapped Fletcher to Thomas, and he reflected a moment. Fletcher had never heard the name before, but here in this man Skyles was the brain behind the exposure. Something seemed to identify this fellow in Fletcher's mind from among all the others outside. He was the only man out there with a truly menacing personality.

Already, however, Fletcher had learned that his tale was not overwhelmingly convincing. It simply appeared to be a question of who could bluff with most force.

FLETCHER STEPPED BRISKLY to the door and opened it suddenly.

"Skyles!" he called out sharply. The long, cadaverous man slouched in. His hands were slightly smudged with blue pencil, and his clothes were spotted here and there with glue.

"I am Bill Skyles," he announced as he looked from the one face to the other before him without getting any sign of sympathy and then his gaze strayed into Bland's office, where it seemed to stop fascinated at the surprising presence of Miss Van Mortimor here. Gloria did her part nobly. There was enough scorn in the withering glance she gave Skyles to intimidate an iron man.

"You dirty rat!" Fletcher flared, now letting his passion blaze, "the only reason I do not give you your just deserts with these hands," his hands doubling and twisting as he spoke, "is out of consideration for my sister. Come clean! What's behind all this?"

"Well," said Skyles, "I see from the looks on the faces around here that it is all up with my job, so I may just as well get a little satisfaction out of this swift 'How do you do' and 'good-by.'"

As Skyles spoke the upper lip of Fletcher stretched into a white, thin line.

Skyles went on: "I have a pretty fair nose for news, and I smelled something fishy about your return from Europe and your actions since. I took a long shot in the dark on those headlines and blurbs of mine! If I was right, you couldn't deny it, and I would have scooped America. I have been watching you, Mr. Van Mortimer. You're a queer duck, and my nose tells me," he pointed to it vulgarly, "that there is a big story lurking around you somewhere. This was just the first shot, but it looks like I missed the bull's-eye from the hell of a row you are making. A pig that is stuck right, no matter how big he is, doesn't holler at all; he just rolls over and stays there." Skyles frankly leered at Mr. Van Mortimor.

Fletcher was experiencing a sensation akin to the desire to murder, but he had in mind what he had previously decided upon, a policy which he considered a far more effective way to rid himself of this scavenging pest. His upper lip merely became whiter and thinner until it appeared just a bare thread, as he said:

"I can wipe your yellow paper off the face of the map. I can blacklist you from your filthy employment in this country. In short, through the courts and otherwise, I can ruin you and break you horribly. Regardless of any rights that you may have, I can incarcerate you until you rot, through my power alone, if I wish! The alternative is that you leave America, forever—and at once!"

"How shall I live, and what will my family do?" Skyles asked calmly.

"A rat like you can live anywhere. As for your family. I'll pay them in installments the value of your stock in the paper. If you take them along I'll have it sent to them. Do as you please about that; but be out of the country in thirty-six hours or by everything in hell, I'll smash you!" Fletcher turned to William Thomas. "See that he does this or I'll finish up you and your yellow rag. Now get out, both of you!"

"I must say," commented Skyles sarcastically, "that it is kind of you to pay my traveling expenses where I am going!" And two men slunk away to settle some difference of their own. Gloria timidly emerged.

"Sigmond," she ventured, and as he faced her, she nervously jumped.

"You are not—not yourself," she stammered. "Let me get a doctor?" At no other time could he have been so abrupt and cross with her, but something stronger than himself was urging him on. For a second he saw Gloria only as a part of the problems confronting him.

"Young lady!" he declared. "This is a business game, and from this moment on, I am going to be on the job. In the future, you amuse yourself!"

"Goodness!" she flung over her slender arched shoulders as she staggered out of the office. "You *must* be my brother!"

THEN HE DISMISSED the others concerned and invited in the gentlemen of the press from all the other papers who had, during the interview, been carefully excluded.

"Mr. Van Mortimor," Fletcher announced to them, "awaits with the keenest interest the forthcoming disclosures about himself in the New York *Morning Star!* Possibly he is not well acquainted with himself and will learn many interesting things about himself!"

The reporters left, laughing hilariously. The papers were full of ridicule of the silly story about him. On top of that, the *Morning Star* printed its full apology, and publicly thanked Mr. Van Mortimor for not prosecuting them under the "regrettable" circumstances.

The columnists and humorists of the whole country widely caricatured this incident. Such expressions as "Is Sigmond Van Mortimor himself? I'll say he is!" and, "As sure as Van Mortimor is himself!" became by-words and a part of the slang of the nation.

Edmond Fletcher, nevertheless, pondered gravely over his wonderful success on the very brink of failure. "So shines the truth," he mused cynically and then he caught himself, "but maybe things like this can only happen when its candle power is weak!"

The rest of the day of his signal victory he worked with an iron grip on his actions. One in his position must be very careful what he did or his generous acts would jump up and wreck him.

While lunching with a railroad official that week he had a very peculiar experience. A thought came to him and provided such a shock that he dropped the day's work precipitately. It was the doubt whether he had done all this absolutely unassisted. Maybe there had been some lashes of the phantom whip behind him driving him on to his mad conduct. This violent, avenging wrath he had exhibited was not altogether natural to him.

What a genius this fellow Van Mortimor must be! "Of all possible things," he worried, "I believed my mind was at least my impregnable castle in which I had undisputed sovereignty, yet I can't be so sure of that now, for it seems that this Van Mortimor makes me do what he wants me to, when he feels it necessary!"

Fletcher knew he could handle tangible things, but what about such occult influences as had seemingly been at work within him? He determined to run things more firmly still, lest this mysterious influence should increase its sway over him.

A different, sterner Edmond Fletcher dined with Gloria for many evenings. He slept peacefully at night and felt better in every way while he was keeping up the hard pace. Best of all, when he retired he felt free from Sigmond Van Mortimor.

Gradually Fletcher's great business went ahead. He shook off his sentimental fancies and redoubled his efforts.

But the most appalling thing everywhere to his sensitive nature was the exploitation of the workingmen in his organizations, and their lack of foresight. Fletcher knew that for the average family man to lose employment or meet with illness meant that the wolf was instantly crouching at the door. How he would like to see every one of his employees self-respecting and financially secure!

ONE THING, THOUGH, was noticeable. Fletcher was instilling a new spirit into the men. Crack trains were coming in everywhere on the dot of the hour. Great freight movements were proceeding punctually. Farmers, all about over the nation, found empty cars on the sidings for their produce as if by magic, and the country was getting real service from his systems. One incentive for this was that the men were taking pride in the personal leadership of this strenuous young magnate, who, no matter how hardboiled he might be reputed to be, was violently on the job!

For some time he kept his face set to his task, driving things through by the sheer power of money and will force. Kindness was one luxury that he could ill afford. If he was ever generous again he must wear steel gloves, for the objects of his liberality would jump up and bite his hands—or Sigmond Van Mortimor would do it for them.

Then one night he sat watching Gloria contemplatively. How careful he must be if he ever stood a chance of getting her. Yet only a worm working on a mulberry leaf with patience made a silk gown. Patience was needed; he must not do anything rash, just do the best he could from day to day, and some day his very own Gloria would emerge from the mulberry leaf of his labors.

Gloria climbed over on the arm of his chair and began studying him. Fletcher wondered if she was reading his thoughts correctly.

"The other day," she said pensively, "you called me 'Honey.' It was peculiar—but nice, Sigmond. Just what did you mean?"

Fletcher became nervous. It was easy to tell from Gloria's soft eyes now that she was engaged in the further consideration of the strangely contradictory feelings which he also aroused in her. Almost simultaneously now would come those wildly sweet flashes of feelings from her which so secretly brought that baffling question for her: "Was he her brother?"

"Just that," said Fletcher quickly. "But how are you getting along with this Martha Adams, the social service worker you've employed to investigate some of those cases over in the tenement district?"

"Martha and I are accomplishing a lot!" declared the winsome young lady. "However, some of our cases are terrible disappointments. You would be surprised how thirsty our very worst cases are! Often we find that we are only helping the bootleggers in their vicinity."

"Um-m-m!" he answered, but delighted to find something safe and sensible to discuss.

"So," said Gloria wisely, "we have decided not to help people who aren't willing at least to try to help themselves."

"Fine!" complimented Fletcher. "But that's the trouble with most unfortunate people, in the first place—they won't help themselves when they have an opportunity. I wonder—I do wonder," he pondered aloud, "if we couldn't make some improvement on the usual charity systems. If a fellow could just hit on it, there must be some way of playing on human nature to make people help themselves!"

Fletcher was deeply absorbed for a few minutes. Suddenly practical ideas were breaking upon him like shrapnel. A ray of light was coming to him by which he could help all his many employees.

"Wonderful little Gloria!" he proclaimed excitedly to the dainty slender creature, all curled up like a big kitten and half sleeping beside him. "I see how I can really help people, even against their own wishes!"

An engulfing emotion, was flooding Fletcher's innermost being. As ever when deeply moved, he trembled and his eyes became moist. This bold young dreamer was beginning to vision how he could actually do something for which his heart had so long striven in vain.

Gloria awakened, looked up at him in a puzzled manner. "I do not think I understand!" she said.

"But I do!" cried Fletcher exultantly. "You see it is fine to put people on their feet, but they should be able to stand alone after you do that. Now I have found a way of sort of propping them up so that they will stand up, whether they really want to or not! This is too good to keep—I must get busy at once. I shall explain it all to you and show you how it works a little later. Now, let's retire so I can get up early in the morning!"

"I suppose that is right!" said Gloria dreamily, "but all I know positively is that you certainly are a very sweet brother!"

13

REMOLDING THE WORLD

FLETCHER REVIEWED HIS business handiwork the next day. His great machine was working as a unit. Thanks to the efficient work of his staff in carrying out details, everything was so beautifully dovetailed and organized that his slightest wish, once expressed, reverberated to the farthest ends of his vast enterprises and rippled back promptly in complete execution. He tuned up his solid organization a little bit here and there, where he might expect some friction, and sat back in his chair satisfied.

The whole octopus of his double's fortune was pulsating with new life in every tentacle, and all the great Van Mortimor wealth was actively ready for him to use in molding some things nearer to his own heart's desire. First he contemplated he would make a few strokes beyond the desire for gain, and I see if he could not sound some new harmonies for his employees in their bungling human relations. For at last, he felt, Fletcher knew how to go about that too!

That night, up in the playhouse, he worked out his first big stroke and discussed it with Gloria. She was also enthusiastic at its prospects as she came to realize them.

"You see, it is like this," he summarized. "We must begin

to help people practically, otherwise our efforts and funds are thrown away, just as most charity fails of its purpose. Thrift is the first practical step to comfort and happiness among working people and I have caught an idea by which I can force people despite—or through—their own nature to practice thrift with our help. I can make most of all our employees independent and self-respecting in no time. This is going to cost us something, but it will be worth all it costs and may even prove profitable. I am sure I can do something worth while for all of us!"

Then he went ahead and showed Gloria how he had worked everything out for this. When he finished he exclaimed jubilantly:

"Can you imagine how much happiness this will bring?"

"You are now your own true self," she praised, "my old Sigmond. If you can make them any part as happy as you make me, this will be a sweet old world!"

But that night he was a little restless. He had some anxiety about putting this potent thing into execution. Where would his own impetuous nature lead him? Van Mortimor must be lurking around somewhere, nor would he be too well pleased with his proxy's present intentions! This revolutionary thing which he had planned for tomorrow necessitated a large cash expenditure, and it might very probably bring this eventual catastrophe down quickly upon him. Where would his uncontrollable impulses to help people finally land him.

THE NEXT MORNING Fletcher was in the office early, lest his resolution weaken if he considered too long its personal consequences. It was surely inviting personal disaster from the power behind him. Of the things that might happen, he rather hoped it would bring Van Mortimor out into the open—if alive. Fletcher felt himself fairly intrenched now, and Van Mortimor would have to admit that Fletcher's stewardship had been permitted.

Once fairly begun, Edmond's scheme would carry itself along, while he dealt with Van Mortimor at any personal cost. So it would be if he came out in the open; but Fletcher did not fear that half so much as what else Van Mortimor might do! From what he knew about him, it was far more likely that Van Mortimor would mete out from his mystic ambush some diabolical punishment concocted at his leisure. Be that as it might, this thing was too big for him to consider selfishly. He would take chances on his fate.

Within his first hour of business he issued this astounding bulletin throughout all of his enterprises:

Effective as soon as arrangements can be perfected, this organization will give each employee earning under three thousand dollars per annum, who is accredited by a duly constituted bank with saving ten per cent or any less amount of his salary, a sum equal to one-half of such savings.

This additional sum is absolutely donated and deposited to the employee's credit in his personal account, on conditions entered into between the employer and employee, namely, that the employee cannot withdraw this money, either his special personal savings or our donations, in part or in whole while in the service of this company, except with the consent of the company, which will be freely given where and whenever any real necessity arises.

This is designed as true life insurance. It really insures life while living, for those who accept its benefits, the people making under three thousand dollars a year, who most need such a safeguard. It is presumed that all making over three thousand dollars a year have sufficient of the wolf in them to keep the kindred animal away from their door themselves.

Not one of you employees is to be put under the slightest obligation to save, and it is purely optional with each of you whether you do so or not. This simply means that we will absolutely give you regularly every pay day one-half of what you permanently save.

SIGMOND VAN MORTIMOR.

"Now watch them save like beavers, just as they work," Fletcher chuckled merrily after this was posted. "Their very selfishness to get that fifty per cent will make them forego extravagances, as nothing else on earth could do. It isn't so ruinous to us either, considering that ten per cent of the highest salary is only three hundred dollars, which means we can only pay out a maximum of one hundred and fifty dollars, just a decent bonus, to one man in a year. But it sounds like a tremendous gift to the employee, and in its results it is," he craftily reflected, "for he has saved at least twice as much as we gave him, and with compound interest he will find himself respectable and on the road to independence before he knows it."

However, though scattered bonuses had frequently been given to special classes, no one before had ever dared to give a great bonus daily, and to all workers generally.

Instantly the office was a storm center. Fletcher had never guessed that he could start such a bedlam. Every one in the place was busy at telephones and interviewing a frantically interested mob. Fletcher was besieged by all who thought they had a chance of getting his attention. Both telegraph news tickers were devoted to details of this gift, nearly to the exclusion of everything else.

Fletcher, with some misgivings, turned to the opening clicking of the stock ticker. Ah! here was the real answer to what lie had done if he could just interpret it aright.

Beginning at this moment the answer would start and it would all be discounted on the stock tape months in advance of the actual results. If he could just feel this pulse of the nation today, tomorrow, this week, and read the true results at once—then there would be further selfish opportunities which would please Van Mortimor himself.

THE MARKET OPENED hesitantly and then the avalanche of selling stunned Fletcher. In lots of thousands of shares the sales came, his stocks holding as fast as they could, but gradually receding—then there was a lull and the selling and prices strengthened slightly.

"Ah!" he grinned as he half-guessed the cause for this and his breath came a little freer. "The professionals, the wise boys, sold the market short against the news, and there's been some little liquidation. Now they are all wondering just which way the cat will jump and they are afraid of supporting orders from me. In the next few days we shall see what the minority interests do with their stock in all these companies in which I hold control! If they sell, prices will go lower and I'll get bargains, according to my way of thinking."

Thus, while he put through a great heroic good, another spirit within motivated him to profit selfishly by it and he listened to this second inner voice just as gladly as the first. Such is the nature of us all.

To his brokers, and particularly old Morton's frenzied request for advice, Fletcher said laconically:

"No supporting orders! The situation is well in hand."

He refused to see officers, directors, and stockholders, no matter how big their holdings in his companies. Knowing what to expect from these people he had issued a blanket reply for all of them which was nearly as insulting under the circumstances as if he had sent around a handbill to them. His message was:

> All great pioneer benefits entail some sacrifice. I stand to lose more than all of you put together and am absolutely within my rights. If you are not with me, sell your stocks.

And with that stereotyped message behind him, he left the office at noon, through for the first day, leaving pandemonium to reign in that short street called Wall which has a river at one end and a graveyard at the other.

Gloria had all the "extras" awaiting him. Reading about her brother in the papers had become a steady diversion with Gloria in Fletcher's absence. For her now he had a sort of dual personality; one was this kindly good fellow with whom she spent such a big part of her time, and the other the vainglorious demigod of industry who could be relied upon to give one a thrill almost every day in the news.

Gloria had a letter from Martha Adams, her social service worker, explaining some special work and some new arrangements she had made for her many patients. Much to Fletcher's delight Gloria had planned an expedition to inspect the patients and see that they wanted nothing. As

Fletcher was very busy she invited Myrtle Marbleton and Count Rononotski to accompany her.

Myrtle came very near accepting, as of course she relied upon Van Mortimor's cheering presence in this obnoxious undertaking. When the personnel of the expedition was made known, she was nearly stricken with apoplexy, considering the number of conflicting appointments which she found in her engagement book.

Fletcher did not leave the house the next day; and that afternoon Gloria and the count, closely followed by the detectives whom Fletcher had been careful to provide, came in exhausted from their efforts. In appreciation of his helpfulness Fletcher and Gloria insisted upon the European's dining with them. One had to admire his sportsmanship. He was a good fellow at heart and Gloria was very close to that organ indeed, for more reasons than he had originally intended. At dinner the count voiced weakly:

"Mr. Van Mortimor, you know it—I would help them as I could for your sister. But the next time I dress like a truck driver and wear one Red Cross sign so that they will know I am a non-combatant! Too many things they happen accidental-like!" He inspected his clothes for spots and nursed his toes under the table.

"But it is a wonderful country, *n'est-ce pas?* No matter how miserable the people be here, they have a keener sense of humor than I."

After dinner Fletcher slipped away to his rooms and left the count with Gloria for an evening which he certainly deserved.

FLETCHER TOOK THIS opportunity to study seriously the press comments about himself. He hadn't realized what a pandemonium his action could start throughout the whole nation. The papers varied widely in their opinion of him. But the consensus of opinion was that he had acted rather foolishly in view of his previous sane and rigorous policies.

Capital was unanimously bitter in its denunciation of young Van Mortimor's "suicidal liberality." Great industrial leaders contended that if he established this silly precedent, men would be clamoring for the same benefits from competing companies, and that there was no telling how far this thing might spread. Fletcher keenly enjoyed this vein of thinking.

A socialist paper acclaimed him as a money baron with a spark of intelligence, but doubted that his men would really get the money as freely as it was promised. And here was something small but powerfully significant: the Roundhouse Union of Racine, had elected him an honorary member. He made a note of that. Those boys would get an inspiring wire of acceptance from him.

But all the other harsh criticism wore down Fletcher's spirit. One can assert that he is immune to others' opinions and remarks, but each lash flicks on the raw, each criticism sinks a little barb in his consciousness and depresses one, just as every one feels a sense of exhilaration when praised.

Fletcher had a much better criterion than the news by which to judge what he had done, but this was not blazoned in the papers. Thousands of letters and messages were flowing into the office from employees, thankfully anxious to get started saving. As against this, the prices of his securities were slowly, but steadily declining on the exchange. Fletcher glanced over the stock tables gloomily.

Surely this thing would bring Sigmond Van Mortimor

down upon him, but where was he? Last night Fletcher had been in mortal terror, yet nothing had happened, and today, so far, there had been no evidence of his ghostly shadow. If anywhere, Van Mortimor was probably very near Fletcher, right here in New York!

But this Van Mortimor was no ordinary antagonist who could be easily seen. He might at this very moment be watching him and coldly calculating some torture in which he would take a ghoulish delight at just the most opportune time. Sitting in his very comfortable seat Fletcher shuddered to think that most anything horrible might happen to him at any minute now in these luxurious surroundings!

He arose and inspected the window fastenings, and minutely went over the upper floor of the apartment. Fletcher didn't see how he could sleep without ventilation and yet he scarcely dared leave a window open.

Near one of the windows, partially hidden by the side drapery, he found an ingenious device recently installed for controlling the heat of the radiators concealed under the window seats. By a thermostatic arrangement the heat was controlled automatically at any degree it was set.

This intrigued him. He set the hand up ten degrees and he could hear the steam charging into the radiators. He pushed the hand violently in the opposite direction and the temperature soon got chilly, compelling him to reset the heat indicator. It greatly interested him—this small delicate instrument having such perfect control of all the cumbersome steam-fittings and power which went to make up the heating system.

This clever little mechanism stealthily throttling, propelling, and gauging all the heat, reminded Fletcher very unpleasantly of the way Van Mortimor invisibly regulated his proxy's conduct and emotions to suit his own desire. The very stars were set against Fletcher now! The pressure he would feel would make him writhe for his last offense! **FLETCHER COULD NOT** sleep well during the night. He purposely left on a light, and only had one of the windows in his bedroom open, just a little from the top. During the early hours he woke up suddenly with a sense of something burning his hand. Then he felt very foolish, for he was standing over by the window with his hand on the heat regulator.

Evidently he had been playing with its indicator in his sleep. Never had he been given to sleep-walking and this new experience rather nettled him. The steam contrivance must have strangely fascinated him. It was very late and still, but the light was burning as he had left it.

The much disturbed young man turned the lever up sharply. The heat charged up with a gentle pulsating sound. It was unpleasantly warm. He turned the heat off. Then he thought he heard faintly the notes of the blanched face coming from his window. But it was not distinct. Probably he had only imagined this, he reflected, as he had just quickly turned down the steam and the radiators were under the window-seats. That might account for what he had heard, but he wasn't sure. He got down on his hands and knees, and putting his ear as close as he could to the pipes listened.

How silly he was—suppose some of the servants saw him! Getting up, he looked searchingly at the tiny indicator which had such a powerful grip on the steam and such a suggestive and irritating influence over him. Fletcher did not like the thing and a fury surged up in him against it.

He would order it removed, for he couldn't tell whether he heard the guttural notes of his avenging Nemesis or not with such a weirdly gurgling thing in his bedroom. It was useless to try to sleep. He dressed and unnoticed, slipped out into the night, but he did not go far, for fear of being caught unprotected by the great thrill pander who followed him.

He soon came back and lay down in one of the rooms below where they had not yet installed that infernal device which softly pulsated and gurgled so humanly.

With the day Fletcher's fear somewhat abated. Darkness and fear, light and self-confidence are so inseparably interlinked in our understanding. He disliked to disrupt the household with his eccentricity and give in to what was most probably only a figment of his imagination. Then, too, the strenuous market of which he was now the storm center distracted his attention from this haunting fancy at home. There was no use worrying about Van Mortimor in that maelstrom. Time enough when the thrill hound came!

Fletcher had a premonition that there would be no doubt about it when Van Mortimor came this time—he believed he would know it as a man might feel the touch of a thousand needles. So he slept with his door open and lights on, and kept a servant in his rooms on the pretext that he wasn't well.

Meanwhile throughout the ensuing-week, the strain of the falling stock prices became terrific. Pressure was being brought to bear from every source upon this wild young capitalist to support the market and not let his securities

go lower, for they were now leading the whole list downward. But he sat maliciously inactive, and silently watched
the tape, while he rigorously counseled his soul to wait for
the utmost bargains. To do this he had to steel his heart
against all entreaties.

BUT EVEN AS he schemed so Satanically, this adamant
young financier took every short-cut and precaution for
putting his new pet philanthropy into operation. Within
a few days he had it so generally authorized that it would
be in evidence on every pay roll of all his many enterprises
that week even if hell must burst with it.

He, who had been so easily seen, so likely to drop in
anywhere, had become a recluse hugging his ticker behind
tight-locked doors, while all the world could praise him or
damn him as they wished.

Now came the day! Friday, it was, and truly a black one.
It was about two o'clock as Fletcher watched the tape
sullenly. He had believed for five consecutive minutes that
his stocks were scraping bottom, as low as they could be
carried at this time.

Then and then only did he begin to buy cautiously, and
all the time that he was buying, he kept answering desperate appeals for the support of the market with his cryptic
reply that he wasn't interested in the gamblers over there—
meaning of course on the New York Stock Exchange where
now he was the very biggest speculator.

The bargains Fletcher got were thousands and thousands of shares of America's greatest corporations. He did
not bid up for anything. He just took them quietly at the
last sale or under as they were offered, his sly purchases
almost unnoticed in the day's demoralization of values.

But to his chagrin the market did not firm up after he had bought absolutely all he wanted. On they came, these avalanches of big selling orders. Prices sagged lower.

Now he gave forth the news that he was supporting the market—blatted it over the news tickers—rushed it through the wires over the country, inasmuch as he had his chosen line very fully purchased.

Yet still the stocks came for sale until he was forced really to support the market, and now he stood desperately overbuying to protect himself. Soon his brokers were frantically taking everything on his rushed orders to stem the tide and hold his already swollen purchases from further depreciation.

Never during that awful day did Fletcher know how much he bought. He only knew that he was still within the cash assets of the Van Mortimor fortune, as magically calculated by his feverishly working corps of secretaries from moment to moment.

An hour and twenty minutes after the exchange closed, which was twenty minutes after four o'clock, the ticker was still running, despite the emergency use of the most abbreviated code: it was that far behind, but it closed steady for the last ten minutes on his herculean support. Blankly he stared at the prices which could not go lower—that day. Most of the Van Mortimor fortune was spent for securities which must be paid for by fifteen minutes after two o'clock Monday.

The door of Fletcher's private office opened without formality, and there stood old Wilkerson, the president of the bank.

"Your requirements here, sir!" he cut in brusquely,

"surpass even your credit with this bank by one half million dollars!"

"Get it!" spoke the young financier coldly.

"No, my boy!" answered this staid old veteran of innumerable big loans, "this is a poor time for you to pull your bold authority on me! I don't have to listen to you!"

"Why?" snapped Fletcher.

"Because the legal limit for your credit with this bank is reached; and there is another reason why you shouldn't ask this of me as a favor!"

"Well—spring that, too!" demanded Fletcher breathlessly.

"Because," Wilkerson said kindly, coming around to put his arm affectionately on Fletcher's shoulders, "I have already personally arranged your little deficiency here! By Gad, it does my heart good to see you working—just like the old man, you are, pulling off stunts and running everybody ragged when it's nothing but a blind for you to steal control cheaply of some of your competitors in all this excitement! I know two or three big corners in stocks will show up soon!"

WILKERSON STALKED OUT in high satisfaction before Fletcher could thank him, but this wild young financier went ahead thinking confusedly. Corners nothing! He had not stopped to concentrate all his buying on two or three important companies in this demoralization, as he might well have done, so that he could now engineer corners and run the prices up to break even in any event. He was just desperately overburdened with his own and all other good stocks—a bull on America and that was all!

At ten o'clock the next morning prices would move

again. If they held or went up, all would be well; but should they go much lower not even he could support his tremendous line of stocks for many minutes more. This stupendous business organization and all its wealth of which he had had sole charge would be wiped out!

Suddenly Fletcher clutched his desk with both hands, for faintly but distinctly the weird cry of the blanched face rang in his ears as his true situation flashed upon him. In that instant he painfully saw that the entire Van Mortimor fortune was threatened with ruin, while Edmond Fletcher, through the commissions accredited to him in the office of Morton, Keene and Company, was a wealthy man!

Let Van Mortimor come and give him his just deserts quickly, Fletcher inwardly moaned. He deserved the worst that the outraged owner of this fortune could possibly do to him. Scarcely cognizant of his surroundings, he made his way down to the car and was driven home in a daze.

Fletcher tried brokenly to explain to Gloria the frightful thing he had done, how they might be poverty-stricken through his acts; but she could not understand and insisted on sticking by him in all events.

"I know," he informed her contritely, "come what may, where I have enough to insure you a living," and in his heart he thanked providence for that positive proof of his real identity which was so safely tucked away in a safe deposit box to be opened on his signature.

"You mean to insure us a living!" she insisted. "With everything else gone, happiness may still exist for me now, but not without you, my dearest!"

"Don't, Gloria," he pleaded, "you make me ashamed of myself, you sweet, wonderful girl. But you don't know what you say! You are simply repeating the fool ideas that I have given you."

While they dined, he mustered courage to ask:

"Gloria, may I make a silly request of you?"

"Certainly," she agreed readily, "anything you wish."

"Would you mind if I had those steam regulating devices taken out of my room at once if possible?"

"Not in the least," she responded, no little surprised, "but don't you like them? The workmen went to terrific pains putting them in a few days ago under a big engineer, who was sent here from Chicago especially to install them in this apartment just for us alone. No one else in the building has them! I don't know how we could get them removed instantly."

"Then we can't get them out tonight," he spoke sadly, "but forgive me; it is just a queer fancy which I have taken against them," and they both laughed nervously.

Fletcher excused himself and retired early, worn almost to the breaking point under the strain. His servant in the next room, sleeping there by his orders, annoyed him moving around, and Fletcher snappishly dismissed him for the night, ordering him to stay away. Before long, he rather regretted this, but his pride prevented him from shilly-shallying before a menial.

HE SHUT HIS bedroom up tightly. All doors leading into it he bolted, and he locked the windows securely. Then he tried to sleep with the lights on, but he could not manage to doze off. The light irritated his overwrought nerves and he felt he would suffocate without fresh air.

In desperation he raised one of the two windows just a little. The steam regulator unfortunately was between

"Can't you see? I am not your brother!"

them, so that he could not avoid its being near the one he opened. He turned off the lights and fell like a dead weight into bed, for he was completely worn out.

Strange to say, sound sleep came to him, the sleep of the exhausted—sleep as of the dead who know no worry.

It seemed, hours later, that from the depths of an all-pervading slumber he found himself floating on the bosom of a river or out in a boat somewhere, for it was very moist all about. He dreamed that he was proceeding slowly through a murky fog. He was in the tropics, he supposed, for it was warm, even sultry. Fletcher was puzzled about where he could possibly be traveling, as he had no boat lines to worry about. He thought he would ask somebody to explain it all.

Now all at once, as occurs in dreams with reason and fantasy combined, he found he was alone in some strange sticky hot place. In an effort to free himself Fletcher wandered about blindly, pushing through dank, wet, clinging undergrowth. It was everywhere.

Suddenly he heard the horrifying notes of the blanched face. Then he stopped breathless with terror. Better to suffer anything than to encounter the fiend. It was getting dreadfully hot and he felt that he would suffocate if he could not get out of this sweltering and engulfing bog.

Then, squarely in front of him, loomed up Van Mortimor with a malicious leer upon his chalky face; and he held high in his hand that haunting steam gauge with pipes swinging from it gushing fire and steam. These the fiend turned upon Fletcher as His Satanic Majesty, Van Mortimor, gave forth a sardonic howl of delight.

Fletcher crumbled under the pitiless assault. He was being roasted alive as the maniac basted him with the fire and live steam from the gushing pipes, in a wet and sticky hell.

The pain seared him right and left as he screeched out in agony, for he was fully conscious now and this was no dream! His yells were getting fainter, already scarcely audible. He was suffocating. In his anguish he even realized that he had locked his doors on the inside, and that he was powerless to open them.

YET JUST AS the burning inferno enveloped him he could hear frantic pounding on the door. With a terrific impact something came crushing in. Air, air, worlds of cool air flooded in; but he was unconscious. He was gently carried out to Gloria's tender ministrations, while the steam was hastily shut off from below.

Lying in Gloria's rooms, the setting of so many happy moments, he was found to be scalded and burned almost all over his body, for he had been unable to protect himself. A physician was tediously and carefully plastering some

greasy balm over his skin. He had to be nearly mummi-
fied to live.

Fletcher revived momentarily as a measure of blessed
relief came to him, and with swollen eyelids he painfully
blinked at the anxious crowd about him. The sensitive little
"sister" was sobbing her anguish.

"What happened?" he asked faintly with quivering lips.

"Some wretch broke the automatic control device off
the wall and that opened the steam valves. Your bedroom
was flooded when the steam came on this morning," they
tried to explain.

"I shouldn't have left the window open," he said wanly.
"Any evidence of the intruder?" he mumbled.

"None," replied a detective, "unless you can remember
giving some person this. One of your cards—we found it
on the window sill."

Fletcher beheld across the pasteboard:

SIGMOND VAN MORTIMOR

He shrank back from it in mortal terror as they carefully
and sadly prepared him for the hospital.

"Oh, yes! Van Mortimor," he cried in sudden delirium. "I
am sorry I didn't get to see him, but you must get somebody
in my place. His fortune is at stake. Get somebody just like
me. It's quite the regular thing." He raved on.

"Poor dear boy," sighed Gloria, tears streaming down
her face, "and he wanted that horrible thing out last night."

Day stretched after day, and then weeks passed as he lay
helpless, unconscious the greater part of the time, in his
suffering from his burns and a general nervous breakdown.

Hard as they fought against it, pneumonia set in from the scorched condition of his lungs.

In an all-consuming service Gloria Van Mortimor did practical things which had previously been undreamed of by her. She alone must feed him and wash his face. No one but she must be permitted to touch him more than absolutely necessary. What did mere doctors know about how gently he should be handled? Were not her hands infinitely softer than theirs? Theirs might not be tender enough. In her now truly was aroused the eternal feminine.

Horrible were Fletcher's ravings. He continually feared he would be poisoned. "The Borgias have me!" he would shout, "but only the brother is venomous!"

He examined his food minutely and, holding a clear glass of water up to the light, he would study it intently for the palest of discolorations before he dared drink it. To please him, Gloria had all his food searchingly examined and she would try to allay his fears by tasting it in advance of him. But this would throw him into paroxysms of fear, and his innate character was vividly shown, in that no matter how much he feared the food himself, he would let no one else, however humble, taste it before him.

"This is my gamble only," he would hysterically cry. "Do you think I am an ingrate?"

BUT TIME HEALS or kills all things, and in Fletcher's instance, slowly the pain from the scalded places abated, the overwrought nerves became firmer, and though he could not move, and still had the pneumonia, his intelligence at last emerged out of chaos. They had kept all news from him; but now that he was himself mentally they saw it would be worse to withhold information than to give it to him.

Gloria had assured the patient repeatedly that everything was well, that there positively had been no wolves howling at the door which she had noticed! Bland and the secretaries had often tried to convey to their audacious leader that the market was better, but in his feverish state it had been hard for him to understand how such a thing was possible; for even in his half delirium he knew that they would not have told him the worst if it were true.

A day came, though, some six weeks later he was permitted to run exultantly over the stock report page of a newspaper. What he found there was too good to be true. The market for his securities was up an average of ten points from the dreadful low at which he had loaded up so heavily.

He took some gigantic profits on a part of those great purchases and settled back in bed, his mind eased for the time being of his very greatest fear. If Van Mortimor had any interest at all left in worldly goods, Fletcher had certainly garnered an astounding supply of them for him! He did not know how much he had bought on the break, and it would take the boys at the office a long time to compute exactly all he had gained.

Dr. Bates had practically given his entire time, simply lived with him. By some strange telepathy the good old family physician also seemed to suffer equally with Fletcher through it all.

So the days ran along as Christmas approached. Gloria's only aim in life, it appeared, was to get Fletcher home for the holidays. How one's view can change. Here was this wonderful brother of hers, one of the most eligible young bachelors in the world, and what a social season she had planned for him in which he would have been lionized! But now she had dropped all of those plans entirely, and the confusion of the hospital and her anxiety about him had caused her to forget even her personal invitations and engagements.

14

STRANGE CHRISTMAS VISITORS

CHRISTMAS WAS ALMOST at hand, and each day Fletcher grew stronger as if Gloria's unconscious prayers were being answered. Subtle emotions often enter into trivial events and make of them epochal occasions.

Gloria Van Mortimor had been reared virtually an orphan and her great wealth had served to make her a singular one in some respects. There were some bleak little spots back in her life that must be lived over again, since at the time the circumstances of her childhood had precluded her from ever enjoying them.

Every recent Christmas since she had settled upon her way of celebrating it, had found her alone with her Christmas tree and surrounded with reminiscences of what this day had meant when she had a dad, and Sigmond was a big playful boy.

Then, years later, dad left her and Sigmond; and, against her pleadings, they took him, all that she had left, this dear dreamy-eyed brother, far away from her. She always bought him a gift, however, and placed it on the tree, aside from the formal ones which they at first exchanged across the ocean.

She had some of the dolls which her mother had given her, particularly "Psyche," a big beautiful bisque one, and these, together with treasured things that she had received from her father, she grouped about her tree and kept her trysting place with memories alone each Christmas, looking at the gift for her brother and wishing he might be there to receive it. Then her heart always broke and she cried in her loneliness.

Too wonderful to contemplate—for this Christmas she would have him, her brother! By every means, she must get him home! For did she not have a rendezvous with love?

Under these circumstances Fletcher came home on Christmas Eve, making the event real for Gloria.

The Christmas spirit was upon him also and he wondered absent-mindedly why Gloria kept so busy away from him, with her door closed so very formally. Finally from his rooms he peeped through the keyhole into her boudoir. On her bed were a dozen dolls of all sizes. "So that is what she likes!" he smiled to himself.

Fletcher carefully made his way down below and ordered the car. The servants bundled him up and the ride was exhilarating, as his motor nudged through the heavy traffic to the best toy shop on the avenue. A hasty consultation with a magical engineer of toydom produced a good suggestion! From what he had seen Fletcher naturally wanted the finest and prettiest doll obtainable. This order fairly kindled the toy wizard into a flame of inspiration.

"WE SHALL MAKE of it a masterpiece," he promised, "a work of creative art! A truly lovable doll, and a highly complimentary gift to your sister, would be an exact likeness of the young lady! We shall produce a miniature Miss Gloria Van Mortimor!"

Pictures were obtained hastily. There were many strange doings in the Van Mortimor play house that evening.

Snow was gently falling on the window sills before Fletcher closed his eyes. He was content with all the world, and tomorrow would be a white Christmas.

The next morning early, ever so early, for Gloria could not sleep, there came a knock on the door between the rooms, and Fletcher jumped to the entrance, for fear she would see in prematurely.

"Merry Christmas!" sang a glad little voice. "Come through this way to our Christmas tree. Just put on a dressing gown. I cannot wait for you to dress!"

Fletcher put on some things quickly, and went through Gloria's bedroom to the parlor of her suite.

Before him he beheld Gloria in a gorgeously flowered kimono, seated before a fairy Christmas tree, resplendent in ethereal frost and sparkling silver. It was not yet dawn and mellow candlelight from its verdant branches cast a glamorous flickering softness about, which made Gloria the picture of a saint at a shrine, while she again kept her tryst, and this time so rapturously looked upon a true Christmas tree, one which could be shared. Radiantly, she turned to Fletcher.

"Come sit close to me on the floor and just be foolishly happy. This is so much ours alone that no one else must even see us now."

Fletcher dropped down beside her and gave her a big hug. Silently, half in awe of what was around him, he had a vision of the innermost workings of her strangely famished heart. No one but himself, who had been partially admitted to her tenderest feelings, could have guessed what lay buried under the cool exterior of the little heiress.

"Open up your presents, Sigmond, just as you used to do for dad and me," her soft voice quavered, "and so long ago for—for mother."

Her grateful hand trembled, as she delicately pushed to him in their proper order boxes, each containing a present which she had kept for her brother from one to twelve years.

"Hurry," she said, while he undid one gift after another, "you are a little late. I have had merely to look at them for so many Christmases."

We are all children at heart and such is the spirit of Christmas. For a little while these two wiped out the callousness and selfishness of adult life and reveled in the mythical existence of childhood.

Gloria's happiness was complete, except that suddenly there came over her face a slightly blank expression, which Fletcher immediately caught and correctly interpreted. It had just occurred to the winsome little lady that her remarkable brother had not given her anything.

Fletcher instinctively glanced over his shoulder. They had been so absorbed in their own affairs that they had not noticed the approach of an eavesdropper, although the eavesdropper had had a very hard time getting in. Behind Gloria and Fletcher, and all rapt attention but so begrimed and dirty that he was scarcely recognizable, sat a great, big, shaggy dog.

Gloria had turned around sharply, following Fletcher's startled expression.

"Heavens!" she cried. "What is it and where did it come from?"

"My Lord!" exclaimed Fletcher, "that is Belshasher!" At the mention of his name the big dog came galloping upon them. He waded into them with such force and scattered their presents so effectually that everything was chaotic for a minute.

"Down, Bell! Down, Bell!" frantically yelled Fletcher, and at last the big dog subsided from his strenuous greetings, taking up a position half in Gloria's lap with his head cocked wisely to one side at Fletcher. Sometimes all academic discussions about our relationship to animals can be very easily settled by a mere reunion with an old pet. In this instance it was hard to tell which expressed the greater affection for the other, Fletcher or the dog.

PARKINS, VERY DEEPLY distressed, presently appeared in the doorway.

"Oh, sir! Beg pardon, sir!" he stuttered. "How did that dog get in here? I have put him out of the house a dozen times!"

"Where did he come from?" asked Fletcher eagerly.

"I don't know, sir! He jumped off of the dumbwaiter this last time! He rode up on the groceries and I was chasing him in the picture gallery when I heard him crash in another direction."

"Don't chase him any more!" said Fletcher, both he and Gloria laughing. "Leave him here with us. I think he has earned a good rest!"

The butler limped away in outraged bewilderment.

"I can't guess how he found us," commented Fletcher blankly to Gloria, "but that old rascal you are nursing is my very own dog, Belshasher!" The old rascal barked again at the mention of his name. "See how he knows his name? I'll show you all of his circus tricks later. You probably want to get rid of the mud of our early caller and then come into my rooms. I have something for you that you may like!"

"Let's take his mud along! I can't wait!" said Gloria, but she was inspecting the old and obviously unpedigreed dog thoughtfully.

Belshasher, possibly thinking it meant breakfast as of old, joyously led the way.

Fletcher among other things diffidently presented his small but rather unique surprise, the artistic miniature likeness of Gloria Van Mortimor. Gloria in all anticipation undid its elaborate wrappings carefully. Then she tenderly brought out the beautiful little reproduction of herself. She fondly held this marvelous creation of her own self in her arms and studied it, nearly overcome with emotion.

"Little Gloria," she breathed ever so softly, as she held it close to her and looked up at Fletcher, her eyes showing her gratitude, "how sweet she is!"

In rapture she carried her gently—ever so gently—over to the window, straight into the full light of the breaking dawn as Fletcher followed her. He was struck with the new and wonderful softness in Gloria's countenance as she gazed upon her little Gloria in her arms.

"Sigmond," she perceived suddenly, "she has blue eyes!"

Fletcher reddened. That confounded toy artist had worked wonders from pictures, but he had not discovered the true color of Gloria's eyes and he had taken a chance on their being the same as her brother's. Fletcher's small surprise had proved a boomerang.

He was so genuinely embarrassed that he would have been forced to leave the room, but for the quick assertion of the eternal feminine in Gloria Van Mortimor. Gloria was in every sense a woman and she possessed the full complement of the complex emotions of her sex. Every Christmas Day about this time for many long years she had cried in her bitter loneliness and now, for the very extreme opposite reason, she was also crying. Edmond hurried over to comfort her.

NO EXPLANATION COULD be found of Belshasher's startling appearance, and Gloria, with that usual complaisance with which she shrouded all strange occurrences, asked none. But along in the afternoon she dropped a remark even more amazing to Fletcher than the dog's coming.

"Sigmond, dear," she said, gently chiding him, "you peeped at my Christmas tree last night." And when he glanced at her in frank astonishment: "I saw you in my room after I had retired!"

"Oh, Gloria," he declared, "you are mistaken!"

A look of wild alarm came into her sensitive countenance and quickly spread into one of positive terror.

"Don't! Don't!" she cried out sharply. "Sigmond, you scare me! You wouldn't joke with me about a matter like that, would you, dear? Tell me—you must tell me that you were in my room about one o'clock!"

A cold chill crept up Fletcher's spine as she gave way to her fears; and he answered her numbly:

"Yes, dear! Yes, yes; forgive me, it was I. I couldn't wait to see what you had for me!"

The little lie worked wonders and restored her composure nearly at once. But the distressing coincidence left

Fletcher unsettled. Was Gloria dreaming or was there some connection between two weird occurrences in the same night and on Christmas Eve? Anyhow, he had Belshasher again without having to make any apologies about it, and that was something.

The first time, however, that he was alone Fletcher made use of his private telephone line. He called the kennels where he had left Belshasher for safekeeping and he inquired about him.

"Don't argue with me," said the landlady's firm voice, which he knew so well, "you took the old dog away yourself!"

Fletcher dropped the phone and fell back faintly into his chair. He was curiously disspirited after dinner. Only Gloria's cheering presence made the silly struggle in which he was engaged seem worth while, and possibly he paid her a little too much attention that evening.

"Isn't it sweet to be home again?" she said, rather late, when he attempted to kiss her good night.

After being with him so continuously at the hospital Gloria now seemed to forget the little point of etiquette which had been seemingly emphasized by the weird voice. Grasping him around the shoulders with her soft, clinging arms, she looked longingly into his face as he tried gently to disengage himself.

"Sigmond," she asked pensively, "where is my old Sigmond who was so good and sweet to me, who did not mind sitting up ever so late with me, as on the first night up at Cleborough?"

"Oh," he answered considerately, but still trying to free himself, "I suppose your old Sigmond gets caught in the dark of the moon sometimes, where you can't see him so well!"

Very close to him, he saw in her eyes a flicker of ecstasy which he felt sure no girl could feel for a brother! In her gaze was all that ardent rapture which has a way of welling up for the first lucky one of a girl's choice! Something within Fletcher relented. He realized there was actually nothing in the whole world comparable to having this exquisite little creature beside him.

"But, honey," he went on, "sometime, somewhere, somehow, the old moon will shine again, ever so softly, for us!" His voice unconsciously carried far more meaning than the words.

"ON OUT ACROSS the golden Pacific, which is merely a step for us," he mused aloud to her, "are beautiful little tropical islands with pink coral beaches; and on them there are no tiresome railroads, or banks, or selfish people, or—anything else that we have to contend with. There, I imagine, the moon would shine the very softest and the sweetest."

"How wonderful that would be, to run away!" she whispered.

A tumult of thoughts were turning about in Fletcher's tired mind. "Chuck it all! What a relief it would be—and to have her, too!" The idea was very enticing indeed, but it occurred to him that as surely as Belshasher strangely slept in his bedroom, the most sensible thing Edmond Fletcher could do was also to go to bed.

"All right, honey!" he answered carelessly. "Life is such a grand adventure that you may be asked to twiddle your little toes in the pink coral sands almost any time now, but it is getting late now, and I am tired. Gloria, dear," he stated emphatically, "I must retire."

"Don't!" she begged.

"Why?"

"Because I can't give you up!"

"Annette," he called out, and the maid appeared. "Miss Gloria wants you. Good night!" he said as Gloria made a face at him.

But that was not all of it as he found out. About an hour later Fletcher was awakened in bed.

"Move over!" came Gloria's voice in the dark, and he nearly swooned as he felt her delicately lovely, warm body cuddling up to him.

"Gloria Van Mortimor!" he exclaimed. "Suppose the servants see you? Are you crazy?"

"The servants didn't see me!" pleaded Gloria. "I have them locked out of here, and if you will just keep quiet no one on earth will know I am in here with you."

"Honestly, dear, sweet little Gloria," he said tremulously, "tell me truthfully from the bottom of your heart why you do a thing like this?"

"Because," she answered plaintively, "I can't help it! All else there is for me that I can think of is not worth staying away from you—and if I am bad, forgive me, I am what I am and I didn't make myself this way! All I want is to be near you—just let me sleep close by your side," she sobbed as she hugged up closer to him. "There can't be any wrong in this! You are ill, and I am so awfully afraid in my room! I'll be so quiet and so very good if you will just hold me here in your arms."

Fletcher dared not move or speak again, but he tried to

collect his racing thoughts, for he needed to think fast now, if any one ever did. Gloria, however, took his silence for consent. She remained with him! And then, to Fletcher's great wonder, she went happily asleep—almost at once!

There they were, he realized, locked up together all alone, and no one on earth could know it!

Under the bed was a sudden low, sharp growl. Its dismal significance set Fletcher's teeth on edge. Belshasher had sighted the unseen. Fletcher felt a cold chill leap to his throat. A breath of icy air swept over his face as though a door had been suddenly opened. Across the room stood the blanched face of his other self!

Pallid and haggard, like a wraith from another world, it rested in his doorway. Some stray moonlight from the hall framed the phantom in a gray shroud. It was calmly contemplating them.

FLETCHER, IN SOME manner, fell onto the floor. He desperately pulled himself over the door-sill into Gloria's room. He hoped this mad ruse would draw the pale specter after him.

A horrible tragedy was imminent, and he wanted the gruesome details out of Gloria's sight.

But the apparition wavered at his hasty retreat—silently turned as if disappointed in some particular! Fletcher, spellbound, watched it sadly fade away. It appeared simply to float down the stairwell outside.

At his feet was only left Belshasher crouching in fear, moaning pitifully. Fletcher snapped the light on.

Gloria sat up in his bed confusedly. "Oh, Sigmond," she moaned, "I had a bad dream!"

"Yes, I know," he said wearily. "Let's trade back rooms, Gloria. Would you mind telling me what you dreamed?"

He eyed her anxiously.

"When I came running in I was so happy to be with you! Everything was delightful, and I was so contented there by you. I reached out to hug you, and something touched me, oh, so very lightly, on the arm.

"I looked up, and there was a beautiful butterfly playing around over my head. I tried to catch it, but my arm hurt me, and then I saw that the pretty butterfly was an ugly wasp and it had stung me! Ugh!" she said. "That wasn't a nice dream."

"Gloria," exclaimed Fletcher, "your arm is bleeding! Let me see?" And so it was. Fletcher examined it carefully. On the tender flesh of Gloria's white arm was a single drop of blood.

She was scared speechless. Fletcher brushed away the drop with his handkerchief and disclosed a little pin prick; nothing more.

"Just a tiny scratch," he said. "Put some iodine on it! Now, Gloria, is that absolutely all that you saw tonight?"

"Yes!" soberly stammered his formerly vivacious little companion. "Is that not enough?"

"Uh-huh!" answered Fletcher, in one respect greatly relieved. "Gloria, I don't propose to understand such things as have happened tonight; but you would better keep Freeda in your room after this when you are afraid in the dark. Please, whatever you do, don't chase any more butterflies in here!"

Gloria went very silently into her boudoir and closed the door ever so softly behind her.

"That's a damn good ghost for me in some particulars!" said Fletcher aloud, and disheartenedly threw himself back into bed.

So finished Christmas Day for Gloria and Fletcher.

But, ghosts or no ghosts, there followed some wonderful days for Gloria and Fletcher, between whom a deeper and deeper intimacy continued to develop.

Always there hung something of the glamour of stolen fruit about his having her now, and possibly that made her appear all the sweeter to him. Fletcher had frequently to restrain himself from making violent love to Gloria. He wondered daily if he should not throw over everything and take her as his very own.

She seemed so acquiescent in his every mood now that he believed his transformation of her was about complete. But he did not dare to take the desperate chance of Van Mortimor's vengeance, unless he was absolutely sure of his lovely little ward, Gloria.

WITH THE NEW year Fletcher returned to business cautiously, devoting only a few hours daily, as his strength permitted. Everywhere out on the far-flung stretches of his railroads the men were becoming more dependable as their welfare was becoming more or less automatically assured.

Nearly all of his people were taking-advantage of the savings bonus. The small thrifty element had gobbled up the opportunity he offered at one gulp, and by their quick action had led the crowd. With widely varying enthusiasm, and actually painful reactions among the most extravagant, nearly all were saving the full ten per cent; for if they did not, they suffered a real cash loss of the bonus from Van Mortimor. This urge to save was all-compelling. People's jealousy, selfishness, and even viciousness were turned to account to make them help themselves against their own weakness.

A queer part of it, too, was that once a man was in the employ of any of Van Mortimor's companies, and started this insidious thing, every day put him so much deeper into it that only a fool could quit. These earnest workers were now, clicking off their various tasks with clocklike precision, and naturally great corporations, so sound at the bottom, went ahead powerfully.

Nevertheless, a very disturbing factor rankled in Edmond Fletcher's breast while his health returned. It was that he had somewhat lost sight of the more serious phase of his singular position in this eccentric genius's shoes.

Dr. Martel had said that Van Mortimor would probably act like a snake in alternately charming and scaring a bird, until he was ready to strike the final blow. Van Mortimor was certainly doing just this to him! But what Fletcher desired more than anything else was, in so far as it was possible, to anticipate in advance specific moves of his phantom master. Thus to some extent he might be able to protect himself.

Late one night Fletcher locked himself in his rooms and took the history of the Van Mortimor case from his private safe for some careful analytical study on his part.

Slowly it occurred to Fletcher that love and fear, two greatest of emotions, had struck simultaneously in him the very first night up at the Cleborough estate; and that everything else which had happened since then had actually been a variation of love or fear playing in him, while both grew stronger within him all the time. Love and fear were the keynotes of this beast's operations against him, and they ran consistently through everything. There was reason in this madness, after all!

Then, as Edmond Fletcher sat there brooding his true predicament dawned upon him. He could see clearly that, though his petty initiative and drive toward business power might at times irritate or even appease his crazed master, for the most part all that was incidental and mattered no longer anyhow.

The real, the logical stage for love and fear was and always had been set around the exquisite little Gloria. Now he could see that the big show, indeed the main event for which Van Mortimor had staged so much, had begun in earnest!

Now, indeed, it appeared to Fletcher that Sigmond Van Mortimor had the situation well in hand for wringing out exquisitely morbid thrills from his puppets' actions. Out of his present acute relations with Gloria, Fletcher recognized that some thrill-stuff would arise deliciously morbid enough for even this jaded master. Of course, this human anaconda had no other disposition to make of Fletcher finally than to try to finish him off with a nice thrill murder at the very end.

15

TORMENTING JOY

AS THE DAYS wore on the strain of this watchful-waiting attitude on Fletcher's part toward Gloria became almost unbearable to both of them. The holidays had increased their intimacy to such a degree that her solicitude for him and her desire to be with him every possible moment were pathetic. It was hardly fair to her, he thought, to let her go on in this way, continually intoxicated and tormented by strange insuppressible emotions which she could not possibly understand.

Then, very much as if some invisible stage manager in the great wings was pushing the next character upon the scene, Fletcher one evening had a caller.

Count Rononotski asked a private audience with Fletcher, and he was received alone in the drawing-room of the playhouse. Candidly and honorably he asked Van Mortimor's permission to sue for Gloria's hand.

Fletcher was stunned by the abruptness and frankness of the fellow in stating his business so openly, but, after a fashion, he was also inclined to admire him at least for his sincerity in the matter.

"Count," he answered deliberately, while the very thought of what he was saying cut into him cruelly, "I am willing to give you the sporting chance you seem to deserve! It is all up to Gloria, and you have my permission to have her if you can—provided that you will give me your promise that you will ever remember who she is! She is an American girl, and does not by any means fall under the Continental standards for handling women." A dry smile came over his face. "It's a considerable responsibility to which you aspire. If you get her, she'll have to be your sweetheart always as well as your wife, or she won't understand at all and it will be all off with you!"

"I promise solemnly," pledged the count, "and you overwhelm me with the liberality."

They shook hands in a jovial manner as befitted two such high adventurers, but the masked one, Edmond Fletcher, retired at once, in uneasy sorrow, to the seclusion of his rooms.

Hours later came a gentle tap upon his door, and Gloria was admitted. She sank on a cushion at Fletcher's feet and lifted up her large eyes appealingly.

"Sigmond," she remonstrated, "you gave the count permission to ask me to marry him!"

"Yes," replied Fletcher, not meeting those eyes of hers, "that was the only thing to do. Such decisions are up to you."

"You put me in a strange position," she confessed contritely. "I do not suppose that I am capable of loving any man, and yet I want a home"—her voice became very low—"a distinguished husband, and little children to love me. Money is of no importance in these great things, for I have too much of it. The count has some truly fine points of character, such as are rare in men! That much I have

learned from you. The count might give me all the happiness I require, except that I have no affection to return
for his. However, even that might come in time but for
one insurmountable difficulty—I could never leave you!
I admire the count and strangely I should trust him, but
when he touches my hand there is no romance—no feeling in it. You, my own brother, look at me, touch me even
accidentally, and bewildering sensations, ever so sweet,
pulsate all through me!" She dropped her eyes, and her
clear complexion flushed.

FLETCHER, YEARNING FOR her from the very depths of
his soul, could not trust himself to speak. "Sigmond! Am I
unnatural? Why do I have these uncontrollable impulses?"

"Gloria," he said, "the count is a gentleman, and I
suppose, in my own fool way, I shall always try to be something of the same sort. Do not let me influence you in the
least! The way of the heart is weary, but it is not too long;
you will find your happiness somewhere—somehow! I do
trust, Gloria, you will recognize it when it comes!"

"Never with the count," she asserted brokenly. "I admire
him, but that's all there is in me for him or any other man!
He is just the latest of a string of men from whom I have
fled since you kissed me that first night at Cleborough. I
have refused this really fine man—he sails tomorrow.

"Lean over and kiss my hair, Sigmond, just once, to help
me forget. How could he know what was wrong with me?"

Fervently, Fletcher kissed her lustrous hair, drinking in
its luscious, natural perfume, to him like fresh red wine.

Fletcher caught up her hand.

"Gloria!" he said. "You have made me promise not to

discuss this matter so many times that I do not know how to make you understand me!

"But when you feel it so strongly, can't you see the simple truth? *I am not your brother!*"

Out of her tears, Gloria sat up, one slender arm akimbo, an elbow on his knees and a hand on her face, while she looked up into his eyes thoughtfully several moments without saying anything.

Then she darted instantaneously to a standing position, her lithe little body taut and erect. The storm of dejection which had swept over her was gone, and her radiant self was brightly shining forth again.

"I must study that over with 'Little Gloria,' my little Gloria with the blue eyes," she avowed playfully as she hurried away, suddenly bashful, but smiling happily again.

16

THE REALM OF FEAR

FLETCHER'S SECRETARIES WERE shortly buzzing with activity. This Van Mortimor carried knightly adventure and high ideals into business. For the moment Edmond Fletcher was taking men out of themselves and giving them a glimpse of faith in the ultimate good in all things.

Late one afternoon he sat at his desk well pleased with the progress he was making.

"Cablegram in code, sir," announced Colston Floyd, placing a message before him, "which we can't possibly decipher."

It read:

3 P.M., 10 Feb. Paris.

Following my nose. Smell so strong trail not much trouble.

SKYLES.

"Personal code, thank you," said Fletcher, remaining, by a great effort, outwardly composed. "I'll take charge of it."

Then he thought hastily as the door closed on Floyd: "Thank goodness, he closed the door sharply!" If it had been shut softly, Fletcher would have screamed. For the full realization of what he had done now broke upon him. This message was from Bill Skyles, the scandal-hunter whom in his anger he had crushed and banished from the country. Now he understood Skyles's taunting remark that day about its being very kind of him to help defray the expenses of his banishment! Skyles knew where to go!

Would his pitiless revenge on this poor, foul-mouthed news editor prove his own undoing? He thought morbidly: "I have ordered my coffin in advance from Skyles!"

Fletcher miserably slumped down in his chair and buried his head in his arms. What a fool he had been! Right at the very apex of his accomplishments an ugly storm of his own making was brewing close behind him! Great fear settled down upon him then and made of him a weak, sickly thing.

Angrily he braced himself—disgusted at the fear he could not avoid or conquer. Masking his face as best he could, and pretending a calmness he did not possess, he summoned Bullard Bland.

"Bullard," he confided, "I need you now desperately! Read this message from Bill Skyles, whom I drove out of the country. Give me all that stuff you looked up on him before. Get all the personal information you can about him from our old files to help you; then pack your bag for Paris. Sail next steamer and employ any service you need over there to shadow his every movement. Just keep me advised and stand ready for summary action!"

"Mr. Van Mortimor," responded Bland as his eyes ran over the surprising words before him, every moment adding to his wrath at the insinuation upon his generous leader, "if you should have to ask me to burn down a cathedral over there I would do it rather than refuse you! There may not be much to me, but you can use me and depend on me just like a dog does on a bone! And anybody that can get any meat off me after I am through obeying your orders over there, is welcome to it!"

A certain grim humor had visited the visages of the two men. With no further discussion they parted. Fletcher knew that in the whole world he could not have had a more trustworthy or formidable emissary for this delicate mission and also he knew that—maybe he might have to use him!

THE THOUGHT WAS so consoling that he turned his mind to Gloria with even pleasurable feelings for the immediate moment. After all, why not live madly, happily, to the utmost of his heart's desire, each hour that remained?

In all of his more serious moments, however, Fletcher's mind was inescapably focused upon the unrelenting Van Mortimor; and the long hours late at night grew longer in which he secretly studied the phraseology of "The History of the Van Mortimor Case." This had become really an evil bible with him, for though he found nothing but hell in it he ever hoped to be able to glean something of positive advantage to himself from this frank medical statement about his invisible master.

Late one night he had finished reaching a part of this morbid record and had just closed its worn covers, when he turned slightly and glanced at a picture of Gloria, placed there on the table by her own hands.

"Ah! So sweet," he mused half aloud, "she is worth anything! If I but knew I could have her for a little while I'd sacrifice the rest of my life and end this silly torture!"

It was getting very late and he was so very tired; he

scarcely had the energy to retire. He leaned far back in the soft comfortable chair in which he was sitting.

Fletcher's attention was arrested nearly at once by a slight movement of the window sash. He was about to give the alarm, thinking that some burglar was jimmying the sill when the window came slowly up, moved noiselessly by an unseen hand!

In the opening he saw evolve a conglomeration of colors, which gradually took the form of a human being. It moved silently as the wind and was wafted over opposite him where he could plainly discern the blanched face of himself projecting from a dazzling-hued Hindu robe.

The iridescent colors of the mystic garment played about crazily before him in the dim light. The face was the same one he had seen in his bedroom window at Cleborough, and here at Christmas, only its expression was different now—the blanched face was leering at him. On its features was a look of unutterable contempt and gloating hatred! Fletcher felt rooted to his position, and this gloating countenance held him spellbound for a dreadful second.

The ghastly apparition raised its gaunt open hand. It dashed its palm forward, cutting the air in the direction of the table—and the light instantly went out. Dismally now came the harrowing weird cry of this dread thing from out of the darkness! Low and shrill it was as if the thing were exultantly whistling while contemplating some dire act.

"What are you? Are you dead? Are you alive?" cried the distracted young man, speaking by a mighty effort.

"You know who I am," answered a sharp voice, interposed between snatches of its weird dirge, "I am Sigmond Van Mortimor, whom you fear! Whether I am dead or alive doesn't matter, for you, my very counterpart, live for me. But be careful what you do!" And there was a whistling, sneering interval before the Thing went on again:

"You trifle with your petty life. Off the ledge outside the window, the pavement is hard and cold," stated the sepulchral voice oracularly. "Beware how far you follow me! Sit still or run from me as you did at Christmas! Never be so foolhardy as to try to run after me! I am always with you, my fool, to study you and punish you if needs be."

"What do you want me to do?" quavered Fletcher, for he knew not how to deal with a thing like this.

THE SHRILL, DISMAL notes took on a tone of fiendish glee, after a chilling pause had ensued, and then:

"You know what I would have you do. Do it—or how bitterly you'll suffer! Run this fortune like a man; stamp men down, tramp them down, and make them pay, as the world has ever been run, so that men will say I am dominant, a master on earth. Nasty little spill you nearly had, following your fool bonus scheme, wasn't it? You should have learned a little lesson from that. Fear alone turned the trick for you! Fear of the loss of savings and the little premium you gave your employees was all that made them come across so nobly!" The ghastly voice chuckled in glee:

"Whose word now is worth the more in these affairs? Mine or yours? But play the game more safely. Use fear alone—make every one fear you! Fear is the master of all men and gets more results than anything else on earth! Fear of the hereafter! The masked face! The hooded power of some secret order! That is what accomplishes great results—the fear of loneliness and desertion!

"If you want results inspire sufficient fear and all things

will move with alacrity to accomplish your ends. As you fear me, make all men fear you! Of such is the secret of mighty human endeavor. Thus, too, I shall run it all." The thin queer voice chuckled ghoulishly as it shrilly trolled a few bars of its weird gloating cry.

"You can supplement your means of fear by a neat little trick! Marry Myrtle Marbleton! She even desires you!" the rasping voice again chuckled. "Ah! There's a fitting mate for a ruthless dictator. Thoroughly disillusioned, wrung dry of all sloppy sentimentality; shoulder to shoulder, she would apply the social scourge while you cowed them in business. A courtship with her or any other woman is disgusting to me, weak and vulgar since you buy them anyway! However, it is expected. You might usefully bring your predilection for such philandering into play there and if I ever supplanted you, then, even such a sniveling worm as yourself would have been of some service to me in return for all I have done for you!" The voice now came hollow as if from the depths of some desecrated tomb as it went on:

"You contemptible ingrate, Christmas gift ghoul that you are! The circumstances of your mission places a delicate girl, my sister, near you. Ha! Ha! You may play with her much as you wish—that's part of my sport! But touch her and I'll kill you, snuff you out as I would an odorous smoking candle! Ever shall I be with you, as you will know!"

The voice blurred. Fletcher was repeating the words. Was he going crazy?. Was his other self within him doing the talking? Was he talking to himself? He could hear the weird notes of the blanched face now receding toward the window! He heard a slight grating noise—was the window going down? He didn't know. Whatever it was, it had passed away and he was so comfortable; such a relief that this monstrous thing had gone—and he knew no more.

FLETCHER WAS AWAKENED by his servant, who shook him gently. "It is nine thirty in the morning, sir."

Fletcher looked about him, stupefied. By his side on the floor lay the history of the case, which he hastily picked up. The window was down.

"Did you turn off this light?" he asked, while he tried to grasp the situation.

"No, sir," answered the valet, "the light was out when I came in."

Fletcher attempted to turn it on, but found the switch was already on, but the lamp or connection was dead. He pushed the button off and on again in vain.

"Take this lamp out and get another one for the room," he ordered the servant.

Something on the table caught his eye and held him spellbound. Gloria's picture lay face down. It might have been a dream, but how did that, too, happen? Dazed by his night vision of horror, he made his toilet for the new day.

Was his mind disordered? Had he seen an apparition or had Van Mortimor been physically present? Was this Van Mortimor working some Hindu magic upon him in this phantasm of fear? He shuddered at the weirdness of what little he knew of the occult. Those sinister dark stretches of the human mind from which could be conjured such black magic, into which it is very unhealthy for any one to penetrate. Surely he little desired to enter into such a realm, but how else could one defend himself from such a subtle and obviously powerful influence as was now bearing down upon him?

Consider it as one would, there had been indicated to Fletcher in no uncertain terms what was expected of him; and there was no doubt that to win Gloria, his fondest fancy, would call down upon him swift and horrible destruction.

"Always shall I be with you. Make them fear you even as you fear me! Of such is the secret of mighty human endeavor." The words still rang in his ears.

For several days this held sway over him, coloring all his thoughts, distracting him with strange black moodiness. No matter how it had come, the phantom's message had been delivered, and the words of it were indelibly imprinted upon Fletcher's brain. The very worst of it all was that Van Mortimor might actually have been present! This fellow's life was a drug dream; he was not like ordinary mortals.

One evening not much later, he sat brooding after he had eaten dinner. Gloria was sitting near him pretending to be reading, but he knew she was not. She seemed to partake of his moods and when he felt at his worst he knew she was simply contriving to remain silent which was a hard thing for Gloria to do at any time with her interesting relative. He was wondering what she might be thinking of him, too, when a servant announced:

"Miss Marbleton."

Gloria arose and smiled an apology to her brother, but the man added:

"To see Mr. Van Mortimor—excuse me, sir."

Gloria stopped shortly as though some one had struck her, and Fletcher felt as guilty as if he had intentionally

hurt her. However, he quickly assumed an impassive countenance and strode out of the room.

MYRTLE WAS WREATHED in smiles when she met
Fletcher. In fact, her obvious pleasure proved very alarming to him.

"Isn't the new freedom delightful which we women
enjoy today?" she cooed after the exchange of some pleasant remarks. "We women now engage in business, do just
as we please, and meet men on an equal footing in every
other way, don't we?"

"Yes, indeed," he politely stammered, trying to guess all
the while what had brought her here tonight. He knew
Myrtle was not interested in the modern freedom of her
sex. Her practices, though as old as the race, gave Myrtle
much better than an equal footing with men.

"May I discuss a matter of business with you?" she
begged ingratiatingly.

"Certainly," he replied, and from him emanated very
much the attitude of a banker eying a customer about to
request a loan.

"We both have large fortunes. They should be united,"
she said sweetly. "It would put us in an enviable position. I
have no embarrassment in proposing such a sensible and
expedient matter. I assure you, no sentiment need enter
into the affair!"

Fletcher was studying her with narrowed eyes and
Myrtle, who had lighted a cigarette taken from her hand
bag, was regarding him languidly through little slow puffs
of smoke.

"Pardon me, Myrtle," queried Fletcher breathlessly, "but
by any chance did you have a dream?"

"Oh! My word, no!" she gasped, leaning over until her cheek nearly touched his. "No, I did not have a dream about this. But, of course, we shouldn't lose any emotional flavor that we might happen to find, should we?" His senses, it seemed, were being narcotized and deadened as she swayed toward him. He was being lulled into forgetfulness by the powerful appeal of her voluptuous body, which it was his ghost-commanded duty to take! If she, too, had dreamed, the spell would have been complete. But suddenly Fletcher caught himself, and sprang to his feet.

"Well—if that's the case," he spoke decidedly, "I'll take this—er—business matter under advisement." By his attitude he dismissed Miss Marbleton in the same fashion as he would have terminated an unpleasant conversation at his office.

He shuddered to think of what might have been the consequences if she had not intruded that false note, by admitting that she had not been supernaturally directed to come for him!

Myrtle left the apartment obviously disconcerted. This man was a perfect enigma to her, and she did not know whether to be elated or depressed at the indecisive outcome of her unconventional venture.

But Fletcher, turning back upon the threshold of the room, met a young lady of a more positive disposition. It was Gloria, and her face was livid with anger. It was obvious to him that in some manner she had been listening. She was so badly agitated and he was so nettled that he merely waited coldly for her to say something. He had not long to wait.

"You have given that awful woman an excuse to invade

our home!" accused Gloria haughtily, but her feelings broke
over. "Haven't you guessed that for months I have been
keeping her away from you?"

"I had no reason to expect this," he answered sadly, "but
be reasonable—Myrtle is your friend; and if I am only your
brother, why should you be so angry?"

"Myrtle was my friend!" she corrected him. "But she is
one no longer, because you are mine! And no one else shall
have you—even though I certainly do not want you now!"
She sulked like a spiteful kitten.

"Be still or I'll kiss you," he flung at her deliberately; yet
he was just a little uneasy about her temper.

"Just dare try it," she flared hotly, "and I'll scratch your
eyes out!"

"Gloria," he asserted calmly and evenly as his face
became very serious, "don't ever talk to me that way again.
I mean it!" But far down in his heart he thought how black
the world would be in the short time he had if she became
cold and impersonal to him as she was to most people.

Gloria, fuming with dislike of his actions, considered
even in the depths of her peevishness how terrible it would
be if this wonderful brother turned against her and then
he was so masterful—she shuddered—what might he not
be expected to do to her?

NOT ANOTHER WORD was spoken, and very formally
they left one another at the head of the stairs in the play
house. Each went to his own broodings which were only
about the other. But it further unsettled Fletcher, this rift
with his object of all desire, and he wondered whether Van
Mortimor was in the offing again, whether Bland would be
able to handle that detestable news-monger, Skyles, whom

he had foolishly set on his own trail. His mind raced along from one fear to another. While he tossed about in his bed that night he dreamed that he was on a voyage and a shoal of sharks was following his ship.

The next morning starting for the office, for the first time that he could remember, Gloria did not appear at breakfast and the food was tasteless. He gloomily sauntered down to his car and just out of habit looked high up to her window. A little hand waved ever so faintly. His heart bounded upward!

"Hurry along," he spoke to the chauffeur. "It may be that I am late!" Fletcher forgot almost at once about Myrtle. But his mind did dwell upon the dream of the night before. He tried to put such silly things out of his senses, but he worried, "Could they be sign posts of my dread? Sharks following me at sea!"

On his way down town he felt a compulsion to count automobiles waiting for the traffic signals, to determine if he were riding with units of thirteen or a multiple of the number. Various premonitions, to watch for symbols of superstitions, which ordinarily would not have bothered him, bobbed up in his mind.

A cat, black as midnight, darted out of an alley and ran along the pavement with the motor. He found himself watching its untoward movement in actual horror! Would it by chance pass in front of him? Happily it stopped and turning sharply around walked lazily away! "That's the spirit," he soliloquized. "I don't need any black felines to cross my pathway now!"

But before he could begin the day's work at the office he had the operator get Gloria on the phone.

"Gloria, I just wanted your encouragement," he stated, "before I begin talking to all the people that are waiting to see me down here. I saw your hand wave from the window and I concluded I could ask this of you?"

"I did no such thing," she declared indignantly. "I did not!"

"That is all right," he affirmed merrily. "I saw you, you dear little storyteller! Now what are you going to say to your poor brother who has to carry on world affairs without the encouragement of his stanch little partner?"

"Understand, I dislike you," came back spiritedly, "but no one will know it and in business, at least, I am for you to the limit!"

"That's fine of you! Thanks!" he answered, and hung up the phone.

"Another one of those cablegrams, sir," announced Colston Floyd, "in your personal code, sir!"

Fletcher opened the missive and read:

> Bombay, March 5.
>
> Pardon me for crowing. This trail leads to a feast. I am going to spread-eagle down soon if I can beat a certain vulture to it who is hovering over the prey.
>
> SKYLES.

Things went black before him, and he felt once more the terrible smothering feeling of close places. The next he knew he was faintly drinking a glass of ice water which some one was holding up. He weakly made his way to a window which was pushed open for him by many hands.

He motioned them back, all these many enthusiastic

assistants. They stood respectfully on the other side of the room awaiting his better disposition while he drank in the cold clean air. It partially refreshed his lungs and cleared his mind.

For another instant he stood there deeply meditating like some young soldier of fortune who read impending disaster in the glowering skies; and then he acutely realized that if he was to accomplish anything at all he must drive hard before the storm. His shoulders came back and he turned sharply; in an abrupt manner he dismissed the respectfully curious crowd behind him.

But by the time he reached home that evening the full realization of his misfortune had once more borne down his spirit. He looked pale and haggard. Gloria, reproachful no longer, was half frantic at his unusual appearance. Her recovery from her anger in view of this new development in her brother's "health" was wholehearted. She simply threw her arms around Fletcher's neck and wept, declaring that she had been petty and that she did not care what happened so long as she could have him well. Then she wanted to know if anything alarming had occurred at the office today.

"Nothing! Nothing to worry about!" he asserted, most unconvincingly, as he sat down, clasping her comforting little self close to him for a moment.

17

THE GHOULISH DIRECTOR

SINCE HER CAPITULATION after the quarrel, Gloria had been exquisitely delightful to Fletcher. Her affection for him had become so ripened, so complete, that at times only the scandal from Skyles which hung like a shroud over him, and, through him, over the whole family, kept him from making a desperate attempt to snatch her out from under her brother's fangs, as dangerous to them both as that might have proved.

Illustrating woman's sweet inconsistency, or stratagem of reason as the case might have been, coincident with her surrender, Gloria had asserted a very positive little proprietorship over Fletcher's most intimate affairs.

She developed an inclination to talk too much about his being her very own, and to ask his opinion of herself much too frequently.

She evinced a very keen interest in doing all Fletcher's personal shopping. She read every little thing of his that lay around, and when she would get cuddled up in his lap, as she quite too often did now, she would playfully go through his pockets.

Inasmuch as Edmond fell more deeply in love with Gloria daily, all these trivial attentions from her pleased him immensely, but then too they accentuated his desire for her and his permanent worries, which day after day only made worse as time passed and nothing definite was heard from Van Mortimor or Skyles or Bland.

Fletcher realized that he was not fully recovered from the dreadful ordeal of the steam pipes. He did not dare trust himself under any great strain very long for fear he might break down—even go mad. He knew now what Dr. Bates had meant when, so long ago, he advised him, above all things, just to he himself.

Until recently he knew that he had, for the most part, a very clear mind, but now the agonizing suspense of all things, these troubles and unknown perils were shaking it. After every previous flagrant act of his, Van Mortimor had evidenced himself in some manner, but at present, though Fletcher had continued handling the family fortune to his own taste, though Skyles was bearing down upon him, and though Gloria cared so much for him now that she was pathetic to behold—yet Van Mortimor did not show himself in the slightest! All too well Fletcher guessed what was coming. His horribly subtle master was quietly coiling to spring upon him.

He knew that the great climax in this hideous drama was approaching. Everything was rounding in on him to crush him for the superlative thrill of his drug-crazed ruler, who would certainly manage that affair. The worst aspect of it all was that so many weird things had occurred and such horrible fears were beginning to surround every further effort upon his part, that, like water continually dripping upon a stone, it was telling on him. He could not keep his senses straight much longer for the big ordeal with his cruel master.

Soon Fletcher was having impulses to count houses in a row, people in a group, callers at the office, dishes served at the table, and, in short, anything that might total up to thirteen, or a multiple thereof, with the idea of avoiding the Judas numbers. If he started a computation and was interrupted, he did not feel comfortable until he had counted it over again.

That he should be swayed by such irresistible feelings gave Fletcher much concern; and yet too there was a sense of singular logic about it all. This Van Mortimor would be just the type to play with him and finally dispose of him in some very subtle manner by heinously perverting the very forces of nature to trap him. Therefore Fletcher felt that he must study any apparent evidences of such things which seemed to abet the monstrous phantasmagoria of hope and fear in which he was enmeshed.

Strange to say, despite industrious efforts, he did not find many thirteens; then again these doleful digits would turn up most unexpectedly in the most uncanny fashion. **AT LAST SOME** news from Bland pierced the gloom. It was forwarded up to the play house one night, and Fletcher avidly read:

> 3—16.   Bombay, 9 A.M.
>
> Roosting and dining with the crow. Has full knowledge, but is completing proof by following itinerary which leads to New York. As his co-worker suspicion allayed. He is surely covered. I stand out here awaiting any orders, but watch out in New York. The great danger lurks there. Occulists here

secretly communicate with party in question in New York
and contemptuously say greater forces than Skyles handle
the matter. Weird business. No New York details obtainable.
Advise me.

BLAND.

There was some little measure of relief in finding that
Bland had the confidence of Skyles and that therefore
Skyles lay in his hands at least for the present; but the reference to the occult in the message and its absolute confir-
mation of Van Mortimor's presence hovering over him
here in America actually gave corroboration to his worst
superstitious premonitions.

So gently and feelingly did Edmond Fletcher stroke
Gloria's hair late that same evening while she out of habit
now was cuddled up to him and reading some poetry, that
she intuitively glanced up and caught his eyes hungrily
drinking in her loveliness.

"Why," she asked, "are you so tender tonight, Sigmond?"

"I guess, darling," he answered, "it is because I love you
so much!"

"Ah!" she said dreamily and her hands attempted to close
quickly the book she had been reading as if she would hide
a page that her thoughts applied to him.

"Wait!" he exclaimed. "Give me that book!"

It was by Edgar Allan Poe, and opened at that bitter
lament. "The Raven." Gloria's fingers rested pallidly upon
the last three lines of that poem:

And the lamp-light o'er him streaming throws his shadow
    on the floor;

And my soul from out that shadow that lies floating on the
   floor
Shall be lifted—nevermore!

"Don't read such things as that!" he cried out. "Oh,
Gloria, you must not!"

Fletcher took the little volume away from her, kissed her,
locked his doors, including the one from Gloria's rooms,
and wearily threw himself into bed.

There he lay—after midnight it must have been—and
he could not sleep. Down on the floor below was a large
and invaluable antique grandfather clock with cathedral
chimes.

He heard its melodious voice chime one o'clock, softly
but solemnly as if it sounded an epochally sad hour in some
venerable ecclesiastical pile. Then in the same solemn tone,
"two—three—four"—it could not be any such hour! With
his predilection for counting things he counted on, until it
sounded, "nine—ten—eleven—twelve—thirteen!"

Frozen with terror, he sat up stiff and cold in bed. Was
some mystic force, associated with his demon shadow
warning him and chanting the very end?

AT LENGTH SOME soothing reason came to the relief of
his distracted mind and numb, cold body. He would examine the clock in the morning. In any event, come what
might, he might just as well sleep. He covered himself up
and peacefully dozed off.

But Fletcher began dreaming immediately, utterly
melancholy dreams. No such vulgar terrors as sharks
followed him now. No, these were much more poignant
and excruciatingly sorrowful. In some strange white coun-

try by the sea, he could hear a cathedral booming a vast dirge, while he took eternal farewell of a weeping Gloria, made fantastically beautiful by surrounding blossoms. They were blooming everywhere about her, out of season, and out of reason, for there was snow upon the ground!

Later, in the strange changes of his dreams he was floating in the sea all alone, being carried out—out—and away on the tide to some bourne unknown.

The next morning at breakfast he could not get the clock off his mind, particularly because he had not heard it strike after arising.

"What is the matter with the hall clock?" he casually asked, attempting to appear self-collected.

"It stopped at one o'clock last night," Gloria replied, nervously avoiding his eyes.

Something in her manner caused him to inquire:

"Have you seen it?"

"Yes—but I knew it had stopped before I looked," she explained uneasily.

"How?" he insisted.

"It struck too many times for a clock, then—nevermore. I listened all night."

Half chilled in this sunny spring morning, he went to the office, only stimulated by the impetuous kisses of Gloria still warm upon his lips.

Sitting at his desk and alone, Fletcher took Bland's cablegram of yesterday from his pocket. He read it over carefully several more times. Again he had this scandal-mongering rat Skyles within his hands, and he could do exactly what he wished with him through Bland, if he acted quickly!

The public reads of some murder in the newspaper, some tragedy which the police and the press are never able to clear up, and which forever goes unexplained. Fletcher, from his keen knowledge of life, knew how many of these came about.

The subject of the tragedy was most often blackmailing some one of importance to a point where life became unendurable. As the sorely harassed victim of the blackmailer made one painful sacrifice after another to appease the unspeakable leech, the blackmailer only grew worse in his demands, until the world became too small for the two people to continue to live upon it. Of the two alternatives—to take this rotten blackmailer's life or accept inevitable ruin—some powerful men chose practical and expedient measures, and that ended it. Nothing was left but a mystery, a forever unsolved case for the public.

Fletcher rather imagined that Van Mortimor in his place would thus deal summarily with Skyles, but, of course, this news-scavenger's yellow tactics were directed against Edmond Fletcher and that complicated the matter. Regardless however of what Van Mortimor would do to Skyles, Edmond Fletcher's fagged brain concluded he would handle this as his own private affair.

HE COULD NOT conceivably let considerations for the devilish Van Mortimor enter into personal affairs of such paramount importance to himself! No matter what might be expected of him, and no matter what the necessity for it, the idea of his own snuffing out a life was repellent to Fletcher. In his mind, to kill a man under any conditions was about equivalent to destroying a world for as he saw it each man is unto himself the center of a universe.

The thought weighed so heavily on him indeed, as to resemble the presumption of considering oneself a god in meting out such mighty extinction.

"Neither I nor Van Mortimor is so big as all that, regardless of what he may think about it!" concluded Fletcher. "Maybe I can handle this hound for bad news some better way. Anyway, I'll give him a fair chance for his life! Of course," he soliloquized sadly, "that is more than Van Mortimor is giving me; but such is my decision. It stands!"

Then with trembling hand, but firm resolution he wrote out what he could intrust to no other. There went into his personal code:

BULLARD BLAND,

Bombay,

Just continue splendid work. Get everything you can, all he finds out, and prepare to warn me against the time when he strikes at me. Above everything, do not hurt him. Some occult signs here. Give me anything available on the subject.

S.V.M.

But to Fletcher's amazement and horror, there was no answer to his cable, that day, or the next. As days passed, he cabled again and again, all in vain.

For a month or so complete silence brooded over Fletcher. He gave no more attention to business than was strictly necessary that he might listen all the better. But nothing was heard from Bland! Or Skyles! Or Van Mortimor!

He lived like a wary swordsman ever alert for the first thrust of death, but with him it was worse than that. His

sole weapon was his wits, which he must keep ever sharp-
ened against the unseen—for his real and biggest enemy,
the brilliant Van Mortimor, himself always invisible, fenced
only with the unknown.

Fletcher sought light and public places for safety. He
became acquainted with life around exclusive clubs where
men stare at one another and all things in perpetual bore-
dom. He took his relaxation, if any he found, in solitary
splendor at some showy hotel, always alone, but nevertheless in the brightest dining rooms where he would be
closely surrounded by many people, and guarded by a little
army of detectives.

In desperation about this time Edmond Fletcher took
up a sport, of sorts. But he did not pursue it around the
Polo and Racquet Club where his presence would have
been so highly appreciated. He went secretly to a private
shooting gallery which he had purchased, and he employed
the best sharpshooters available to coach him. He spent
much time at this and became highly proficient.

But he believed that if he wished to live, he would have
to hit a more difficult target than any he found there—and
that his test would come very shortly.

18

SPRING

FLETCHER BUCKLED HIMSELF down determinedly to strengthening his business machine. He did not see much of Gloria except at breakfast, and he knew this was wise just now, in view of the impending scandal from Skyles, and the proved fact that Van Mortimor was here, no doubt hovering ever closer over them.

However, one of these days at noon, the warm spring sunshine a little too enticingly flooded across Edmond Fletcher's desk at the bank. It was really too beautiful for him to remain indoors. Although he knew it was not the thing to do, something deep within him called insistently for Gloria and the open country of Westchester. He impulsively got the bewitching little lady on the telephone and asked her to go for a drive. She accepted gladly, but just a little hesitatingly, he thought. He supposed he had startled her with his sudden attention.

When he entered the apartment, Gloria handed him a cablegram, rather timidly, too. It had been forwarded up there, was opened, and was from Bland. He did not care if Gloria had seen this because it was in code.

The cable informed Fletcher that Skyles and Bland aboard the steamship *Latronia* were nearing the port

He struggled desperately under the deadly thing.

of New York, and would dock some time Friday. "Our messages must be intercepted," said Bland, "because I have received no answer from you for many weeks."

This jolt would have thrown Fletcher into a sweat of apprehension but for the remarkable change, which was manifesting itself in Gloria; and that, on the very instant of his noticing it, turned his attention from anything else.

Gloria had not happily run up to kiss him, as was her invariable custom. Nor did she ask him the contents of the cable, which certainly was to be expected; and when he reached out to touch her, she very shyly drew away from him!

"I read the message," she broke the news simply. "I made a copy of your personal code very recently, so that I could find out what was worrying you." His concern about Gloria mounted until it effaced all his own apprehension. How cruel it was of him if he had let her into his terrible fears at this late hour!

Gloria had turned away and was pensively staring out the window, one small foot tremulously tapping the floor. He stepped up awkwardly behind the demure little person and placed his arm around her. As if she had been some beautiful stranger, she darted from him in dismay, only stopping in the doorway to look back very timidly. A crimson flush was spreading over her features and he beheld this new and elusive Gloria in rapt astonishment.

"Why, Gloria!" he exclaimed. "What on earth has come over you?"

"Don't be silly," she smiled, as if possessed of some sweet and secret knowledge. She turned her face away from him. "Let us get out in the lovely sunshine. It is so close in here!" And out of the room she went.

IN A MOMENT she was back. A stunning spring coat, gay-hued, fluttered around her when she tripped ahead of Fletcher to the car. Now and then she was glancing over her shoulder at him diffidently as if she were half afraid of this slender, erect young man with the solemn mien behind her.

"Where to, sir?" asked the gold-emblazoned starter.

"Give us a long ride along the Hudson," Fletcher suggested absent-mindedly.

It was May-time. As they swept into the invigorating open country, the scents of the blossoming and budding trees—peach, apple and cherry—and all the green and growing things, were wafted to them on a warm southern breeze from an ever-changing panorama of colorful landscape.

Every so often Edmond Fletcher caught Gloria Van Mortimor studying him as some beautiful woman might

covertly look upon one when she thought herself unobserved. Oh, how careful he knew he must be with this
delicate-spirited girl!

Fletcher nonchalantly lay back in the cushions, apparently content with all the world. They must have been
quite a distance out now, for they had been speeding on the
perfect billiard-table road up the Hudson for over an hour,
their motor humming dreamily, musically, like a swarm of
woodland bees.

"Gloria," he suggested casually, "we are near Cleborough.
Would you like to see in full dress the woods in which we
rode last summer?"

Her eyes met his and wavered uncertainly.

"Yes," was all she said and it seemed that it was with a
mighty effort that she said so much.

Fletcher spoke into the tube and soon they were winding
gracefully up the parked ribbonlike roadway which led to
the great house on the crest of the hill at Cleborough. His
eyes feasted hungrily on the familiar scenes which unrolled
before his gaze. Memories crowded in upon him of all the
happiness that he had discovered here, of all the high hopes
that had been born in these surroundings.

The cars pulled down to the edge of the great woods
far behind the house, where Edmond Fletcher directed
them to wait. Edmond and Gloria sauntered into one of
the magnificent trails over which they had joyously ridden
the past year.

About them clung that fresh clean odor of budding
things and reborn life. A little beyond them the long, clear
waterfall broke over its precipice and went sparkling like

silver far down below to a pool where they could faintly hear its murmur upon the rocks.

Near them was the great trunk of a fallen tree which made a natural seat.

"Come," he called out when he noticed this, and confidently took her hand which thrilled him with its soft warmth. She did not withdraw it, and her slender little fingers trembled.

THEN THEY WERE at the body of the tree trunk and something had to be done. It was much too high for Gloria comfortably to seat herself. Fletcher grasped her firmly, a hand on either side of the lovely slimness of her waist, and he bounced her up there!

"Don't!" she cried out. However, it was too late. She was prominently displayed on the big log and blushing profusely. Fletcher vaulted up beside her. He still avoided her eyes, but now it was not from any fear about how she felt for him! He felt sure she really loved him with a love that knew that "he was not her brother. Gloria on her high perch was vividly publishing her mind! And, it seemed, she did not know what else to do about it! What an exquisite feeling pervaded Fletcher! What a beautiful and glorious thing it was to live!

Her eyes met his and in them was the irresistible soul-offering of this maiden for her lover. Such wholesale self-abandon deserved more attention than he was giving Gloria!

As she melted into his embrace, her warm lips pressing one cheek and her tender arms about him caressing the other, some great void in Edmond Fletcher was completely filled—some great growing gap in his nature was blissfully healed over. Nothing was said for awhile; but sometimes lips have little use for words.

From where they were sitting, through a break in the woods, was barely discernible in the far distance the east terrace of the grand house where this idealistic romance had started.

"My very dearest," Gloria whispered ever so gently as she looked in that direction and her eyes closed. "Kiss me as you did on the terrace the first night we met. I have thought and dreamed of it ever since."

At last they found time to talk a little, but in view of what she so earnestly said, it seemed trivial for Fletcher to be inquisitive immediately.

"From here," she insisted, "we go as one! You must never have any more fears, because if you love me, nothing can take me away from you. My love, you can do as you wish with me from this moment on! Unless you tell me in so many words that you do not want me, you will always have me!"

"Don't, don't, Gloria!" he exclaimed.

"Let me say it all, dearest! This is the last time I wish to assert myself! Look into my bare heart. It may help you. Even if you told me to go, you could always have me back, when you wanted me! Why lie about the nature of a woman in love? It seems wrong to say so, but even if you did not marry me I should be the same to you! You've taught me that one alone, no matter how self-sufficient, is incomplete in this world; and when one finds the missing part, the great thing is to hold together at any cost."

"Gloria," he said very thoughtfully, deeply moved, "among my many premonitions, something seems to tell me that you are as clever as you are lovely. Such humility usually accompanies wisdom. When did you really know that I was not your brother?"

"Only this morning! Dr. Bates came up and informed me! He told me that I was only your adopted sister!"

"What?" cried Fletcher in astonishment.

"Look!" cried Gloria, drawing a letter out of her dress from somewhere near her heart. "Here is what he gave me! Haven't you yours? Here, read it quickly!"

IN THE UNMISTAKABLE bold script of the grand old man, Phelps Van Mortimor, Edmond read:

My darling Gloria:

This letter will be given you by Dr. Bates in whom I have full confidence, when he feels that you have attained womanhood. Though I have been blessed with worldly goods as few men ever have, there are some elements of evil in passing so much on to my posterity. Yet I wish to act fairly in the matter.

I very well know what pitiful wasters men may become who receive too much unearned wealth, with nothing to do but spend it, and I do not want to burden any man with more than his shoulders are capable of bearing.

Sigmond Van Mortimor is my only child and as a boy he is fearfully weak.

I feel that there should be some check put upon giving him this tremendous power, and I am not satisfied with the ways and means prescribed by lawyers for doing this.

You, dear Gloria, are at least strong, healthy, beautiful and, from the time you were born until this is written, the sweetest little girl on earth! You ought to have been! I picked you out myself from nearly all the fine little orphans in the country when my wife and I decided we needed you. The sight of you is an inspiration of all that is fine and noble and we have reason to believe you may live the part.

You were our ideal little baby girl; and in order that our happiness might be the further served in the same spirit and that the welfare of our son, Sigmond, might the more naturally be safeguarded as well—as I shall presently explain—you were reared as our own daughter in reality.

However, so that you should have all the rights of a child born to us, you were legally adopted in a quiet little town so very unimportant and so very far away that even our name passed unnoticed there. Dr. Bates alone knows this secret. He will give you all details, will tell you that you are of sturdier stock than our own, and that you need only call attention to your adoption record if you ever wish, or need to do so.

When you read this you will be possessed by due course of law with one-half of the Van Mortimor wealth. You will, I am certain, have been a good influence upon our beloved son.

If—and the many dreams my wife and I have had of you seem to promise something miraculous from you—if Sigmond should prove worthy and you should fall in love with him, what more wonderful thing could happen on this earth?

A copy of this letter will be delivered to Sigmond at the same time you receive it. But decide all issues with your own free wills.

Your loving father,

Phelps Van Mortimor.

FLETCHER WAS GAZING blankly at Gloria. "Oh!" she exclaimed, glancing up at him through moist-ened lashes. "Isn't it wonderful for me that you still want me! Now I can breathe again without my throat aching. You see, I had been trying all this time to puzzle things out, absolutely convince myself one way or the other about you—and it was only this morning that I succeeded in understanding the whirlpool of my own feelings. When Dr. Bates gave me this letter I realized how simple it all was."

A haunting sadness came into her soft eyes.

"A year ago when you returned from France, my true love had come to me! No wonder you affected me so!

"You were really that all-wonderful one to whom I should have freshly given every intimacy in my nature. You understood our love at first sight, without any letters to explain it, as I should have done! And you tactfully made up fairy stories to prove our true situation! I am a sorry ideal for you!"

She buried her face on his breast. "And I have been so immodest, that this morning, when I received the letter, I feared that you, my very dearest, would not want me now!"

"My exquisite little girl!" said Fletcher tenderly, "let me tell you how badly I want to get rid of you! Always have I followed in my day dreams an ethereal little maiden of such surpassing loveliness that her soul matched her beauty! A golden little sweetheart, gorgeous as a peacock, and yet one who could be implicitly trusted, whose sense of honor and delicacy were so high that I need take counsel from her rather than ever criticize. And impossible as it may seem, wonder upon wonder has brought her to me—in you!

"Don't worry about those other little things! As a matter of fact I am still not Sigmond Van Mortimor!"

"Ah! Sigmond," she stopped him; suffused with happiness, and put her slender pink fingers over his mouth. "I know you were rather wild in Europe, but you have certainly proved worthy of all the love I can give you, so don't spoil my happiness by speaking of such awful past things!"

Rapturously they wandered back to the cars, with not a care on earth. Life for them was just to be something better than a reopened Garden of Eden.

When they emerged out of the woods Fletcher looked up at the clear blue sky. Well he could face heaven with his highest hope so joyously fulfilled. But even as the lightning of their love had so vividly flashed, now came its thunder!

Far over Fletcher's head and circling about was one lone vulture. That Gloria was an adopted daughter, had not changed his relations with the true Sigmond Van Mortimor in the slightest. It possibly added relish to the man's fiendish work.

Gloria, running playfully ahead, was snatching up daisies and wild flowers, which she capriciously tossed, like some nymph of the woodland, in a 'little path,' before Fletcher.

"What have I done?" came down the question bursting into his consciousness like a bombshell as his normal senses returned. Of all things that he could have perpetrated, this surely was the most despicable to his other self, Sigmond Van Mortimor!

He suppressed his feelings, at least outwardly, and catching up with Gloria, they strolled together hand in hand. BEFORE THEM NOW lay the big old house, with the east terrace plainly disclosed to their view.

"Look!" discovered Gloria, "some one is on the terrace. I

wonder who it could be? The house is still closed." So there was. Fletcher could easily see a man, dressed in dazzling white, standing by the balustrade.

"I cannot understand that," he replied slowly. "You run over to the cars and have them wait for me. I shall cut across here and see the caretaker about this! That house, you know, is very dear to us!"

There was an added interest in this investigation for Fletcher. Why should any one wear such brilliant white clothes? It was too early for flannels or ducks, and these were too white for them anyway. If foreign strangers were at the house they might throw some light on the one and only Van Mortimor, and Fletcher dared neglect no clew now, no matter how trivial, on account of his great new responsibility.

Edmond Fletcher saw no further signs of life as he approached the mansion. The caretaker's quarters were locked. Evidently the man's whole family was taking a holiday, and Fletcher would have to look about for himself. With the strange tail-dives that his mind took into superstition, he reflected that today was Thursday, the 12th of May. Fletcher was glad it was not the thirteenth, as he gingerly came up the terrace to prowl around the old home of this stock which dealt so potently with the destinies of the living even after they were dead!

But what pleasurable memories this place could excite in him! He was visiting the very spot where he had first kissed Gloria. Fletcher ascended some stone steps and was surprised to behold some chairs on the terrace as though they had lately held occupants. He walked cautiously toward them. On the balustrade lay a powerful pair of field glasses. This was getting very mysterious!

In front of him now one of the large French casements leading inside was open. Some intruders must be in the house. He felt a vague uneasiness, as though this might have something to do with Van Mortimor, and so he dared not summon his servants and detectives from the cars, Fletcher let his curiosity take him into the house. First he peeped covertly through the open French glass window. He could see or hear nothing, and since it only went into the main hall, he softly stepped inside.

Even that near the spring sunshine, it was dark and rather spooky as all closed houses are likely to be. He held his position for a moment thinking something might turn up, but here was only silence—and the silence was deafening for Fletcher. When his eyes had become accustomed to the dim light in the hallway, he saw that the door of the library was flung back. Since a heavy velvet rug extended from where he stood to its entrance, he decided his footsteps would be sufficiently muffled to enable him to view the interior of the open room.

Guardedly, stealthily, he moved toward the library door, thankful that the heavy-piled rug deadened his footsteps and that it was so dark in the hallway that no one could see him. What little light there was in the whole house came from the open library door.

Finally he reached its entrance. First he noticed that the curtains at the top of a window had been undrawn. That accounted for the gleams of daylight. Then, chilling him to the marrow, he saw in a mirror directly across the room from him a half profile of himself! It was very sallow, haggard, and white in the dim illumination, but it was a horrid caricature of himself!

He would have believed that by some optical illusion that it was himself, too, since it was reflected from his own direction; but this figure was sitting down. Fletcher was still standing, but he did not know for how long that would be! Even in the paralyzing fright which instantly gripped him, he tried to reason.

From where could the reflection of the blanched face be coming? His eyes painfully surveyed every inch of the deeply shadowed library, as they worked back to the door-way in which he stood. Horrifyingly, it dawned upon him that Van Mortimor was seated with his back to him at a table just inside the door—so near Fletcher that he could easily touch him.

He made his way outdoors in a panic, to the blessed sunlight and fresh air, as fast as his legs would let him!

A SICKENING DREAD pervaded him. Sigmond Van Mortimor, if not always with him, had now returned in the flesh. He had been right with him, today of all days! The binoculars still lying on the balustrade told their own disquieting story. Thus were the beady eyes of this modern demon upon him all the while today! Now Edmond Fletcher understood the figure in snow-white whom he and Gloria had seen on the terrace; no doubt an Indian servant or conjurer, who always wore snowy-white. It all pointed to the awful mysteries of Indian magic.

This was no place for Edmond Fletcher. He hurriedly ran from the terrace, closely hugging the side of the house. He made strenuous efforts to compose himself before reaching the motor cars.

Ah, the old war-horse, Phelps Van Mortimor, had had great vision to see trouble ahead! But, of course, he could scarcely have foreseen a thing as bad as this! The benign influence of the grand old man was now forever gone. Another had taken charge, and what a wretch he was!

At the very moment Sigmond Van Mortimor, the last of the line, sat in the old family home, using it as an ambush while he leisurely plotted a final orgy in the torture of a human victim!

If it were not so, why did not this living ghost come out in the open and meet his dupe? For the malignant spirit was indisputably present! With Fletcher's own eyes he had seen him—the blanched face in the flesh!

At last he succeeded in burying his turbulent emotions, and at least outwardly quieted, joined Gloria in the leading car.

"Everything is well," he explained bravely, "friends of the caretaker!"

Soon they were putting distance speedily behind them. This was very much as he would have had it, but he knew flight would be futile in their case. Again a different little Gloria sat by Fletcher. She chatted merrily, indeed, about the future, so well was she satisfied with it—but her partner in this could only force smile after smile. As they neared the city, he declared: "Gloria, I am stopping at the National Club tonight."

"Oh, Sigmond!" she pleaded. "This is the very first time that you have stayed out all night since you came back to me! If you stay away from home I am afraid you will get that queer feeling again that you are not Sigmond Van Mortimor!"

"Remember what you said: 'From now on,'" he reminded her, smiling nervously. "It is for the best! Anyway, unless you can give me some better advice, a brother goes out when a sweetheart comes in!"

"Ah, well!" she agreed resignedly.

FLETCHER TALKED TO Gloria several times on the telephone that night. Although he had other reasons for absenting himself from the playhouse, it was rather consoling for him to realize that it would be difficult for even a Van Mortimor to pull off one of his fiendish stunts at such an exclusive gentleman's club as this which he had chosen tonight! However, he slept only fitfully after many stiff drinks had drowned out a stark, blanched face that was staring, staring, forever staring at him and gnawing its presence into his heart.

Edmond Fletcher had a distinct premonition that his end was close at hand. He knew by intuition that something monstrous was going to happen the next day, something was coming from which he could not possibly run away! The mine for this atrocity had been planted squarely within himself!

The blanched face with the brilliant intellect had merely been using him as the subject for the most dastardly experiment ever practiced in human emotions! Even as Dr. Martel had predicted, this degenerate human fiend had, like a snake, alternately charming and torturing a bird, simply worked upon him, the gullible victim, storing up within him enormous hopes and fears—of course, with no other purpose in view than ultimately to kill him by touching off this accumulation of high explosives and thus completing the weird drama for his superlative thrill.

Fletcher's taking Gloria for his own today must surely have signaled the attainment of the height of hope in him in this intoxicating and gruesome test of love and fear. It would surely provoke the fiend to bring up his full forces on the other side—to strike the fatal blow! Had not Van Mortimor himself intimated as much? Some things are so plain that they hardly need a ghost to tell us, but Edmond Fletcher had even seen his other self that very day!

As the well-meaning young impostor went back over all things in retrospect, it was obvious that he had just been led into a magnificent trap with an exquisite and innocent little girl as living bait.

19

FRIDAY, THE THIRTEENTH

EDMOND FLETCHER LAY abed late the next morning, for he slept much more comfortably in the warm sunlight which flooded his club bedroom from the high windows. Light of some kind had come to be essential to his ease and daylight was so much more soothing than the electric light to which he had become so accustomed. He had so much to fear from darkness! Actually the morning sun shining fully in his eyes only soothed his aching nerves, so far had his sensibilities been distorted in this supersensitive realm of emotion.

The telephone jangled shrilly by his bedside. It was as if the voice of his strident fear itself were within the instrument. Every noise, every sound now had some distinctive character for him! He must expect to hear the vindictive cry of the avenging face at any moment now, since Gloria was his own.

All the other sinister signs had been but omens— outcroppings of something he did not understand, heralding a greater and more peremptory warning! What he dreaded most of all now was the depraved hunting cry of Van Mortimor himself, which always came when he was in action—that yell from the hidden depths of the occult.

This time Fletcher did not see how he could conceivably protect himself against the attacks of perverted natural forces which would surely accompany it. How dangerous it was for him even to stir out of bed this day! Any step might be toward his end!

His nerves were breaking so badly and his resistance to terror was weakening so rapidly, he wondered if Van Mortimor intended to kill him with violent fear alone! Would merely the coming of this murderous warning touch off something already loose within him and plunge him into sudden madness? Indeed, such would be a most subtle assassination and strictly according to the medical prophecy of the case!

With all this sunlight, he finally decided he could answer the telephone.

"Miss Van Mortimor on the wire, sir," announced the club operator.

Oh, what a relief that was!

"Good morning, Gloria," he called.

Edmond could have smilingly entertained himself with pleasantries with Gloria, even in his sorely distressed condition, but for something else on the wire—a low, dismal howl which set him half crazy. The sound was not mechanically in the wire, but guttural, from something alive—or dead.

"What is that, Gloria?" he asked excitedly. "Can't you hear that awful thing?"

"Yes, dearest—it's Belshasher!" she hastened to speak bravely, but her voice broke. "He has carried on in that wild manner ever since—since midnight! I thought I had him quieted, but when I began talking to you he started again. I have him shut up in your rooms, but he is jumping against the—he's charging the door now! And his howl is getting terrible!"

"Send him out for—for a walk in the park. I cannot bear to hear him!" spoke Fletcher weakly. He was getting deadly pale.

While he finished the conversation, he heard old Belshasher's gradually receding growls. Good old "Bel"! He was doing his best to tell something which he, too, knew. The workings of the perverted forces of nature had not escaped the old dog's love for him. Things were drawing to a close. Even the joy of love in Gloria's voice was blighted by the warning of terror accompanying it.

Fletcher rushed feverishly to his private office at the bank. On his desk was a Marconigram in personal code. He tremulously tore open and deciphered this. Skyles was due and this doubtless was from Bland. He read:

> 5—13.   At Sea.   S.S. Latronia.
> Dock this noon. Give whereabouts to police and bury yourself. See no living creature until I reach you.
>   BLAND.

IT WAS EVIDENT that Bland had grasped a part of the true situation and was still striving to save him even though his hands too were in some manner tied. Again Fletcher looked at the cable, but this time minutely.

"5—13." The mystic date smote his eye. Fletcher's eyes traveled to a large wall calendar. "Friday, 13," stared back at him! Something instinctively told him that he need not worry about Skyles's coming; but he did wish that he could see Bland again—good old Bland, who had been so faithful and who had worked so loyally for him, even in the dark.

It seemed so petty, however, even to consider running away at the very end of everything. It seemed suicidal to start now with such an unevenly balanced baggage of love and fear as he must carry! Any fight that Edmond Fletcher could put up against his great intangible enemy appeared so feeble that he could not conceive of any better place to face him than in the very harness of his business imposture. Instead of calling the police, he shortly scrawled out a code reply to Bland:

> Bullard Bland,
>> S.S. Latronia at Sea.
>> Come directly to my office. Will remain here until you arrive.

He sent it, and now he sat inactive and all alone in the very seat that he had been warned to leave. He would see no one. There now remained only a few hours of precious daylight. Yet, upon the use he made of them he knew his life depended.

Time went on relentlessly clicking off the minutes of the hours, while here he sat inactive and all alone in the solitude of his inner office. For him, no less than the weakest little oriole in the toils of a viper, paralysis was setting in. It was as if he were in a lethargy, but still faintly struggling to formulate some defense against this monstrous unseen thing which was already settling down upon him.

Come what might, however, he determined he would not communicate with Gloria until this horrid thing was over, and that meant, he was sure, that he might never see her or hear her sweet voice again. The more Fletcher left her, the other waif of circumstance, his innocent orphan partner, free from this hideous business, the better was her chance of surviving it!

"What a master is handling me!" was the best his addled wits could muster up. Now at last he caught a broad view of his whole predicament. The idea came to him that while his situation was cruelly oppressive, it must be intensely difficult for another—dead or alive—to maintain! Possibly the phantom whip over him was having some trouble too!

It was as if fate itself had rolled all human trials into one—all a lifetime's hopes of reward and fears of defeat—and of many lives for that matter, rolled into a single supreme test for Fletcher. Now the test squarely faced him, unescapable, demanding that he put forth some superhuman effort as the price of his further existence! But why did Van Mortimor not strike now!

Well, with just a little bit more time, maybe he could put up a little fight himself. What was there still left sound and firm beneath him on which lie could make his last stand against this monstrous invisible enemy? With what straws could he combat him?

FLETCHER HAD CONSIDERABLY strengthened this bubble which his namesake had blown about him. He was, in fact, well intrenched in it if he could just get his enemy out in the open, where he could meet him on fair, human terms. Now a great light of reason broke on Edmond Fletcher which routed all fear from his mind.

Why, Van Mortimor himself had not known until yesterday, when he received a copy of the letter from his father, that Gloria was only his adopted sister! That must have given him an awful jolt, possibly had upset some of his well-laid plans!

Ah! While Sigmond Van Mortimor had made a vicious tragedy of life, a tragedy in which a human being was now being sacrificed, his father, though long since dead, had placed another living character in this very weird play as a check upon Mr. Sigmond Van Mortimor's enormities. An unseen hand no less powerful than the fiend's very own actually operated in Fletcher's favor!

Gloria Van Mortimor, not of this doubtful blood, actually owned one half of this whole great fortune, and, though she did not so much as know it, Edmond Fletcher now stood here as her representative and champion! In these unforeseen circumstances, such would certainly be the wishes of the founder of the fortune.

His situation thrilled him to the core! Now, by all the powers on earth, he must stand his ground and bring up his best shock troops!

Fletcher at once began to think more coherently. First he would wait for Bland; secondly, he would take counsel with Dr. Bates; and, thirdly, he must not let anything conceivable overcome him.

This was his program for the moment. And since he could never again for long avoid the beady eyes that were settling down upon him, the next move was up to Sigmond Van Mortimor. Now, while he waited for Bland, he started methodically clearing his desk of the day's work, to give his painfully strained mind more sane employment.

The sun edged over in the sky. Noon had passed. He knew the *Latronia* had docked.

Shortly his inner door burst open, and Bullard Bland slammed it tightly behind him. He was wildly excited, red in the face, puffing desperately to get his breath.

"Edmond!" Bland cried, rushing to Fletcher and grabbing hold of him, "for God's sake get out of here! You haven't a minute to spare! Come! Come!" He begged piteously, trying to pull what he considered his discredited and hopeless leader away by main force.

"Don't! Don't!" exclaimed Fletcher, indifferent to his entreaties. "If you want to help me, sit down and quietly answer my questions!"

Bland dropped into a seat.

"Where's Skyles?" demanded Fletcher.

"He's through! Got cold feet and crumpled up with fear! Came to me, told me he knew who I was, and begged me not to mention he had anything to do with this matter! He wanted to wash his hands of it."

"What is he afraid of?" asked Fletcher incredulously.

"Van Mortimor!" stammered Bland in an agony of impatience. "I got Skyles down on his knees in his stateroom and choked the truth out of him! He sold his stock in the *Morning Star* twice, and he has been doing this traveling abroad for the real Van Mortimor himself! Was employed by him all the time. But Skyles is scared to death now. He says he's been playing into the most weird game that was ever staged in the world! Come on, Edmond!" begged Bland, with hot tears breaking forth from his eyes. "Get yourself out of here! This is no place for us. You are the subject of a ghastly experiment."

"I KNOW," ANSWERED Fletcher apathetically, "but where is Skyles now?"

"A gleaming white yacht came slipping up to our boat at quarantine and took him off. That's the last I saw of him."

"Was its name the Sylvia?" asked Fletcher breathlessly.

"Yes! Yes! That has something to do with Van Mortimor and the biggest tragedy ever played in human emotions! Come on, Edmond. For God's sake come on out of here. You haven't a second to lose, and this awful degenerate Van Mortimor knows everything! He is due to strike at you any instant now because you made love to his sister yesterday."

"God!" exclaimed Fletcher, burying his face in his hands, "did Skyles know that too?"

"Yes—I searched his baggage while he was at breakfast. He had a radiogram which said: 'Trap sprung, sister taken, climax on, rush ashore, we'll strike together!' Signed, 'Your Host!' Do you want anything plainer than that?"

Bland's voice was choking with terror. "Oh, the horror of what you are doing! Here you are, staying in his identity, in his property, right in his clutches! He'll knock you off with a thrill murder as clean as a whistle—do you want to make it easier for this filthy beast to kill you with some devilish mystic trick?"

"That isn't it!" cried Fletcher. "I am trying to figure him out, guess what he is up to! Where he is now, and how he will strike! Don't get rattle-brained," commanded the victim of it all, growing steadier momently, and holding Bland down now to keep him quiet. "Think, Bland, think for me. I've got to think to live. He would run me down anywhere I go! Good as you are, haven't you a single idea with which to help me face him?"

"Here's all!" said Bland limply. "I can't believe that Dr. Bates is a party to all this blood thirst, and if we could talk to him quickly, tell him the Sylvia took Skyles off my ship, that Skyles is at sea with Van Mortimor, and find out what the doctor knows, maybe we can get the jump on this colossal maniac and somehow be ready for him!"

"Now you are talking sense!" agreed Fletcher heartily as he wiped the moisture from his tense face. "I'll go with you!"

But even as he spoke the door of the private exit in the rear of his room moved slightly, making a faint noise which instantly caught their strained attention. The ashen countenance of Dr. Wendell Bates was peering in at them through a crack in the doorway.

"Come in! Come in!" commanded Fletcher testily.

"God forgive me!" said Bates to Fletcher as he came in, furtively glancing about. "You realize it is not like me to sneak in on you this way, but, honestly, I did not know whether I should find you or your double in your seat!"

"What on earth do you mean?" demanded the young financier, "and let go of my arm!" he cut in on Bland, who was shaking all over.

"I'll tell you all I know!" confessed the doctor. "What a fool I have been! But I have awakened, thank God, to what is really going on here! We've got to talk fast. Do you know what happened to Skyles, the only other one that knows anything about the truth of what is being done?"

"Sure," answered Bland at once. "Skyles is on a yacht with Van Mortimor!"

"Skyles is dead," said Dr. Bates.

"Dead!" gasped Fletcher and Bland together.

"Yes, poor Skyles is dead! I was called to the Jefferson flying field to meet a sinister and queer airplane just a little while ago! Van Mortimor stepped from it and, with a great show of frankness, took me back aboard. 'Make out a death certificate for this fellow,' he said, casually indicating Skyles, who was stretched out on a lounge. 'He died of heart failure.' " The doctor paused to catch his breath, went on:

"Not a mark of violence on the body! Not a trace of poison in his system! I made a thorough examination. He did die of heart failure, but the heart failure was from—"

"Fright!" said Fletcher, taking the word out of his mouth.

"Yes-s-s," stuttered Bates. "How did you know?"

"Never mind!" he shot back. "How did Van Mortimor do it?"

"I don't know!" cried the doctor. "But in some infallible way that leaves no trace of evidence. Van Mortimor killed Skyles in that way and—you are next! Then it is Bland, and myself, I know, for he said—" The doctor gulped.

BLAND WAS CLUTCHING both Fletcher and Bates, huddling them closer to him as if in clinging together there might be some little measure of protection.

"Ah! What did he say?" exclaimed Fletcher earnestly, with a cooler, saner light breaking in his face. "That's what I want to hear! What did Van Mortimor say?"

" 'Now, Bates!' he told me confidentially, 'you see what happens to people who inject themselves into my affairs! You have been a pretty bad offender yourself, by keeping secret until yesterday the information that Gloria is my adopted sister.' I gave him a letter—"

"Yes, I know!" cried out Fletcher. "Go ahead with exactly what he said!"

" 'That little matter of withholding that knowledge from

me,' he said, 'might have spoiled all my plans! But as it is, everything has just turned out perfectly. The big bubble that I have been puffing up in my place is almost ready to burst anyhow. And fortunately he has the girl so anxious to marry me that it won't be any trouble at all after I finish with him. Then I'll have eaten the whole cake of life, and still have it, too! The fortune will be reunited, I'll have a good reputation—everything just as my very d-e-a-r old father so ardently wished! The girl is rather a nice fresh young trick, isn't she?' He ended, laughing uproariously." Dr. Bates was white.

Fletcher was leaning rigidly across the desk. His face had gone livid with anger at the mention of Gloria's name. Would he stand by Gloria! Gloria, who had stood so unquestioningly by him through everything! Before Dr. Bates had finished speaking, his passion had become a cool white heat that glowed in his eyes, pervaded his whole person. His hands unconsciously reached out before him. They were writhing and twisting in agony as if he were grappling with something intangible.

"That beast marry Gloria?" he said hoarsely as if he were talking to himself. "Why—if he dares to touch her—" and his hands and throat became strangely quiet.

"But wait! That's not all!" exclaimed Bates. " 'A little something more will happen tonight,' Van Mortimor said; 'a little loose end in my new plans will be cleaned up this evening, something, Bates, which it would be better for you to know nothing about; and then, doctor, you will have no more trouble at all warding the public off me! I'll have a reputation splendid enough for anybody and I'll live up to it—or at least so every one will think! You're like all doctors,' he flung sarcastically at me. 'How silly you were to have believed that you were smarter than I! That you could "cure" me! I have more brains than any one else in the whole world; I do absolutely as I please and the law can't even suspect me! While you fooled around trying to work your cure, I have simply been using your crazy scheme to play God over another, and build him up to suit myself and the dear public! That's vastly more amusing than all the things you've told me to do! Now there only remains the supreme thrill of puncturing the big bag of wind that is tottering in my place, and I'll step forth in his shining character! Doctor,' he said, 'actually in the passing of my dummy, though the means may be somewhat the same, there is not going to be a fraction of the evidence of disaster as you see before you on Skyles! My dummy's old clothes are all waiting for him, and he is going to kill himself, literally! However, be careful—no interference from you, Bates, or there will be an extra death certificate in my collection!' " The doctor gazed piteously at Fletcher.

"An undertaker was removing Skyles's body, and during the confusion of that, Van Mortimor simply disappeared as he has done many times before! I was talking to him one moment and then he was gone—just vanished behind my back! I searched all over the airplane for him. Ah, me; at last he is a raving maniac, and I have lost all control over him! I don't know where he went or what he is up to; and finally I got up courage to come here and tell you!"

"LET'S ALL GET out of here!" said Bland sullenly. "This will be his next stop!"

"Where can we go?" asked Bates hysterically. "Van Mortimor is everywhere! He is a brilliant roving lunatic with a fiendish sort of insight into men's mind! I never heard of anything like him in all my medical career."

"He is still on that airplane, at Jefferson Field or no matter where it is, even in the sky; he will try to come on it tonight!" spoke up Fletcher firmly, with a desperate look in his eyes. "Thank God I now know where to lay my hands on him! I'll be there to meet him and I don't need any further invitation from anybody to come aboard on my business!"

"For the love of Heaven!" wailed Bates, both he and Bland panic-stricken at the thought of what had been said. "Don't go aboard that plane! I forgot to tell you what an incredible death plane that is! It goes up white and comes down black! When I first saw it, it was a terrible black thing swooping down out of the sky—and then it touched the earth and turned a gleaming white!"

"Please be reasonable!" was all Fletcher said, and that quietly.

"But it did! It did!" protested the doctor obstinately. "I'm not insane—though God knows how long I can say that. If you set your foot in that plane of death, you'll change, too! You'll go up alive and you'll come down dead like Skyles!"

"Bates, I am surprised at you," Edmond declared, even smiling dryly now. "You are the one who has always told me to keep my head clear; now look at the foolishness you are trying to put into it! My mind is functioning perfectly and you are simply afraid of one of your own patients!"

The door opened abruptly and they all jumped. Colston Floyd, the secretary, entered, vastly surprised at the commotion he had caused.

"A message for you, sir!" he explained to his chief.

"Wouldn't have disturbed you, but it's urgent and from home," and he beat a hasty retreat.

Fletcher tore open a dainty envelope and in neatly type-written script read:

> Meet me at Jefferson Flying Field at twilight for an airplane ride.
>
> GLORIA.

"Here is a nice little invitation, too, much as I expected," commented its recipient, and he idly tossed it across the desk to the others. "Of course, that is from Van Mortimor. Gloria never saw it. It is plainly a decoy message, and he knows I am one goose who will come!"

"You aren't going to accept that invitation to die, are you?" asked Bland.

"I may have to!" he mused aloud. "Some way or another that I can't prevent now, he may have Gloria coming on that airplane this evening: and then Van Mortimor understands as well as I do that I will sail with him tonight. Wait a minute!" he exclaimed sharply, and he quickly telephoned home.

He spoke to the butler for a moment and a twitch of pain flickered across his brow.

"TOO LATE!" HE said sadly, and he hung up the receiver slowly.

"Parkins says they are searching everywhere for her. Gloria has disappeared!"

"Oh, Lord! How awful!" moaned the suffering Bland.

"Can't we do something to find her," demanded Bates spiritedly, "and stop her before she goes on the plane?"

"I doubt that very much!" said Fletcher coolly and deliberately. "But what a mistake Van Mortimor is making now! He already has Gloria in charge in some manner that we could not possibly find out, but I am sure he will not harm her in any way until he finishes with me this evening. She's safe until nightfall, and that part doesn't bother me; for the poor little thing is simply bait to get me aboard that airplane tonight! But Van Mortimor's a good fisherman only up to that point! There's where he errs, badly! He expects me to wear myself out searching for Gloria the rest of the afternoon and then come on the plane exhausted, still looking for her. Our time is far too precious for any wasted efforts! I'll come aboard, willingly enough; keep the appointment to the minute; but I am saving all my strength for a rendezvous with life—not death! He little guesses what he is inviting aboard! I am just beginning to grasp things clearly now and I am coming on that plane to fight! This dope fiend, or I, dies tonight!"

"Oh! What a pity!" wailed Bates again. "You haven't a ghost of a chance—with that fiend!"

Bland, though listening intently, had given up all attempt to talk.

"You two can quit thinking altogether if you wish," Fletcher snapped, "but you must obey me! Your lives depend on how well you do it! This fellow is almost a perfect criminal," went on Fletcher. "And he nearly had me today! Without one touch of physical violence he could have murdered me, this morning! I don't know how he killed Skyles; but I do know that only a few hours ago he had me worked up to such a pitch of frenzied fear of him that his sudden appearance in this room would have killed me outright. All that, he could have done through the tremendous power of the unseen, in which he has worked so skillfully upon me! But for me he is no longer an unseen terror."

"You haven't faced him yet!" objected Bates pointedly.

"No, doctor," explained Fletcher. "The brief time in which he could have killed me with mere fear is forever passed. As they say in salesmanship, the psychological moment for getting the order has passed! He has overplayed his hand by letting you two through to scare me further with your tales; and he has made a lot of other wholly unnecessary arrangements for scaring me to death, that seem positively silly to me now! Therein he has proved to me that he has no supernatural ability whatsoever, and I am not in the least afraid of him!"

"Let me tell you about those occult powers—" begged Bates.

"No. Not now," he answered. "I must hurry with anything I intend to do. Van Mortimor thinks he has set a trap for me tonight, but he has really set a trap for himself! I am going to catch him in it just like the dirty snake he is! His greatest power has been that he has worked altogether in the unseen. I have learned a great deal about that in serving my apprenticeship under him; and now I am going to give him a taste of his own vile medicine, that will lay him out cold so that we can deal with him sensibly! Outthink him in his own field. Doctor, what kind of an airplane has he, and how many are in its crew?"

"It's a big Fokker," said Dr. Bates in surprise, "has dual controls, seven or eight compartments—it's a sort of airgoing hotel, a flying yacht. It has two pilots, a mechanic, a steward and two or three other men who all go with it. But it has changed so—it goes up white and—"

"FINE!" CRIED OUT Fletcher, wryly smiling—much to file amazement of the others. "Now where was this air yacht situated on the field when you saw it today?"

"There was a storage shed for housing planes not far from it. I think there was an old office and a reception room in one end of that. In between the building and the plane were some trucks and a fueling station."

"Splendid!" exclaimed Fletcher. "Quick now, Bland! Think of the old days when we were hungry! What we have before us is nothing compared to that—we are fighting on a full stomach now. Quick—" Bland was already out of his chair. "Can you hurry down to that flying field, if possible catch a glimpse of that air yacht, but by all means duplicate that whole crew Bates has described?"

"On my way!" Bland answered, fired with his old enthusiasm.

"And Bullard, old boy!" said his old friend. "Don't let Van Mortimor see you or anything you are doing."

"Not liable to," he growled.

"Come to think of it, don't duplicate the steward! We'll leave him on the ship to allay our host's' suspicions and to lead me to him, wherever he is hidden, when he sails down for me tonight!"

"Boy!" declared Dr. Bates suddenly. "I don't know where we are bound for—it's probably across the bar—but I got you into this, so count me in on the last act!"

"That's the spirit!" cried out Fletcher. "Now we sound like three live men, instead of three dead ones! Bland, work carefully down there. Don't let any one at all catch on to what you are doing this time! By sundown, have your men out of sight, but instantly ready in that shed! You must have two pilots, a mechanic, and at least two others, five altogether, but don't take them near the plane! I'll show up with Dr. Bates and two secretaries, each a plainclothes man! Post a man to delay Gloria if she arrives much ahead of me and then wait for me! I'll take charge!"

Bland rushed out and Dr. Bates fell back weakly in his seat.

"If it were any one else but Van Mortimor!" the doctor gasped.

"No matter what you say," objected Fletcher, "you have heard the only way for me to tackle him! I propose to cut the whole earth and everything else that he can use, right out from under his feet. He will have to operate in very thin air to beat me tonight!"

"That's his specialty!" cried the old physician. "I beg you to let me warn you about that! His father before him had great foresight! He always had his way while he lived, but he died with a big worry. The grand old man wanted badly to leave a living monument behind himself and his efforts, yet he only had one child and the blood of that heir was tainted with insanity through his mother's family! That accounts for Gloria's adoption and the two letters which were intrusted to me for delivery to the children. But who could tell that all these horrible events would follow!" The doctor shook his head dolefully, then continued:

"I saw your face first in a newspaper picture of a group of people, noted your remarkable resemblance to the present Van Mortimor, and kept tabs on you just for the romance of it! When Van Mortimor returned from his long resi-

dence in Europe such a mental and physical degenerate that he could not appear publicly, I took him off the
boat near Sandy Hook to avoid notoriety. It seemed then
that Providence had sent you! I suggested to Van Mortimor that you be substituted for him until I could get him
straightened out, and he readily agreed to the whole affair,
and arranged it himself. He did it superbly, too; but as you
know, from the most sordid of motives, though I thought
he was very liberal at the time. I had him in the lodge in
the valley below the house at Cleborough and he behaved
very well outside of yelling."

"Don't mention it!" said Fletcher with an uncontrollable shudder.

"Well, he didn't bother you much at first, did he?"

"I haven't time to tell you about that. Go ahead!"

"I DIDN'T KNOW there was to be a brain operation and
when all those foreign specialists landed here, Van Mortimor simply disappeared! I couldn't find him anywhere!
However, he turned up at an opportune minute, said he
was very sorry—that he had taken an overdose of dope and
slept for three days in a strange haunt, and he wanted to
do the right thing for you by giving you a general power
of attorney to act in his name and stead for awhile. He
did, too!"

"When and how?" asked Fletcher unbelievingly.

"It's a fact. You have actually had the authority to act for
him up your sleeve all the time, so that everything you have
done for him, if it were ever really contested, is perfectly
legitimate from the very first day you went to business for
him! He put the instrument of your authority inside the

covers of the 'History of the Van Mortimor Case,' and that is the way he made me give it to you!"

"Smart as his father!" exclaimed Fletcher.

"Smarter, in his perverted way," said Bates. "If I told you, he could revoke the authority instantly, and in the meanwhile he did not have you violating the law. It was better for him, too, than if I had tried to have him put in a lunatic asylum. However, I let things run along; I was so anxious to keep you in his place! I hadn't taken seriously Dr. Martel's prophecy that he would start this fiendish playing on human emotions; I thought I had everything in hand and was serving every one's best interests. Van Mortimor promised not to touch you and he never did— but, of course, as I now see too late, he doesn't have to touch you to kill you! He made me believe you scalded yourself in your sleep with the steam pipes; but I suspect now that he did that!"

"Absolutely."

"What a fool I have been! This whole thing is just a cold-blooded experiment in murder on Van Mortimor's part! He is a sadist, one who delights in cruelty. When you stepped in that car last summer on lower Broadway, no one in this world but this fiend himself knew just how thoroughly he took you in charge. Your very thoughts have scarcely escaped his attention since then. And I encouraged it! I wanted to show him how splendidly you were living and cure him by example—and all along he has simply been trying to kill you!"

"I have known that a long time," said Fletcher wearily, and he did not appear to be giving close attention. His thoughts were flying with the man in the airplane!

From then on only snatches of Bates's talk registered in his mind. Van Mortimor, no doubt, had keys to the play house. He was often hidden in that second car which always followed Fletcher!

"He must have tortured your dog and then returned him to you," said Bates, "for the animal goes wild at the sight of him."

"And that," Fletcher checked up, "explains the howl on the phone this morning!"

"I have seen weirdly contorted little dead animals lying about," stated Dr. Bates with a shiver, "on which he must have experimented. But have you any idea why he has been keeping a few buzzards in a coop on the roof of the house at Cleborough?"

"I know what he did with one of them!" answered Fletcher grimly. "He must have been turning some of his buzzards loose yesterday, for one of them circled over Gloria and me just after I made love to her in the woods up there!"

"A man who would do that has lost all human feeling," spoke the doctor solemnly. "You may expect something so gruesome tonight on his new airplane as to be unbelievable! I never saw this great plane before Skyles's dead body was removed from it, but you can rest assured that this air boat has a special death trap aboard for your last torture! How do you propose to catch him?"

"When we sail tonight," said Fletcher grimly, "he can't get off the plane, and I am confident of my own hands!"

"But, man, whatever you think of, he'll think of something better! He is everywhere at once and he seems to know everything! If you should catch him, God help you!

He is slimy and poisonous! He would slip right out of your hands and leave you to die in agony!"

"Not these hands!" spoke Fletcher slowly. "Not these hands which have held Gloria!"

"The real reason you can't possibly win, I haven't told you yet!" and the good doctor hesitated a moment as if he were deliberating whether he should speak of it at all under the circumstances, but he proceeded at last: "The reason I myself am so deathly afraid of this degenerate is that I know something about him that only his physician could know! He has developed some damnable occult power which he picked up in India; it transcends all our knowledge of life and medicine. He is somehow supernatural! As surely as you go on his airplane tonight you will find that no living man can combat him!"

THE DOCTOR'S NEXT words trembled in a queer falsetto:

"You'll find Van Mortimor can't die! Neither you, nor all the ravages of disease, nor all the poisons on earth, can kill him! I swear he has conquered such things and death in all its forms, and he uses them on other living creatures! He is sort of a moral cancer, a social leper, an evil genius among us. He has dissipated enough to kill ten normal men and he still lives! Sometimes he has taken me in a big dim room about twilight and while he has sat in a chair by my very side, he has tossed his head over on the mantel, and laughed at me!

"He says it is only a trick that he learned in India, but I am not so sure about that now! He can take a thousand drops of laudanum in wine at one sitting; and he positively seems to thrive on all of his dope! Though his system is so heavily saturated, I have seen him take doses of strychnine and cocaine that I know no ordinary mortal could stomach and live! If you put a bullet or a knife through his heart tonight, he will laugh at you and go on murdering you, without even needing to use violence."

But Fletcher had quit listening to all this morbid description. He was completely engrossed in something he considered far more important. It seemed that Gloria was now mutely and dumbly calling to him for help!

He sat there before Bates, oblivious of his immediate surroundings, with a mighty effort striving to achieve the impossible. Behind the blank expressionless curtain of his face, Fletcher was tediously weaving a noose for a neck which he believed would hold upon any man or ghost!

"Now, doctor," he finally said, "just come with me tonight, and do not be surprised at anything I may say or do! I can't talk further with you now! I am really sort of a coward at heart, and at times I have to be left severely alone! If I saw very much more of you, or good old Bland, or even Gloria, before my boat arrives, I feel that I'd fall all to pieces! We'll go to Jefferson Flying Field by different routes. You start out now—and slam the door hard behind you! I want to test my nerves."

The door closed behind Bates with a crash, which went resounding up and down the deserted corridors of the great bank like a burst of artillery, and Fletcher was alone!

A LONG SHED, such as is common at airports, ran along one side of Jefferson Field. Fletcher appeared there just as the shadows of the day were falling. He was immaculately dressed in a new flying uniform, as punctilious and conventional as Sigmond Van Mortimor himself could have been.

Two prize-fighters, lately sworn in members of the police department accompanied Fletcher, as secretaries.

Bland and Bates nearly fell upon his shoulders at sight of him. He was taken to the rooms, with which he had been so pleased when he had first heard of their existence. There were three *en suite,* in the end of the shed and Bland already had his new crew corralled in the end room. Fletcher's face was set and impassive and showed no signs of the terrific strain under which he actually labored.

"Have you seen the airplane or Gloria?" was all he asked.

"Neither!" whispered his confidential wizard. Bland, "but here are pictures of each of the airplane's crew. They were all hired here and I hastily borrowed their tin-types from the files of the office of the commandant of this held."

"Fine," complimented Fletcher as his eyes devoured the photographs, without recognizing anything familiar in them.

"Field records," said Bland, "show that this airplane is a huge Fokker biplane recently brought over from abroad. There in the room I have two good Fokker pilots who have flown all types of these big planes and one of them, a man named Koebel, has taken up this very machine of Van Mortimor's in a test flight. Two mechanics and an expert are with them and altogether they will just about roughly fill the places of the men in the pictures with helmets and make-up. They are all old army men, good fighters when trouble starts!"

"Thanks!" answered Fletcher feelingly and he stepped in the room among them.

"Mr. Koebel!" he called out and a stocky airman, with

gnarled hands that seemed especially dependable, stood forth.

"Mr. Koebel," Fletcher said, "we are changing crews in a rush when my plane descends.

"How soon can you have her back in the air again, after I remove the present crowd?"

"Less than ten minutes," he answered smiling, "with the help of these boys!"

"Very well! Then you handle the flying part."

Now he called everybody around him and announced:

"We may be carrying a stowaway tonight. I believe an assassin is hidden on this plane and these elaborate precautions are necessary to catch him. As soon as the plane comes down, one of you meet it and tell the first member of the crew you see that I want him to come over here. Then, one at a time, send them all over here to me, all except the steward! As the places are vacated, casually fill your men in to them, Mr. Koebel; and be ready to take off again, the moment I step aboard!

"When we are in the air, everything is to proceed as naturally as possible and as if nothing at all were expected to happen. There will be, including my sister—let me figure it out—exactly twelve people aboard! Twelve people are to be accounted for and every one of us is to be alert, and on a still hunt for the extra passenger all the time! If we do not find him we'll all retire early and lights will be dimmed; but the signal for the alarm will be for the lights to flash on, in any part of the plane. Then we'll all rush to that spot!

"Understand me?"

Heads were nodding in assent.

An inspiration came to him. He thought of all the

brokerage commissions that were credited to his account in the office of Morton, Keene & Co., and which were his in any event. He said:

"I'll personally pay a reward of twenty-five thousand dollars to anybody who catches the thirteenth passenger who rides with us tonight!" He wondered how Van Mortimor would like that!

An electric tension gripped the atmosphere about them. He called Dr. Bates aside and quickly told him:

"You get in the middle room of the three, and receive the old crew for me as they come off the plane! Have each man strip to the waist for a physical examination as he comes in, and then pass him on into that empty room beyond.

"Tell them it's by my orders! My policemen secretaries will help you, and take care of any resistance on their part. When you have stolen the last man's clothes, come aboard the plane!"

For Bland and Bates, the tension in the air about them had taken on the tautness of a piano string. They listened for the least unusual sound.

Now Fletcher swung boldly out onto the field.

WHEN HE FIRST sighted the plane it was coming like a tiny speck in the distance. Soon with a mighty roar it loomed up like a black cloud in the sky. Suddenly it was describing huge circles over him. It seemed alive, with its great, dark wings and naked head, it appeared a giant buzzard hovering over him. Well he knew that the beady eyes of Van Mortimor were looking down upon him now.

The cold sweat broke out on Fletcher's forehead and he retreated to the shed, wiping this from his brow. He was glad Bland and Bates had not seen what he had.

The ghastly thing landed not far away and the noise of it was quieted as it came racing up by him and the shed. Fletcher nearly fell over backward when he gazed upon the big buzzard again. It had stopped just a few hundred yards from him and it had turned a gleaming white all over! It was resplendent now in its swanlike innocence, to receive its passengers.

However, events moved so fast that his mind could not keep up with all of them. Men were passing into Dr. Bates's room in the shed on the one side behind him, and different men were coming out of Bland's quarters on the other side of him. Some of them coming out had on the clothes of those who had gone in.

A small hand waved from the plane and he stared at Gloria, spellbound. What a slim chance he would have had of finding her this afternoon, for she had been up in the air!

He heard a scuffle behind him in Bates's room. A fist shot out, and now one man would need some real medical attention.

He touched the doorway of the plane by his side. Its wood felt moist and chilly, clammy to his fingers, like the railing of the terrace on the house at Cleborough that first night when he had heard the weird yell from the valley.

Bates and Bland now rushed out of the shed. Fletcher grabbed an automatic pistol from one of his strong-arm secretaries, stuck it in his clothes, and together they ran for the plane.

Just as Fletcher reached the big air boat, he dived down and peered momentarily under its lower plane. The whole bottom of the craft was painted black. It was a simple trick after all.

With his heart a little lighter he jumped aboard the huge deceptive bird of prey. Its engine roared, and they were off. Fletcher and his insatiable shadow were on their way to keep a rendezvous with death in the sky.

There were many places he could have poked into aboard this great luxurious air yacht as they went thunderously plowing into the heavens. But he left the searching to his men, who were eager for the task. They moved quietly about now, apparently attending to their duties while they thoroughly searched the entire boat for their extra passenger.

Fletcher knew it was better for every one to act naturally; in this way they might more easily draw the prince of horrors out of the woodwork or the wings or wherever he might be hiding. For his own part, Fletcher went directly to Gloria, whom he found in a dainty rosewood paneled compartment, forward in the ship.

"Isn't this lovely?" she wrote on a little pad after she was through hugging him. "Where are you taking me? To one of those South Sea Islands you once talked about?"

"Anywhere you say!" he scribbled back after a moment's reflection. He answered her just as if this big white plane with its-seamy underside could take them there. Evidently Gloria had not the slightest conception of the true situation.

However, since they had to have some destination for the time being and he wanted to please her all he could, he wrote out directions for the pilot:

"Take us over the sea to Bar Harbor."

HE HOPED VAN Mortimor would see that; but not certain

other things. He had a feeling that he was being watched, even while his men were searching.

"I have been on the plane riding about since two o'clock," Gloria informed him, "just getting acquainted with this beautiful surprise that you have had built for me, as you told me to do in your message!"

Fletcher smiled faintly, for other eyes than hers. He thought sadly that she must have arrived just after poor Skyles's body was taken off of this "beautiful" flying barge of death, and now it was on another such little errand!

It was agonizing that all his men should not be finding anything!

He excused himself and went back to Dr. Bates.

"Who fell so hard at the examination?" he asked.

"The former pilot of this infernal craft!" wrote the doctor tersely. "He questioned my instructions, and we didn't argue with him."

Bland's face was pathetic. He and Bates were now only wooden men, like automatons they had performed their parts in this mad drama which had no reward but death for them. And now they were simply waiting to be scrapped!

The steward served a generous lunch, which was not enjoyed by any one but Gloria; if the servant was surprised at all by the new faces aboard, he did not in any way show it.

That was the dreadful part of everything—nothing at all unusual occurred! Though Fletcher had taken the ship, his men could not find the thirteenth passenger; and the merciless eyes watching Fletcher were still in control of it all. It was just the same for him, in a racing airplane, up here in the sky, as it had ever been!

Finally Fletcher began to believe that since the life of

this man over him was a drug dream, not like an ordinary mortal's, he was also capable of making his victim live the same thing. Or worse, he might even be all that Dr. Bates thought of him. In any event, Fletcher saw that if he caught Van Mortimer, he would have to catch something as elusive as a ghost!

About eleven o'clock, lie cautioned every one to retire, but remain on the alert throughout the night. Then he kissed Gloria and called the steward to conduct him to his berth.

Fletcher was led down an aisle to a small cabin in the tail of the plane.

The steward remarked: "You are looking unusually well, sir."

Fletcher passed into an oblong room, about ten feet in length by seven in width, which was the last one on the passageway. Any one who had ever read "The History of the Van Mortimor Case" would have promptly recognized the owner of this. The floor the woodwork, and such little furniture as there was, was all of polished ebony, black as midnight.

A little porthole window had lavender silk curtains.

The bed was an ordinary double-decked affair, such as is common on ships, one section below and another directly above, and both supported by simple iron rods or standards. Each berth, however, conforming to the room, was of black wood with its surface highly finished. There was an outside door across the room, but Fletcher did not think Van Mortimor could come from outside this speeding plane; both the top and bottom of it had been inspected since they left the ground.

There was paneling all around the room. Fletcher would have sounded this paneling, but the noise of the motors made such a thing impossible.

He believed more than ever now that invisible eyes were upon him and from behind these panels! He was very careful, however, not to appear nervous or suspicious. He undressed nonchalantly. But in changing to the pyjamas which had been provided for him, he kept his revolver well out of sight when he slipped it into his nightclothes.

Then he acted as if he were locking the door into the passageway, but in reality he left it unlocked; then snapping out the lights, he jumped in bed.

BY SOME LITTLE moonlight that flickered into the room, he was startled to find that the sheets were of black silk. Yet he pulled them over him with the thought he could stand even that suggestive touch for tonight. Then he glanced up, to discover that the bottom of the upper berth was lined with white satin.

This bed was just like the infernal airplane; black below, white above, for one who had to use it!

Nevertheless, he worked his pistol around under the sheets so that it could not be observed, and yet be free for his use; and he waited for the ghost to appear.

It must have been nearly an hour later that Fletcher realized that his body was getting numb. All the lights were out on the great lumbering plane. The noise of the motors, deafening at all times, now reigned supreme. He was very sleepy, his eyes drooping repeatedly; but he had no intention of going to sleep here, and now!

It was nearing the last minute of the day of Friday the thirteenth, for which Sigmond Van Mortimor had made so much unearthly preparation. Fletcher believed the phantom of him, at least, was due before the day was over, even if he had to hop the plane in mid-air to become the thirteenth passenger!

Suddenly a panel in the rear end of his room flew open! His other self, Sigmond Van Mortimor, dimly appeared in the gray moonlight. He must have had some secret control of the machine, for the engines went off for a second. Fletcher's heart stopped; for in that single second came softly one plaintive note of the old cry of the hashish eater!

At the same instant the upper berth began slowly slipping down its iron rods upon Fletcher! Then he knew how Skyles had died of fright, and under what sheets. He was sleeping in an open coffin that Van Mortimor was closing up!

Fletcher was paralyzed as usual in the presence of that half-seen, blanched face. The ghastly visage of himself was leering in upon him now. The stuffy white satin cover above him was so gently and so steadily creeping down to envelop him! The apparition was delighted—it stopped leering, and now laughed contemptuously.

Was not Van Mortimor actually infallible, omnipotent? The lid of the coffin came down, nearer and nearer to the life-breath of Fletcher, who was held so very securely by the fear of this evil power. None of Fletcher's men could suspect his plight or hear his cries, above the roar of those engines.

But now Fletcher made a tremendous effort to stir. He realized he was not altogether being held by fright, for he smelled the odor of crushed peach pits. He knew now that there were fumes in the funeral room.

If he only had a little fresh air, he believed he could move, even in the face of this inhuman white thing, his double. But how could Van Mortimor stand this same air that was choking him? There was a secret chamber back where the fiend was, but the panel between the two of them was open.

Fletcher could see the cruel face of his other self in that other little room. Van Mortimor was bringing out Fletcher's old clothes now, the very ones he had worn up to Cleborough on that first memorable night so long ago.

The lid of the coffin was within a foot of Fletcher's face. Each breath seemed his last. Yet his hand was still clenched upon his revolver. He had succeeded in weakly raising it about an inch under the black sheet. If he could just get the muzzle of the pistol a half inch higher he could dear the foot of the berth and take one dying shot at the pitiless Van Mortimor.

With an effort that brought the blood pounding in his ears he gave the pistol a desperate jerk that raised it a little higher. His deathlike grip held it there, and his numb fingers fired point-blank ahead. The bullet nicked the wood at the foot of the berth, but it also went through the open panel-way!

There was a shattering of glass which he could not hear, drowned out by the sound of the motors, but he felt the flood of fresh cool strength-giving air that swept in upon him. He quickly put another bullet through the little window in his own room and wiggled out from under the falling coffin lid. He hit the floor in the throes of the last life of a cat.

Van Mortimor had ceased his preparation of the burial wardrobe at the first shot. Now he turned upon his victim, haughtily incensed, and advanced through the open panel in a maniacal fury. But Fletcher had nimbly sprung upon his feet and braced himself against the wall.

HE HAD A straight bead down the barrel of his automatic on the demon's heart—but the fiend kept coming, his hands raised in gloating malediction. Just as he plunged into the room Fletcher blazed away. A streak of fire cut the darkness straight and true to its goal.

Then Fletcher understood what Bates had feared.

That bloated white face was laughing at him and still advancing. Leisurely, triumphantly, now. Fletcher pumped the contents of the revolver into its breast, but he knew now that not even the shots could be heard. Resistance was futile.

But now his hands found and touched the light switch. The gloating face showed up in the light with the pallor of a sickly spider, as it closed in upon him. Fletcher threw the empty pistol at its head and missed. Then he flew desperately at the Thing's throat with his bare hands, and failed in his grasp—his fingers only tore feebly against a vest of solid steel.

People were pounding on the door. The lights were blazing, and the door from the passageway moved. With a sudden burst of diabolical strength the phantom slipped from Fletcher's hands and lunged across the cabin.

The outside door flew open, and for an instant Fletcher saw a patch of pale gray sky. Then the air pressure had closed the outside door—and Van Mortimor had vanished.

In the open doorway from the passage were crowded the white faces of Dr. Bates and Bland. They stood there obstinately blocking the aisle, obscuring the view of those behind them, pushing those behind them back up the passage.

Now Bates turned and made frantic signs for all the others to look elsewhere. Then he pulled Bland into the room with him, shut the door behind him, and locked it.

Fletcher was still so terrified he could not believe the spell was broken. It took Dr. Bates to prove it to him.

"Bland and I alone actually saw him go out into the sea," scrawled the old doctor, and he stuck that under Fletcher's eyes.

"My God!" answered Fletcher. "He had on a steel vest, and he went into the sea."

"So much the better," Bates scribbled below; "his body will never float up."

Running to the nearly closed black bed, Bates examined it with horror. He pointed out that three of its innocent iron corner rods were solid; the upper berth had simply been loosened so that the top section could creep up and down its own legs. The fourth post or support, however, which appeared to be identical with the others, and was hidden in the corner, was in reality an electric jack for raising and lowering the heavy upper berth.

Concealed wires ran from this bed to the secret chamber where the control switch was located. When they attempted to close the coffin-berth completely, they found that the top lid of it could go no lower than it had stopped now.

"You see," Bates informed them, while Bland methodically prowled about the cabin for traces of the disaster, "after Von Mortimor had a victim prepared for death he didn't need to touch him to kill him with this contraption. This is how poor Skyles went!"

They discovered a little rubber tube running from the secret chamber, still oozing some faint fumes. The shattered glass told how Fletcher had broken a pane there to get the fresh air that saved his life.

THE GOOD OLD physician had a happy idea next. He fished a prescription pad out of his pocket and scratched his head, thinking for a moment. Then he wrote:

There's no one left but yourself. Van Mortimor is dead. Long live Van Mortimor!

And he solemnly handed it to Fletcher, while he held a finger over his mouth. Both Bland and Fletcher read it and nodded their heads.

Then Bland and the doctor quickly collected all the simple evidences of the phantom's unnatural practices, including Fletcher's old clothes. Then Bates tore into small bits their present conversation, and dropped that, too, upon the little pile. He made a neat bundle of everything in one of the black sheets, and, opening the outside door, he threw this baggage out after its master—far down into the deep.

Thereupon he locked and barred the outside door, shutting the secret panel; pushed the dark upper berth up into its normal position, heaved a vast sigh, and waved the two others from the room.

When Fletcher finally emerged from the vulture's nest he was confronted by Gloria, waiting by the side of his door.

He gathered her up drunkenly in his arms, and weakly reeled up the passageway which was so swiftly speeding on to Bar Harbor. All the boat was now aglow with cool moonlight; his black cloud truly had a silver lining.

They stopped in an observation salon which was a part of this luxurious sky yacht.

He was handed a message reading:

> Captain Van Mortimor:
>
> False alarm! Have had the whole plane gone over again.
> There are only the same twelve of us aboard this ship.
>
> Koebel, Pilot.

Gloria had at once insisted upon getting a basin of fresh water, and now she was tenderly bathing the clammy perspiration from his face. Her gaze followed his, down to the quiet sea gleaming silver in the moonlight, a mile beneath them, gliding by so swiftly and smoothly.

Impulsively Gloria Mortimor seized a pad and wrote in her charmingly delicate hand:

"There's something awe-inspiring about having been 'hand-picked' and then reared like a little princess, for a great purpose. But somehow, with your help, I feel that I have accomplished it."

Edmond Fletcher answered eagerly:

"You have! You have driven the phantom out of the rainbow."